A MODEL AMERICAN

Elsie Burch Donald

BLACK SWAN

TRANSWORLD PUBLISHERS
61–63 Uxbridge Road, London W5 5SA
A Random House Group Company
www.rbooks.co.uk

A MODEL AMERICAN
A BLACK SWAN BOOK: 9780552772129

First published in Great Britain
in 2007 by Doubleday
a division of Transworld Publishers
Black Swan edition published 2008

A CIP catalogue record for this book
is available from the British Library.

Addresses for Random House Group Ltd companies outside the UK
can be found at: www.randomhouse.co.uk
The Random House Group Ltd Reg. No. 954009

The Random House Group Limited supports The Forest Stewardship Council
(FSC), the leading international forest certification organisation. All our titles
that are printed on Greenpeace approved FSC certified paper carry the FSC logo.
Our paper procurement policy can be found at www.rbooks.co.uk/environment

Typeset in12/14pt Bembo by
Kestrel Data, Exeter, Devon.
Printed in the UK by
CPI Cox & Wyman, Reading, RG1 8EX.

2 4 6 8 10 9 7 5 3 1

'You can take a man out of his country, but you can't take his country out of the man.'

American saying

A MODEL AMERICAN

1

SHAKING THE SNOWFLAKES FROM HIS HAIR, WILLIAM Bolton entered the holly-wreathed front door of his Connecticut home minutes before their guests were due for dinner. He had spent the afternoon in Washington and, evidently elated, had good news, he told his wife, bending to kiss her before mixing a Scotch and soda. 'It'll have to keep, though,' he said, glancing at his watch, aware that the moment he started, the doorbell was bound to ring.

'The limousine's coming at seven tomorrow morning,' he announced instead, sitting down, drink in hand, beginning to relax and to mute his energy. 'We won't need any breakfast; we'll get some on the plane. Let's see now: sturgeons' eggs, sunny side up; toast, Melba; champagne; weak coffee, though. You betcha.' He smiled boyishly, the edges of his bright, berry-brown eyes creasing along lines engraved by laughter as much as by narrow-eyed financial scrutiny.

Realizing her husband was tired but hiding it, Marjorie kept up a soothing lullaby of domestic trivia. 'Everything's packed and ready, but will two summer suits be enough? Hattie packed the linen one. I thought poplin would be easier to travel in; it doesn't wrinkle so much.'

'Two's fine. If I need another I hear they run them up in Bangkok, made to measure, in a day for twenty dollars. Might be worth looking at,' the successful venture capitalist allowed, perking up at the thought.

'Sarah called to say goodbye. She was on her way out to dinner with Gordon; they were going to a movie first.' The Boltons' only child had graduated from Bryn Mawr that summer and had recently started a job on *Vogue* magazine in New York. 'She says Gordon thinks Thailand may be getting dangerous, and we should be careful. Americans are unpopular right now.'

'Gordon is an asshole.'

'Bill, dear, Sarah is probably going to marry him.'

'He's still an asshole.'

'He's a little outspoken, I know, a little opinionated. And, yes, I suppose a little full of himself. But he'll outgrow it. Do you think he won't?'

'Does the pope wear a beanie?'

'He's outspoken partly because you intimidate him, darling. He's not insensitive, and if you could just—'

But the telephone was ringing, and answering it, Bill grimaced in mock-helplessness to his wife. 'Business,' he mouthed, settling back in the low armchair, his long legs stretched out in front of him; at forty-seven, he was still a handsome man, and remarkably fit.

Marjorie was used to Business. Last night it had been silicone chips and up-to-date covered markets; and the night before, Bill's favourite venture, Genetech: genetic engineering and research. A guide to Thailand lay on the table and she picked it up. She wished she'd had more time to prepare, but the trip had materialized only two days ago. She thumbed the guidebook's pages. A colour plate showed a pretty girl wearing a spiky gold tiara and smiling that famous Oriental smile. On another page a whole family was piled, laughing and waving, on a motorbike, hugging each other like koala bears. Marjorie counted five. And the smiles and laughter were so obviously unfeigned. Evidently the photographer didn't need to insist on 'cheese', as if to lure out timid or reluctant mice. In the Orient people exuded warmth and gaiety the whole time. It just poured out.

'It will be summer there!' she had exclaimed when Bill first told her of the trip. Snow clouds hung overhead like bulging rubbish bags and the thermometer outside was plummeting below zero. The milk left on the doorstep that morning had burst its bottles.

'They don't have any summer,' Bill had answered cheerily. 'They have a dry season and a wet season. The climate is governed by monsoons.'

'But it's hot,' Marjorie had insisted. 'That's summer. Well, to me it is. Back home you could fry an egg on the pavement in summer, or so people always said.'

And now, sitting before the blazing fire, suspended in a momentary dreamlike state, her husband's voice droning familiarly in the background, Marjorie was enveloped by a sudden frisson of pleasure, a gentle excitement rising like a breeze in a still garden, spontaneously animating all the leaves. The promise of an exotic world, of otherness, of Asia, lay before her like an exquisitely wrapped parcel, to be opened and with an eager curiosity enjoyed. Though in many ways a conventional woman, Marjorie was strangely drawn to otherness, to mystery, to wonder.

'If Colonel Sanders can produce fried chicken pieces in two minutes, Happy Burgers should turn out a burger a minute . . . What's that? Snappy Burgers? Hey, not bad. Could be misinterpreted though . . . You know, "bow wow".' Now both men were laughing . . . 'That so? Well, veggieburgers might go down a treat in LA, but nowhere else on earth that I can think of. Let's keep to "the burgers we all know and love", shall we? At least to start with.'

A pair of headlights had flared like paparazzi flashbulbs in the living-room window, and Bill brought the conversation to a close. 'OK, let's go for it. See what happens.

'That fast-food franchise,' he explained, as they stood up. 'Could be a pretty big thing. Everybody's in a hurry.'

'Which reminds me, darling – I need spare cash for Hattie, just in case. Fifty should be enough.'

Bill produced a Hermès wallet, bulging with greenbacks. In addition to travellers' cheques he had laid on plenty of cash: big notes for emergencies; small ones for tips and other incidentals. The whole world yearned for US dollars, and Asia, despite the spiralling Communist threat, would be no exception.

Ostensibly a product of the East Coast establishment, Bill Bolton was in fact from Oklahoma. For three generations his forebears had scratched out a living on poor and increasingly dust-blown land, until Bill's father, perceiving the future of automobiles, had opened a filling station in the abandoned milkshed at the end of the drive (the family farm was on the main highway). There were few cars about in the 1920s; and during the Depression, even fewer. Times were hard, and young Bolton, like so many others, had learned the value of a dime, if not a dollar. Unusually, he had also learned the value of investment.

Shortly after Mr Bolton opened his filling station,

he had purchased, to the amusement of friends and family, a famously dud oil well from some Indians. Cars needed oil and he was going the whole hog, he told them. In payment for the well he promised the Indians a tank of free gas once a week, for life; and during the Depression their Model T Ford, crammed with men in hats and feather headdresses, was often the only car seen on the highway all day. Everyone always waved.

Bill was in his teens when the oil well suddenly produced, gushing up out of the ground like a geyser over in Yellowstone National Park. War was looming again in Europe, and Mr Bolton decided it was time to sell his investment on. The deal he made was not unlike the one he had struck with the Indians; but it was with Standard Oil, and instead of free gas Mr Bolton took out company shares, becoming almost overnight a millionaire.

So Bill Bolton, if the point were stretched, was second-generation rich. He had gone to Princeton, another good investment, and being handsome and a top football player, possessed of a shrewd intelligence and a jokey, easy-going manner, had made many friends. He and Marjorie had met in Georgia. Bill was in officers' training camp, having left Princeton, and novice officers were entertained by local society. Marjorie's soft Southern voice had hypnotized and her pretty face and Gibson-girl figure beguiled seductively; her hair was like a shining spindle of sunburned gold. Marjorie was warm and welcoming, and she liked to please; all of which had greatly pleased Bill Bolton. While something about her walk inflamed.

Southerners still hated Yankees, and the Eagletons were no exception. Proud but impecunious, they lived surprisingly well on very little income. Money they deemed vulgar, and mercantile values crude. They were tradesmen's values – which the Yankees were, in Southern eyes, to a man.

Bill had smiled indulgently. Georgia was a backwater and the Eagletons innocently treading water. Money was power; it was freedom; a golden cup brimming with the heady nectar of success. Money made America's wheels turn and her factory whistles blow; it kept people buying goods, and more goods being made. In the end everybody benefited. Money was the fodder of a peaceful democratic society; and what was better on this earth than that?

The Boltons were married shortly after the armistice (Bill having narrowly missed active service, which he fiercely regretted) and the couple moved into a small apartment in New York. Post-war America was booming and opportunities rapidly came Bill's way. His Princeton connections helped; so did the ten-thousand-dollar nest egg that was his father's wedding present. A keen sportsman, Bill proved an accomplished angler in eddying business pools as well as white-water salmon streams. In both he relied on instinct, a cool head, patience, thorough research and a good knowledge of the environment. Soon he was making money, a lot of money. His nest egg had multiplied many times over. 'It's a chicken farm now,' he'd written proudly to his father when Bolton Venture Capital was formed.

It pleased Bill greatly that, in improving his own life, he was also improving, through sound investments, his country's stability and future. For Bolton was a good citizen, and he was patriotic. Beneath the chiselled face, greying hair and firm, organizational hand reposed a somewhat innocent and untrammelled heart that on the whole still beat with expectation. Fair-minded, practical and without meanness, no shadow-self lurked, harbouring cowardly or hateful impulses. Bill was an optimist, he was shrewd, he liked action, he was happily married, and he was lucky. Moreover, he enjoyed a battle and he liked to win. Life was, he had decided, a centre-court affair, and he was going to stay there, winning as many sets as possible – for his own good and for the good of all America.

''Fess up now!' James Merriweather impishly declared, when the charlotte russe had gone round. 'You're on some secret mission, aren't you – some little favour for those White House guys? Nobody's investing in Asia right now. They're getting out, not in; it's Chinese takeaway.' James's freckled face grinned boyishly.

'You're right about one thing, old man,' he said, refilling their champagne glasses before answering. 'I did do a deal with the State Department today. That much is true.'

'Oh my God!' Jane Merriweather laid down her fork and, casting her grey eyes heavenwards, addressed the chandelier. 'I knew it. I just knew it!'

'Well, so did I,' declared her imperturbable husband. 'I just said so.'

'Oh Bill, I wish you hadn't!' Jane swept back an invisible wisp of hair – a perennial gesture. 'This dreadful war. You're going to help it along, aren't you? When what we need is to stop this awful killing and leave those poor people alone.'

The remark brought patient and good-humoured resignation. Jane was a liberal and, like the caprices of a senile or dotty relation, her eccentricity, too, must be gently humoured and indulged. Liberals were well-meaning people. No one doubted that. The problem was they failed to understand reality – how life really was and how the world worked: in short, the necessity for *realpolitik*. Liberals took coddled views from coddled positions. They were idealists and they were never tough enough. In a crisis they ran like jackrabbits for the high moral ground and, sitting in judgment at a safe distance like a theatre audience, left the bloody battlefield to others. The dirty work. And it *was* undeniably dirty.

'It's awful, just awful!' Jane repeated. 'A shameful blot on America's history.'

'A just and necessary war, dear Jane.' Bill was light but firm.

'You wouldn't be saying that if you had a son!' Jane had no sons either. Her implication was an attack on notorious Republican self-interest. Republicans never thought about anyone but themselves and, as an extension, their money, its protection, and keeping the roads wide open for making more at any stops along the route. James was an exception, of course. He was a Republican because his family had always been Republican. It went with the package, and they never discussed it.

'Well, I hope I would if I had a son,' Bill answered cheerfully. 'The boy would have to do his duty.'

'His duty might be to speak out against it. The Vietnamese weren't hurting us. We should have left them alone.'

James and Bill exchanged a look of indulgence, as parents might, listening to a bright but uninformed and innocent child.

'The point,' Bill gently reminded her, 'is to stop Communism – and, yes, preserve capitalism. You can't have a democracy without it.'

'Well, if Communism's such a threat it must be very popular, and if it's popular it must have something people like. Surely they've a right to it, if it's what they choose – that *is* democracy.' Proud of her sharp logic, Jane sipped, deservedly, her champagne.

'A good point,' Bill charitably allowed. 'On the face of it. But people can be very naive, especially if they're oppressed and poverty stricken. They can be innocently taken in, like children – their choices impaired by ignorance and double-dip, ice-cream-cone promises.'

'Bill Bolton, that's *so* patronizing. I bet you've never even met a Vietnamese. Or a Communist. You don't know anything about them.' Jane, scenting success, expanded her position. 'What's happening in Vietnam is medieval. It's like Catholics versus Protestants. That clash doesn't mean anything today – and really it didn't then, or shouldn't have. If people will only live and let live, differences like that just die away.'

'I'd say fascism versus democracy is a better parallel,' Bill answered easily. 'You didn't want that to work itself out without any intervention, did you?'

'Well, that isn't the same,' insisted Jane, unable just then to put her finger on the reason. 'Now, where was I?' She frowned accusingly at her champagne; the invisible wisp was again swept back. 'We're damned lucky we don't have any sons, that's what I say.'

An affectionate smile went round the table. Jane had run out of steam, lost track of her badly fraying thread; but now that her views had been vented, they could get on with a pleasant and agreeable evening. Bill took the champagne bottle around again and Marjorie went to get the coffee.

'To answer your question, James,' said Bill, when they had moved into the living room. 'I'm going to Thailand to look at a rubber-tyre company in Bangkok. It's a lot cheaper to make tyres near the source and ship them. And if the business is properly managed – something I mean to find out – it could be very profitable.' He smiled warmly at Jane. 'Nothing more bellicose, I'm afraid, dear Jane.'

'And you had to clear *that* in Washington?'

'Well now, the State Department meeting concerned something else.' He lit James's cigar, and then his own.

'Ha, I knew it!' pursued Jane. 'Now we're getting somewhere.'

'You know Friday is Marjorie's birthday.' Bill blew his smoke out slowly, thoughtfully, in a sort of dramatic pause. 'I was talking to the State Department about that.'

'He's going to buy you an elephant in Thailand, Marjorie. I won't say what colour.'

Bill scrutinized his cigar. 'For her birthday,' he continued, 'I'm taking my wife to Cambodia, to see Angkor Wat.' Then, shifting his gaze, he lifted his glass to Marjorie in a toast.

The effect could not have been bettered: amazement, wonder, admiration, incredulity. Although diplomatic relations with Cambodia had recently been resumed, the country remained closed to American tourists, a fact now chorused by the Merriweathers in duet. Cambodia bordered Vietnam.

'Well, Jackie Kennedy went,' said Bill.

Two years earlier, in 1967, Jackie Kennedy had visited

the famous site, and photographs of Angkor Wat had been flashed round the globe. The ancient temple, among the wonders of the world and so large that astronauts had seen it recently from the moon, was at the time of Jackie's visit glimpsed for the first time by millions of earthlings previously unaware of its existence, the vast ruins gilded redundantly by Jackie's glamour and their inaccessibility. Without any doubt Bill Bolton had laid a jewel before his wife, one sparkling voluptuously with the multi-facets of rarity, power, wealth and high influence.

'Darling! I can't believe it!'

'It sure pays to have the president's ear,' murmured James laconically.

'Or the means to fill his wallet,' Jane couldn't resist adding; then, feeling she was being churlish and unkind, 'Oh, take lots of pictures!'

'I'm simply overwhelmed.' Tears of pleasure and affection filmed over Marjorie's blue eyes.

'That must have cost you a mint, old man,' James confided admiringly, as the couple were leaving.

'It was sort of a package deal,' said Bill.

With raised eyebrows, James grinned, then clapped his friend approvingly on the back. 'You old rascal. Well, be careful; and send us a postcard – diplomatic bag, of course.'

'Goodness, I won't know anything,' lamented Marjorie, as they got ready for bed. 'I'm so ignorant. I won't be able to do it justice.'

Remembering something, Bill opened his briefcase and produced a small, silver-wrapped parcel. It was a guide to Angkor. His secretary had run it to earth in a secondhand bookstore. 'You can read it on the plane,' he said. 'But we'll have our own guide there to take us round. Everything's being arranged through the embassy.'

'Bill Bolton, I'm so proud of you! I believe you can do anything – anything in this world you put your mind to.'

2

A CAR ORDERED BY THE EMBASSY WAS WAITING FOR THE Boltons at Phnom Penh airport, Thailand having consisted thus far of a night's sleep in the airport hotel. Cambodia had to be visited at once; it was a tricky business, their visit restricted to only forty-eight hours.

'Why, it's a tropical Paris!' Marjorie cried out ecstatically. They were driving down a broad boulevard lined with white-blossoming frangipani trees. The centre aisle was planted in French-municipal-garden-style, but the flowers were more exotic and gaudy. It was rush hour and the boulevard was packed with traffic. Instead of droning engines and impatient Parisian horn-blowing, however, a magnificent silence reigned. The street teemed not with cars but with bicycles. Packing the boulevard, they flowed like shoals of darting fish in an unending stream around the car; and Marjorie, feeling by comparison as if she was in the belly of a whale, longed to be more intimately a part of the joyous life around her – to have the freedom of a bicycle or a bicycle-drawn rickshaw; to smell the scent of frangipani blossoms and feel the silky morning sunshine on her skin. To blend in. Especially since everyone looked so happy. Even a man stooping beside what looked like an open sewer was

grinning up at the passing traffic, showing brilliant white teeth.

'If a Martian arrived on earth and had to report back home, he'd say Cambodia was the best place on the planet,' she insisted. 'In New York people always look so glum.'

Bill was studying papers from his briefcase. 'Well, he'd be dead wrong. The French did sort the place out some,' he added, glancing approvingly at the well-kept boulevard, then lowered his voice. 'It's headed down the drain now that the natives are in charge. You mark my words.'

'Oh, Bill!' It was an affectionate reproof.

They had stopped at a rare traffic light. Four Buddhist monks in saffron robes crossed in front of them, their shaved heads shining in the morning sun like polished wood. 'They look like Roman senators in those togas,' insisted Marjorie. 'Only more colourful. And so elegant.'

Bill didn't look up. He knew what Buddhist monks looked like and they were all the same. 'They're beggars; parasites living off the poor,' he said. 'They don't produce a damn thing. Buddhism is one big con, pretending it's some kind of a pious religion.'

Turning off the boulevard, the car entered a honeycomb of small side streets and the ambiance completely changed. It was a shantytown. Wooden shacks were crowded together higgledy-piggledy as if vying for breathing space. Most had shabby courtyards attached – or, more precisely, farmyards, enclosing as they did chickens, dogs, ducks, even pigs. Small children played naked in the dust, scampering under ragged laundry hanging limply in the breezeless air.

'You see,' said Bill in his best I-told-you-so voice.

But the driver, who spoke some English, came to his city's defence. Phnom Penh was flooded by migrants from the countryside, he told them disapprovingly.

'Happens the world over,' Bill replied, with fellow feeling. 'Cities are magnets. People get pulled in and then they're stuck. And so are all the taxpayers.'

But Marjorie thought that even those living in squalor looked happy, part of a lively street culture that bustled with activity, bonhomie and myriad things to sell: fruits and vegetables, batteries, baskets, spare parts, tin ware, bicycles and T-shirts. One man had pulled an old sofa on to the pavement, another a refrigerator, or most of it. In several dark open-fronted shops, bicycle repairs were underway; in others kerosene lamps wrapped in dust-covered plastic hung like bats from the ceiling; while along the busy street threaded erect young women, like caryatids, carrying baskets of food on their heads and dipping gracefully to serve their customers. Princesses dispensing largesse to the poor, thought Marjorie, who was moved to say, 'I guess it's all this sunshine. It brightens everyone's day.'

But Bill, having begun to view the scene, was more pragmatic. A lot of cheap labour was about, and under-employment rife; no unions and probably no rules. Yet the people seemed energetic enough and, given a chance, naturally would want to get ahead. He eyed the scene more carefully.

Emerging from this ramshackle if picturesque quarter, the car proceeded down yet another elegant boulevard, beside which, like a fabulous fairytale road paved with sheets of solid silver, ran the broad and glittering Mekong River – now so familiar to the American public, because of Vietnam. Colourful pennants fluttered gaily from tall flagpoles along the bank, and in the pavement cafés that lined the route, people sat chatting and reading newspapers, as if they were in Paris. It was hard to believe that less than a hundred miles downstream a savage war was being fought. In fact, Marjorie forgot that this was so.

An hour later, the Boltons were sitting at the bar in Phnom Penh's best hotel, Le Royal, waiting for the pilot who was going to fly them to Angkor next morning. The bar was crowded, every stool at the polished hardwood counter taken – the faces surrounding it, a mélange. Two Orientals, probably Chinese, were speaking so loudly they might have been haranguing each other from across a street; yet they seemed cheerful enough. Beside them, a pair of British journalists were complaining of their newspapers' refusal to print a piece 'out of bloody ignorance'; while a tall, white-haired man in rumpled clothes, presumably a Cambodian 'old hand', chatted *sotto voce* to the bartender in French.

Although ten o'clock in the morning, everyone was drinking spirits.

Bill had a noon appointment with Mike Rives, the embassy's chargé d'affaires and currently the top US official. (Diplomatic relations having only recently been restored, no ambassador had as yet been appointed.) Bill removed his wristwatch and reset it, looking at the bar's wall clock. Twelve hours had simply disappeared en route. Would flying the other way round be more efficient? It was worth thinking about.

A young man, slightly built and as slim as a girl, had entered the bar. He wore faded jeans and a cowboy hat that had seen better days and had evolved a highly individual character. A pair of sunglasses protruded from his shirt pocket. His ginger hair was tied back in a ponytail, and a red-and-white-checked scarf like a little tablecloth hung about his neck. Scanning the room, he picked the Boltons out.

'Mr Bolton? Bill Saltman,' he announced,

'Hey there.' Bill stood up. 'Hi ya doin?' And shaking hands, he introduced Marjorie.

'Another Bill,' said Marjorie, smiling warmly. But her husband, who despised the ponytail and longed to give it a good hard yank, thought: Only one is a 'dollar' Bill, though.

'Everybody calls me Salty.'

'Salty it is.' Bill was more than ready to comply. 'Where're you from, Salty?' He hadn't expected an American.

'Wyoming. Out near Jackson Hole.' And answering the couple's polite conversation-making enquiries, Salty said he'd learned to fly because his father, who was a rancher, owned a small plane. In big open country like Wyoming, a plane could be more useful than a car. He'd done some crop dusting in Colorado, he added, 'before heading East'.

'Dangerous work, crop dusting,' said Bill, who liked a man with skills and who showed some daring. Affably, he revealed his own Western roots.

One of the bar girls had come up, and Bill grinned. 'What'll you have, Salty?'

Salty said a beer and Bill said to make it three. Had Salty been over to Angkor Wat recently, he asked?

There wasn't much of a demand right now, Salty replied. Jackie Kennedy was probably the last American tourist.

Bill knew Salty must be impressed that they would be the next, but that he wouldn't let on. Westerners of the cowboy variety never admitted to surprise, or even enthusiasm. Equanimity was their thing – equanimity before man and nature. When they weren't being drunk or violent. The cowboy creed was on the whole no bad thing, thought Bill.

'A guide is meeting us at Angkor Wat,' he said. 'We're supposed to bring her back to Phnom Penh.' Had the embassy told Salty that?

They had. Miss Phillips: an Englishwoman. There was plenty of room: the plane was a six-seater – a Cessna Centurion – and Salty suggested that since it was a day trip they get an early start. The flight would take about an hour; could the Boltons be ready to start by seven?

'Sure thing.' And Bill offered Salty breakfast in the hotel next morning. 'I hear you don't get poisoned in this hotel, uniquely.'

But Salty said he would meet them at the airport. He needed to be there early to get things ready. 'In Cambodia there's always some surprises. That much is for sure.'

3

THE FLIGHT TO ANGKOR WAS DISAPPOINTING; IT WAS being mostly over water. The plane followed the Tonle Sap River, which joins the great Mekong at Phnom Penh, then traversed the long lozenge-shaped lake, also called Tonle Sap, that feeds it. The biggest lake in all Southeast Asia, its vast size is doubled each year during the rainy season.

Salty had offered to fly low over Angkor Wat, but Marjorie said she preferred to see it more naturally, from the ground. She wanted to see the temple as it was meant to be seen; she wanted to be surprised, to have the wonder of it. They could enjoy an aerial overview when they left.

The airport, an unpaved landing strip sporting a limp windsock, with a small shack standing alongside, appeared deserted. But as the plane stopped and its propeller slowed, two men grinning broad Khmer smiles materialized from the shack to help Salty tether the plane down. Near the runway a car was parked, sheltered under a tree. Its driver now ran forward, pressing clasped hands to his heart in a *sompeah*, the traditional Khmer bow of greeting.

'How you are?' he grinned, making on arrival a second dip.

'Oh,' cried Marjorie, 'you speak English. How very nice. Where did you learn it?' she asked a minute later, waiting while Bill conferred with Salty.

'Airplane!' declared the driver, gesturing enthusiastically towards the Cessna.

'Ah,' Marjorie vaguely rejoined.

A motorbike had sailed up, driven by a pretty Cambodian girl, and Salty waved. 'We ought to take off about three – three thirty at the latest,' he told Bill, pulling a satchel from the cockpit.

'Three is fine,' said Bill. Their flight was scheduled to leave for Bangkok at five o'clock. 'It can't take more than a couple of hours to see a temple.'

'There's more than one of 'em,' drawled Salty, locking the cockpit door.

'One's plenty; it's a flying visit.'

A faded charm enveloped the little town of Siem Reap, near Angkor. The French-built buildings bordering the narrow river (Bill deemed it a creek) were a bit run down, their purpose perhaps unclear to an indigenous population whose houses had, from time immemorial, been built on stilts. But life chuntered agreeably along, as the sleepy town either awaited better days or lived dreamily in the present, uninterested in a future so predictably devoid of change. Palms and blossoming frangipani trees lined the river banks, where water wheels poured brimming cupfuls into bamboo gutters in what, Bill pointed out, was an inefficient attempt at irrigation. 'Most of it goes back into the river.'

To the couple's delight, an elephant sauntered nonchalantly down the road, carrying great piles of wood in baskets on its back, and reducing the Boltons' car from whale to minnow.

'Elephant!' declared the driver, grinning over his shoulder, then, dilating on the view: 'River!' And a minute later: 'Boat!'

'This guy's not very verbal, is he?' whispered Bill. 'It's all nouns.'

As the car drove along, people gazed and smiled; the children, like children the world over, waved vigorously, as at a train.

'Hotel,' announced the driver.

'Stop,' said Bill.

The Grand Hotel, despite its imposing staircase, wasn't very grand, but it was spacious, and apparently empty, tourism having virtually disappeared since the war in Vietnam began. Opposite the hotel, Prince Sihanouk's white-painted summer villa looked empty, too. Mike Rives had said the prince was ill; he was going to Paris for an operation. Rives had smiled strangely when he said this, and Bill had taken it to be a diplomatic euphemism for a spree of voluptuous living, out of town.

'Not a bad little place,' Bill summed up as he approached the reception desk. At six foot three, he felt like a Titan amongst this diminutive, ever-smiling race, and brimmed with easygoing benevolence. 'We'll just grab Miss Phillips and go,' he said, before announcing himself to the two clerks bobbing and smiling behind the desk.

With the aplomb of an ambassador handing over an important treaty for imperial ratification, one of clerks presented Bill with a telegram on a little rattan tray.

'It's from Rives,' said Bill, reading it quickly. 'He wants us to take some French guy back with us. His daughter's ill.

'Could you ask Monsieur Dumont to meet us at the airport at two forty-five sharp? This is his room number.'

'Oh, we know Monsieur Dumont, sir. Monsieur Dumont lives in Cambodia. We will tell him, sir.' And they bobbed again, in unison.

'Mr and Mrs Bolton?' The question, lacking animation and unaccompanied by a smile, sounded serious, and the minute Bill saw Anne Phillips he thought, 'schoolteacher'. The young woman's corn-silk hair was pulled back in the tight chignon Cambodian women wore, but to less attractive effect in that it left her equally pale face unframed; added to which, Anne's hazel eyes did not immediately attract attention. Her figure was, however, as Bill quickly noticed, very good. Tall and willowy, she held herself well. But though Anne's overall colouring – hair, complexion, eyes, even her trousers and buff-coloured cotton shirt – faintly suggested champagne, it was, concluded Bill, champagne without the fizz. Decidedly flat. Having shaken hands his mind moved on, and Marjorie, stepping in, took charge of the niceties, smiling her open, welcoming smile.

'I understand this is a birthday present,' Anne volunteered, in a voice that might equally have said: Take the 94 bus to Trafalgar Square. 'Happy birthday,' she obliged politely.

Thanking her, Marjorie suggested they sit down, and Bill, in no hurry so long as everyone knew the timetable, willingly submitted. Coffee was ordered and Marjorie said how welcome a short preview would be; she needed to get her bearings. 'I'm thrilled to be here, but I'm so ignorant. I thought Angkor Wat was just one temple at first, but there are so many!'

'Over one hundred in this area alone.' Anne said that

Angkor referred to the entire region – some eighty square miles – and Angkor Wat to the twelfth-century temple and agreed highpoint of Angkorean art. 'If there's time, we might have a quick look at Angkor Thom, built a little later, and in its day a whole city.'

'Hey!' exclaimed Bill, but without any enthusiasm. Ruins were ruins and one would amply fit the bill. He changed the subject. 'How did you get out to Cambodia, Anne?' He thought it a strange place for a girl to be knocking about in on her own.

Anne looked at him oddly, and a long pause followed. 'I flew from London, but stopped off in India for two weeks on the way. Then I flew from Delhi to Bangkok, and from Bangkok on to Phnom Penh. I came here from Phnom Penh by bus. This is my third visit to Southeast Asia,' she added, scrutinizing her inquisitor.

She must be a very literal-minded woman, concluded Bill, about to rephrase the question. But Marjorie, stepping in quickly, said they had come via Bangkok, too.

'How did you become a guide, Anne?' Bill persevered, aware that the British never told you anything about themselves if they could help it.

'Oh, I'm not a real guide.' The faint glimmer of a smile flitted across Anne's impassive face. 'I don't know what I am, exactly. An art historian, I suppose – I hope.' She told them she'd had a French grandmother who had lived in Southeast Asia when it was a colony. 'She used to tell me stories about it when I was little – such wonderful stories! I expect that was the seed.'

Anne said she had studied history at university, but Southeast Asian sculpture was becoming her speciality. She hoped to publish a book on Hindu religious beliefs, as interpreted by the Cambodians in their bas-reliefs.

'I've taken masses of photographs, but I need to do more research, in libraries. That's why I'm going home. It's extremely kind of you to give me a lift to Phnom Penh, by the way. Getting around in Southeast Asia can be difficult just now.' Which was as near as Anne came to mentioning the conflict raging to the south and east, across the country's borders.

'I thought these people were Buddhists, not Hindus,' observed Bill, polishing off his coffee in two rapid gulps.

Anne said Hinduism had been the state religion when most of the temples were built. Angkor Wat was dedicated to the Hindu god Vishnu. But Buddhism had been around, too, and had eventually replaced it.

In the car she told them a bit more. The buildings were probably temple-mausoleums, although no one knew for sure. Every king had had to build one, and each was a replica of the universe, an earthly model of the cosmic world according to Hindu cosmological beliefs.

'Hey, that's pretty ambitious.' Bill was half listening. They were driving through a forested park of incredibly tall trees, and even Marjorie's attention was diverted. Beneath the trees a number of peacocks walked serenely, dragging their long tails like medieval ladies trailing brocaded trains across a European lawn. Peacocks were indigenous to Cambodia, said Anne, a fact that astonished the Boltons, for whom peacocks were a quintessential avian symbol of Western civilization, their rightful perch a Renaissance garden wall or grandiose château fountain. Suddenly, however, the raucous high-pitched shrieks, so jarring to the tranquillity of formal settings, and so at odds with the creatures' refined appearance, made perfect sense. It was a jungle cry.

'Plenty of good timber about. Is there much logging?' enquired Bill. The tall straight trees, evidently top quality, were extraordinary.

'Quite a lot further north, unfortunately. The Thais are doing it, I'm told.'

Bill, who thought it unfortunate only because the Thais were doing it, made a mental note.

In the high arching branches gibbons, hanging by their long arms, moved sinuously from branch to branch, and beside the road hunched several monkey families, their white faces fixed and unblinking as they stared like wizened children at the passing car.

'Monkey!' declared the driver.

More elephants appeared, sauntering along with their mahouts.

'Elephants!' mimicked Bill.

'Yesss,' murmured Anne distantly.

'It was a joke,' said Bill.

In front of them an expanse of water appeared, glittering in the morning sunlight. The car turned alongside. Buffaloes were wallowing in the shallows, their backward-slanting horns lyre-shaped, their grey hides glistening like the skin of wet hippos. Women washed clothes near by, and a bevy of naked children, bobbing up and down like corks, waved joyously at the car.

'Some washtub!' declared Bill. And turning with elaborate courtesy to Anne: 'That's a mighty pretty lake.'

'It's a moat, actually. It does look like a lake, though,' she tacked on, coolly polite. 'It's two hundred metres wide.'

'Angkor Wat!' proclaimed the driver, pointing to a reddish stone wall beyond the moat.

'Angkor what?' Bill grinned at Anne, who rather pointedly was looking out of the window.

'That's the temple's enclosure wall,' she said. 'It's three and a half miles long.' Facts, she knew, always interested tourists. At least they were something that they could relate to.

The car stopped in front of a huge stone causeway that crossed the moat. Two elephants ambled along it in the direction of the car, and beside them walked several women, wearing bright, pencil-slim skirts that reached their ankles and carrying shallow circular baskets on their heads. A group of Buddhist monks, barefoot, saffron-swathed and sheltering under yellow parasols, accompanied them.

Behind this exotic and informal procession, almost as a backcloth, rose the celebrated temple. Built in three tiers, and fronted by a low and graceful colonnade, the pinnacled mass of engraved and sculpted rock seemed almost to float, like a mirage, against the feathery blue sky, its five oval towers rising at the centre in a magnificent white crown.

'Now that is some temple!' exclaimed Bill, genuinely astonished, as they began to walk across the causeway. Anne seemed to perk up slightly. The enclosure wall represented the outer edge of the world, she informed them. The temple's top level symbolized Mount Meru, the centre of the universe, where the gods lived.

An elaborate stone gatehouse at the end of the causeway proved a feint, because the causeway continued on the other side, crossing a huge grassed-in basin. Equally astonishing was the causeway's balustrade. The railings were two enormous carved and scaly snakes, each a thousand feet long, with seven heads rising up in a giant cobra-like fan before the entrance.

'Hey, Margie, a railing like that would look great at the sailing club, going along the balcony. Try and get some photos. Old Merriweather is afraid of snakes.'

Anne smoothly continued her narration. The serpents were called *nagas*. They were water gods, important mythological symbols.

Another gatehouse of grandiose proportions gave way to a vaulted gallery that, making a sort of hollow wall, enclosed the entire pyramidal edifice in a giant rectangle.

They mounted to the second level and another grassed-in court. The surrounding walls were lined with bas-reliefs of beautiful melon-breasted women, nearly life-sized. The delicately sculpted figures stood in groups of twos and threes, their feet at right angles to their bodies, bare-breasted, bejewelled, and wearing diaphanous skirts. Some held hands affectionately, others fiddled with their hair or headdress, or held a lotus blossom. But all, without exception, smiled. And so, very broadly, did Bill.

They were *apsaras*, said Anne: celestial nymphs, who danced and flew about.

'Dancing girls. Now that's not exactly religious, is it, Anne?' Bill sounded mildly teasing, possibly even challenging.

'Not pious, perhaps,' she answered coolly.

'Yes sir; this is some temple!'

'It's the largest religious monument ever built.' Anne's tone hinted faintly at reproval.

Bill gave her a quick critical look.

Steep stairs rose on four sides to the pinnacled sanctuary. The narrow treads accommodated about a third of Bill's foot. There were no banisters. 'No wonder those *apsaras* have their feet turned sideways, and learned to fly,' he declared, grinning.

Anne produced a thin smile in response. 'The temple is the height of Notre Dame. The two buildings date from roughly the same time.'

The inner sanctum was an anti-climax: the small, smoke-blackened chamber contained a statue of the Buddha, tended by a tiny withered nun, who bowed repeatedly and lit candles. Bill put some money in the offering plate. What was the sanctuary for, before Buddhism, he wanted to know.

They had emerged from the chamber and were perched on the top step, looking down upon the repeating rectangles of gallery walls and to the park stretching to the horizon beyond. A magnificent sight.

'It housed the sacred lingum,' said Anne solemnly, after a pause.

'Is that some kind of relic?'

'A sort of statue, really.' Then, with something like deep resignation in her voice, 'A phallus.'

'Hey, did you hear that, Margie girl? The Cambodians worshipped the penis! Now those dancing girls make sense.'

'Oh, Bill,' protested Marjorie, with affectionate tolerance. 'It was symbolic of fertility, of crops.'

'Honey, it was the god's penis; he had everybody kneeling down before it. Symbolic stuff was real to these people. Isn't that right, Anne? When they worshipped a statue, they thought it was alive.'

'In a way,' she admitted, almost in a whisper.

'It's just marvellous,' Marjorie enthused, as they returned to the entrance. 'The scale is unbelievable! It's unlike anything else on earth!'

Anne smiled at her in a friendly way.

'It must have taken one helluva long time to build,' observed Bill, more impressed than he chose to show. 'Notre Dame took two hundred years, and it's a little peanut compared to this.'

'It was built in thirty years,' replied Anne, almost proudly. Did they want to see the famous bas-reliefs – to her mind the temple's greatest treasure – or have lunch first? There was a restaurant in the hotel opposite the temple.

The Boltons opted for a break.

'So what were these guys really up to, Anne, going to all this trouble?' Bill was drinking an ice-cold beer with relish. 'Whew, that tastes good. Now let me get this straight. These people thought kings were divine and in cahoots with the gods, or that their ancestors were; and if the temples were kept going, as a sort of shrine, then the kings would be immortal too, which is why every king had to build one. Sort of like the pharaohs. Is that it?'

'Something like that; but no one really knows. When Westerners discovered Angkor, the Khmers had forgotten most of their history, and claimed the temples had been built by gods.'

'Well, you can see why.' Bill was gazing thoughtfully about him. 'I mean, look at these people. They're all so *little*!'

The bas-reliefs – half a mile of them – were indeed extraordinary, but the pervasive element of the fantastic bewildered. In one huge panel men were fighting monkeys – and losing; in another they fought comical gremlin-like demons. Some gods had several heads; others several arms; while some men and animals appeared to have exchanged their heads.

'The gods sure do have a lot of arms.'

'They have a lot to do,' Anne answered, deadpan.

Bill knew he was being patronized, but even so it was a good answer, he decided. Droll but practical. He couldn't have bettered it himself.

Most extraordinary was a panel called 'Churning the Milk Ocean'. A long line of perky-looking men, almost life-sized, faced each other in what appeared to be a massive tug of war – their rope a huge snake or *naga*, forty metres long. Fish swam below their feet and tiny *apsaras* fluttered like butterflies overhead. At the centre, between the opposing teams, a larger figure, Vishnu, stood grandiosely on the back of a turtle. The turtle was Vishnu, too, said Anne, in one of his incarnations.

The story she related was equally bizarre.

An assembly of gods and demons had been churning the milk ocean for a thousand years, hoping for an elixir to make them immortal and incorruptible. But getting nowhere, they had finally appealed to Vishnu, who told them to churn together, rather than competitively. They did, but the churn's pivot, a sacred mountain turned upside-down for the purpose, began to bore a hole in the earth, and the mountain started to sink. Then the *naga* got dizzy spinning back and forth, and vomited poisonous venom. But the god Siva drank the venom, and Vishnu, not to be outdone, offered to underpin the mountain by standing on a turtle.

'Standing on *himself* as a turtle,' Bill corrected.

'The *naga* coiled around the mountain once again,' continued Anne. 'The gods and demons pulled, and the mountain started to rotate. They churned the milk ocean for another thousand years, and finally the elixir was created.'

'Was it butter?'

Anne merely said that many treasures had resulted, including a three-headed elephant, a sacred cow ('About time,' said Bill), and the birth of the *apsaras*.

'Hurrah! Bring on the dancing girls. But you know what this is, Anne? It's a comic strip. It may be the very first comic strip ever made.'

'Such wonderful imaginations!' interjected Marjorie.

'But why go to all this trouble?' pursued Bill, who could think of a dozen things more useful: toilets, tables and chairs, a ground floor to their houses. The Khmers had none of these.

Anne said one theory was that, believing reality and symbols were interchangeable, the bas-reliefs when finished were deemed to be alive.

'Now that's a lot of fun,' admitted Bill. 'But it's kids' stuff, really, thinking you can make a picture of something, and suddenly it's for real. Like riding a broomstick around the backyard, convinced it's an Indian pony. These people never grew up, that's all. Could be they didn't live long enough, running around like a bunch of ants, building all the time.'

'Such wonderful imaginations!' Marjorie repeated. 'It must have been marvellous to stand here and see events from legends and the past come alive before your eyes like that.'

'Yeah, like an early movie,' declared Bill. 'Only it wasn't.'

When they reached the causeway it was nearly three o'clock and their driver, standing at the end of it, looked nervous.

'Airport!' declared Bill, bounding into the waiting car's front seat.

'Goodbye!' answered the driver, grinning, and jumped in as well.

'God, what a country,' whispered Bill, turning to Marjorie in the back seat. He was shaking his head. 'It's one big fucking joke!'

4

YVES DUMONT STOOD WAITING UNDER A TREE. HIS LINEN suit was badly crumpled, his thin grey hair protected from the sun by a vintage panama. A suitcase, large, battered and old-fashioned, rested on the ground beside him. He wore no tie and the edges of his collar were slightly frayed, the lining exposed in places. Dumont was in his sixties; a large man: corpulent, big boned, his stomach protruding precipitously over his belt. His face, bronzed by long exposure to the sun, had probably never been handsome: it was moon-shaped, the broad nose flattened like a spent prize-fighter's, the mouth a thin horizontal line that tended neither up nor down. But Dumont's eyes attracted strong attention: pale as sea-washed pebbles, the pupils mere pin-pricks, they seemed impenetrable. It was like gazing into milk glass; and yet Dumont's own gaze was focused and remarkably intense. It was impossible to tell if he had been waiting for some time, or had just arrived.

'Great to meet you, Eve!' Bill, heartily shaking hands, was privately astonished at the name Dumont so off-handedly had pronounced. The French were a poncey bunch, all right. 'Welcome aboard.'

'Neither I nor my valise is very compact, I fear, but

store us anywhere and we almost certainly will stay put. I am most grateful to you,' he added, picking up the heavy-looking case.

Tempted to give the old man a hand, Bill suspected it would not be well received.

'You have enjoyed your visit, I trust?' Yves continued, as they walked towards the plane, where Anne and Marjorie waited.

'We sure have. That Angkor Wat is some place!'

'Ah, indeed. Everyone is awed, as almost certainly we were meant to be,' acknowledged Yves, his fluent English sailing on a current of mildly French rhythms and European vowels. He smelled faintly of alcohol.

'Yeah, those guys had some big ideas,' said Bill. 'And the power to put them into practice. That's the awesome bit. Lots of guys have big ideas, but putting them into practice like that is pretty rare. That takes some doing.' As a venture capitalist, Bill viewed his own job to be precisely that.

Yves nodded. 'Fortunately the pleasure of ruins requires only the imagination,' he genially observed.

'Well now, Angkor Wat is pretty much intact,' replied Bill, a little firmly. Not one to get sentimental over ruins, he wanted to make that clear. If something was a ruin, in his view it ought to be rebuilt, or else the materials should be used for something else.

Salty had arrived and, lightly kissing the pretty girl who remained beside her motorbike, walked quickly towards the plane. There had been an accident on the road, he explained, shaking hands with Yves and hurrying to untie the aircraft's tethering ropes. The hut was closed, the two attendants nowhere in sight. As Salty inspected the plane and checked the oil, Bill stored the extra suitcases in the hold. Then, everyone having been introduced, they clambered good-humouredly in, Bill sitting up front next to Salty in the co-pilot's seat, and Yves at the very back, in a seat behind the women.

They were airborne in minutes, the Boltons straining for an aerial view of Angkor Wat; and almost immediately it lay beneath them, grandiose and improbable, trumpeting man's victory over nature in what, after nearly a thousand years, remained a continuous and hard-fought battle.

Salty flew so low that they could see delighted faces on the causeway looking up, everyone shielding their eyes, pointing and laughing. A second later, ruins on an even larger scale appeared, apparently the fabulous Angkor Thom. Then the plane swooped heavenwards and, levelling out, sped across the dark umbrella of the jungle canopy.

The Boltons had asked Salty to return over land, not water, if possible, so they could see the countryside. And Salty, with time to spare, made a brief loop, taking in the Kulen Hills to the north, where the temple sandstone had been quarried, then headed east, away from the lake, before turning south.

Thick tropical forest surrounded both Angkor and the Kulen Hills, but beyond it on either side was spread a magnificent chartreuse carpet of brilliant neon intensity: Cambodia's rice fields, yet to turn softly gold for harvest. Skimming across the luminous fields, divided by dikes and framed by scattered fringes of palms, the airplane crossed another, this time narrow, belt of forest, beyond which, raw and red like the gash of an unhealed wound, lay a stretch of ugly and unkempt savannah. The result of recent logging.

Completing this leisurely detour, Salty dipped a wing, banked the aircraft, and straightened it out to begin the journey south. But as he did so the Cessna suddenly spluttered and began to hiccup. Like a colicky infant, Marjorie thought. And Salty, leaning forward, duly patted one of the cockpit dials. The needle bounced and wavered, but the hiccuping continued.

In quick succession Salty checked the carburettor heat and the magnetos, then deftly switched the airplane's fuel tank over. The colicky hiccuping stopped. But so, although it took the others a moment to notice, had the Cessna's noisy engine. For a second the silence was welcomed in the cramped and crowded cabin.

'Mayday! Mayday!' The words, for a split second, suggested celebration as a plausible explanation. Salty, speaking into the radio microphone, was calm and unperturbed, even matter-of-fact. But he was peering hard at the scrub-covered savannah below.

'Mayday, mayday. Can you hear me? Over . . . mayday . . . over . . . over. Fucking hell.

'They've siphoned off the gas,' he announced, almost as an aside, the radio microphone still held to his lips. 'Mayday . . . mayday. Hey, *answer the phone, somebody*!'

Marjorie leaned forward to touch her husband's shoulder, but the seatbelt didn't allow it. Anne, sitting very erect beside her, was staring straight ahead. Transfixed by the slowing propeller, she was praying that, should they crash, she would die instantly.

The men scrutinized the terrain.

'There to the right.' Yves was leaning forward, peering out of Marjorie's window. 'It is a logging track, I think.'

Squinting, Salty nodded and fixed his eyes, hawk-like, on the narrow red band running beside the forest edge. 'Try and relax, folks; it's safer in case of impact. Could get sort of rough.'

Anne tensed more tightly. 'Oh God, let me die quickly,' she begged.

Their landing strip selected, Bill reached his hand back over his shoulder, and Marjorie again leaned forward. They gripped, held fast, reluctantly separated.

Though still able to manoeuvre the eerily silent plane, Salty knew that it was not for long; they were rapidly losing altitude. But keeping the Cessna's nose slightly tilted up, repeatedly adjusting the angle of their descent, he aimed the aircraft at the logging track.

Flying by the seat of his pants, thought Bill with admiration.

The plane's wing flaps were partially down, and for what seemed an incredibly long and dreamlike time there was total silence, rigid suspense, as Salty edged the Cessna into position over the logging track.

Bill wondered fleetingly why men held their breath in crises. Were they preparing to run? They were themselves trapped, powerless in a tiny cage, a leaf pushed along by the wind, drawn irresistibly towards the earth by the Circe-like pull of gravity.

'Dear God, let death be quick!' prayed Anne.

Deep ruts were now visible on the track, crisscrossing clumps of tall grass, as the plane, floating gratuitously on the back of a breeze, sailed lower and lower, the dark wall of the forest rearing up alongside in a dubious welcome.

Suddenly an earthquake shook the crowded cabin. The Cessna bounced in erratic leaps, hitting ruts, catapulting over others, scything the scattered clumps of grass and laying them flat. The wing flaps fully down, the air whooshed like a hurricane and the speed seemed to increase.

'Y'all hang in there!' shouted Salty, gripping the stick hard.

The Cessna began to slow down, the bumps became less riotous; order was being re-imposed. When suddenly, without any warning, the aircraft veered, skidded precipitously, and spinning out of control left the track, jolting, bucking and shaking, to rush helter-skelter, head on, towards the black screen of anarchic jungle.

The horror, the horror! Kurtz's famous words filled Anne's terrified mind.

Marjorie had covered her face with both hands.

A terrific jolt threw them forward against the seatbelts; another catapulted them back again. The careening plane shivered and pitched, swayed wildly; then, rearing up like a frightened animal, tipped sharply to one side and abruptly froze, as if it feared to venture any nearer to the forbidding jungle.

No one moved. Stunned, bruised, badly shaken and reluctant to engage reality more fully, they sat there, still as death.

The entire event had lasted about five minutes, but those five minutes had compacted lives into dense primordial cells of suspended time, vulnerable and potentially highly explosive.

Marjorie started to shiver. She fumbled to release her seatbelt and, leaning forward, this time lightly touched her husband's shoulder.

Bill's hand closed tightly over hers, quelling like a fluttering bird the tremor that had taken demonic possession of her hand.

'You have landed us well and safely, Mr Saltman.' Yves's deep baritone resonated reassuringly through the cabin, as he wiped blood from a cut on his wrist before rolling the sleeve down to conceal it discreetly.

'Thanks,' returned Salty, monosyllabic as ever. 'Looks

like we got ourselves a busted tyre.' And throwing open the cockpit door, he leapt agilely out.

'We'll help you change it!' Marjorie called out after him. Her elbow stung sharply, having banged against the window frame, her knees ached and she was breathless. But the wonder of their survival had begun to penetrate, and she was waxing jubilant.

As indeed was everyone.

Alive. Unhurt. It seemed a miracle as, climbing from the cabin, they wordlessly helped each other to descend. Yves, the last one out, had the support of both men, given his considerable weight. The plane was tilted at a perilous angle.

Silence sown in shock now blossomed as ecstasy and, feet planted firmly on the ground, they turned in circles like bemused dervishes, for some reason looking up thankfully at the sky and smiling foolishly. A euphoric moment.

But Anne, standing apart, was staring fixedly at the jungle, and Bill, noting her stricken face, came over and patted her reassuringly on the shoulder. 'You'll be in Phnom Penh for dinner tomorrow night,' he offered warmly. 'A flat tyre's nothing but a pinprick; happens all the time. And folks are always running out of gas.'

Anne smiled vaguely, as from a great distance. But a minute later she seemed to relax a little, and her arms, previously tightly clutched across her chest, fell limply at her sides. The dread and sinister apparition of Mr Kurtz that had filled her imagination with a dark and inchoate fear had begun to disappear, the image fading in a ghostly retreat back into the lawless interior of the jungle.

'I am alive!' Anne told herself. 'I have survived. The sun is shining, the sky is the bluest I have ever seen. My whole life is before me, a twice-given gift, and I won't waste it. Not one single minute.' She felt such energy, such joy, a sense of being alive, the intensity of which she had never before experienced. 'Everything is so wonderful,' she beamed, turning to Bill and Marjorie. 'It really is. It's simply glorious, isn't it?'

Bill suspected he had a hysterical woman on his hands, but Marjorie, reading his thoughts, suggested they were probably all in shock, even if they didn't know it. She nodded meaningfully and with a smile towards Yves, who was stomping about in an Indian war dance, his feet having gone to sleep.

Spontaneously drawn together, the women moved a short distance away from the plane, and within minutes were absorbed in a sympathetic examination of each other's darkening bruises, confiding in urgent whispers their previously imagined fears and declaring with bursts of feeling their immense relief – creating instinctively, as women will, the courteous and sympathetic groundwork of a civil society.

'I thought I was going to die,' admitted Anne, who, staunchly atheist, forgot that she had prayed.

'I was so worried about my daughter!' Marjorie announced. 'So afraid she'd be alone in the world.'

'One wouldn't want to be stuck out here, and wounded,' Anne observed, following her own particular apprehensions. Anne was squeamish; even the sight of blood made her feel faint, and despite a rational and highly disciplined mind, she panicked easily.

'No, you would not!' Marjorie warmly agreed, and expanding almost girlishly upon their good fortune, they hurried off towards a nearby bush, and stood guard for one another.

The men had gathered around the plane's left wheel,

where Salty pointed out the puncture. He could fix it, he said; he had a kit. But first he must try to establish radio contact.

Bill, opening and closing his hands to exercise cramped fingers, looked quickly at his watch. He estimated there were about two hours of daylight left. Even if Salty's earlier call had got through, a search party wouldn't set out before the morning. Methodically Bill addressed the future: telephone calls, rescheduling, possible trouble over visas, the waste of time involved – and time was money. The Thais would wonder tomorrow morning when he didn't show up. But having lots of time themselves – and therefore very little money – Bill knew that they would wait.

Without saying so, everyone had accepted that they would be staying the night.

'We will need firewood,' offered Yves. 'To keep mosquitoes off.' He and Bill headed towards the forest, leaving Salty in the cockpit, chart in hand, trying for radio contact. But half an hour later, when the Cessna's battery failed, Salty had still not got through. With the women's help, however, he managed to repair the punctured tyre. The plane was in fine condition, he told them, straightening the wheel strut out with several blows of a hammer. 'The minute we get ourselves some gasoline we'll be on our way.'

Dragging back dead branches from the forest edge, Yves and Bill broke them over their knees to build a fire. The women spread out groundsheets from the hold, together with the tarpaulin normally used to cover the aircraft's fuselage. Unpacking Salty's camping kit they set out plastic cups and plates, metal cutlery, a kettle, salt and pepper. Marjorie, reminded of playing house as a child in Georgia, was beginning to enjoy herself. That make-believe could be more satisfying than a real event gave her momentary pause, and she thought fleetingly of what Anne had said about Angkor Wat's bas-reliefs and the appeal of their imagined reality.

Salty produced some biscuits, bottled water and half a dozen chocolate bars from a plastic cooler, together with a supply of jerky wrapped in plastic: dried venison, he explained to Anne, or the Cambodian equivalent. He said jerky was an American pioneer tradition, and still popular out west: the stuff would keep for years.

When night fell – and it was sudden – the little party was gathered on the groundsheets, away from the fire; and, with the possible exception of Salty, they were immensely pleased with themselves. Their suitcases had been left in the hold. They could easily improvise; and besides, they might be required to leave in a hurry the next morning.

Salty had also produced a bottle of whisky, and it went round and round. Little effort was made at conversation; exclamations sufficed and banalities took on new life, for mood governed everything, and it remained euphoric. Marjorie declared the jerky better than the marinated venison at Lutece, a favourite restaurant in New York, adding, 'How fortunate we are!'

This was enthusiastically endorsed. They were having a grand and serendipitous adventure. They had survived a terrible crash with hardly a scratch, the tyre had been repaired, the plane was ready for take-off the minute some gasoline arrived. Meanwhile they were a convivial, close-knit little band, sharing common ground and bound by common interests. In it together.

For better or for worse, thought Marjorie; just like in a marriage. But she refrained from saying so.

Even Salty admitted things could have been worse; while Yves, puffing on a thin-stemmed pipe, his pale, pebbly eyes blearing myopically in the firelight, declared the atmosphere to be in the key of A major, that of some of life's finest music. And when Bill, pouring his third big whisky, blurted cheerfully, 'Hell, here I am, a big shareholder in Standard Oil, and stranded out here because we're out of gas,' even Anne laughed. The remark, although puerile, had something profound about it, too – or seemed to have: a bittersweet irony, coating one of Nature's little practical jokes, of which this seemed to be a fine example.

It was decided the women should sleep in the plane. If not exactly able to stretch out, they could at least curl up in not unreasonable comfort. The men would make do on the groundsheets.

Goodnights were bidden with warmth and genuinely felt affection. Their luck brilliantly turned round, they had had, as Marjorie now beamingly declared, a very nice day.

Salty was the last to retire. Checking the fire and the plane's tethering ropes, he set out bottled water, propping it safely upright between three cooking pots; then, rolling up an old anorak, he made a pillow and, before lying down, carefully stored his pistol, a loaded Colt .45, beneath it.

5

UP BEFORE DAWN, HUNG-OVER AND HUNGRY, THEY watched the sun rise. Marjorie said it looked like a fried egg.

'Sunny side up,' observed Salty, poking the fire's ashes with a stick and throwing dry grass on top to get it going. Following which, the women heated bottled water and made tea. There was powdered milk and sugar, and the biscuit tin went round again; but everyone was subdued, confessing openly to headaches. Marjorie retrieved her cosmetic case and handed out aspirins.

After breakfast there was nothing to do but wait, watch the sky and listen. Bill wagered they would see a plane between nine and ten o'clock – nearer to nine if Salty's mayday call had got through; the Cessna's silver fuselage, shining in the morning sun, would attract attention, even from a great distance.

But by eleven o'clock there was still no sign, and by noon they were hungry again. The biscuits and jerky went round and were finished, as was most of the bottled water. Salty produced three more chocolate bars. Badly melted, they were none the less delicious. But the sun was cooking more than chocolate bars and, moving the groundsheets, they gathered under the aircraft's wing for shelter, like chicks huddled beneath a mother hen, peeking out periodically at the sky.

Yves was the first to hear the sound of an engine.

Jumping up, everyone furiously scanned the sky, now partly obscured by wispy chiffon clouds. The sound was coming from the right direction – the southwest – the decibel level rising and falling as the aircraft tracked purposefully back and forth, east to west, at high altitude.

'Why aren't they flying lower?' Marjorie wondered. 'They ought to be looking where we might have landed. We wouldn't land in the jungle; we couldn't have.'

'Perhaps they're fine-combing the whole area from a bird's eye view,' suggested Anne, removing her floppy-brimmed khaki hat and using it as a fan.

But the sound became fainter, the combing – if it was combing – continuing south, instead of north. And then suddenly the buzzing stopped altogether, like a bee that has found a desirable flower and settles greedily in, to the exclusion of all else.

No one spoke. Rather they continued to gaze vainly at the sky, across which the thin tissue of cloud had begun to spread in an unfolding canopy. Anne thought she heard a faint buzz, but no one else did, although great efforts, even a few imaginative leaps, were made to that effect.

Salty hadn't joined in the speculation, aware that having made a loop north and to the east, they were considerably off course. A rescue team would almost certainly search along the Tonle Sap lake, or in it, that being the more usual route.

Marjorie pulled out her camera and took some photographs.

A sort of contact had been made, Bill reasoned: their absence had been noted and reacted to, people were looking for them, it was only a question of time. The embassy would be pressing the authorities, and privately Bill believed that if the search party was too small or inefficient, Mike Rives would insist Cambodia send its air force out – provided, of course, Cambodia had one. The Boltons were not people you forgot about, and their disappearance having been reported, the press would leap on it, putting further pressure on the Cambodians to get their footling act together. While *in extremis* – Bill felt a puff of pleasure at the thought – the White House might order a squadron over from Vietnam. Suddenly the proximity of that war enormously reassured. Competent Americans were in the vicinity, thank God!

It was now four o'clock. Pulling a machete from the hold, Salty went off in search of more wood. Yves had settled down with his pipe under the plane's wing. Sitting cross-legged, Cambodian fashion, he looked reflective but content. The others resorted to books: Marjorie studied her guide to Angkor Wat and Bill became engrossed in a James Bond thriller, while Anne, with some reluctance, opened *Mrs Dalloway*. She had been saving it for the long flight back to England, and might have nothing to read if she finished it too soon.

Anne was fairly happy. She believed that in the circumstances they had got off incredibly lightly. The crash could have been serious, the resulting situation a horrendous nightmare. Yet the biggest impact so far had been a small shift in perspective. At Angkor, she had been desperate to escape the philistine and facetious company of Bill Bolton. Taking him around the temple had been like showing Picasso's *Guernica* to an Eskimo. Why, she wondered, were Americans sometimes so uncultured, and American men often such adolescents? Like wine without the sugar necessary for fermentation, or yeastless bread unable to rise, something was missing. It astonished her that Bill Bolton had managed to make – as he so obviously had – such a very great deal of money. But then, investment was really a form of glorified gambling, and America, where it was endemic, one vast casino, with Wall Street where the biggest games were played. No wonder something was missing from the American male's make-up, when life was fundamentally about playing games. You placed your bets, put your money where you hoped to win more money – it hardly mattered exactly where that was – and if you won, declared triumphantly that you had capitalized on your investment.

Games no doubt developed many gamesmanlike skills, but they did not develop character. Rather they, and the money they produced, in shielding from reality actually *stunted* growth. Unless you went broke, of course. Broke in America Anne imagined to be a challenge of overwhelming proportions. With so few safety nets it would be sink or swim, make or break, and that could well deliver an excessive, possibly even fatal dose of reality.

Marjorie was different. Although well cocooned, she was by nature sympathetic, and sensitive to nuance; she cared about people and she welcomed culture. Her heart was in the right place, her instincts happily rooted, if in need of more intensive cultivation. Marjorie was naive, but Anne liked her. In truth, she no longer actively disliked Bill. Like all children, he required indulgence and a bit of patience, but he meant well. What was more, he had been kind to her. And leaning back against the Cessna's tyre, cushioned by the gallant loan of Yves's discarded linen jacket, her perspective comfortably back in place, Anne opened her book. 'Mrs

Dalloway said she would buy the flowers herself,' she read.

By the next day they were virtually out of food; suitcases littered the ground and bits of clothing were draped across the airplane's wings in a vain attempt to keep the sun at bay, transforming their narrow shelter into a colourful Bedouin tent. The women had promised to remove the clothes at the first sound of a plane, so that the Cessna's fuselage could catch the sun, becoming a shining beacon. Earlier they had boiled brackish water, collected by Yves along the forest edge, and been able to wash. Bill alone among the men had shaved. At mid-morning an airplane had again been heard in the southwest, but it had kept to the south, this time in a repeated north–south trajectory before once again abruptly disappearing.

Salty allowed that the rescuers were probably searching around the lake for signs of wreckage. He didn't add that, finding none, they might cruise over the jungle, quiz a few peasants in the surrounding fields, then give the whole business up. Bill's optimism prevailed, but Salty felt obliged to point out that, as they were east of the normal route, their rescue was bound to take more time, and he suggested matter-of-factly that they take a few precautions regarding stores, and in particular water. 'We could be here a few days,' he drawled, tipping his hat back and squinting up reflectively at the clear sky.

The others for the first time began to examine more carefully their surroundings.

To one side of the track the savannah stretched in a ragged line to the horizon. Patchy with emerging growth and clumps of tall grass, it was devoid of shelter, an ugly man-made scrub of desert. Salty's chart showed a broad and uninhabited plain beyond it.

To their other side, several hundred yards away, lay the jungle: strange, romantic, ominous; a sinister world without the benefit of sunlight; the abode of wild beasts and poisonous snakes, of dense and exotic vegetation, a world without paths or order or any regularity. A pristine world, predating Adam; and, far from being a proto-paradise, profoundly threatening.

Yet beyond the forest lay the luxuriant rice fields they had seen from the air. Where there was rice there were people, also water, and presumably gasoline. Salty's chart showed the rice fields to be only three or four miles away, tantalizingly near, yet tightly cordoned off behind the thickly meshed and possibly impenetrable jungle barrier. Their party was ostensibly hemmed in.

At dusk the men began to forage for food and firewood along the forest border. Salty had set some snares the previous evening, and when two brilliantly coloured bantams were produced, the looming feast successfully blotted out all mounting worries and discomforts. Another bottle of whisky was produced: Bill's duty-free; but the threat of dehydration invoked discretion, and Anne suggested that the whisky be rationed, to make it last. The proposal, badly received because of latent implications, was none the less grudgingly accepted.

Salty, busy rolling a cigarette, refused his share. He rarely drank spirits, he said; the previous night had been an exception. Yves, however, downed his thimbleful in an eager gulp before taking up his pipe, and he and Salty puffed reflectively, smiling at each other in obscure accord as the others sipped their whisky in minute draughts, like butterflies sipping dew drops off a leaf, so desperately anxious were they to make it last.

Yves had discovered jackfruit. It was the first time the Boltons had eaten it and they found it delicious, and surprisingly meaty, the taste similar to bananas. Yves said the presence of jackfruit and a few palm trees meant that at some point there had been habitation, maybe by hunters who had visited the area regularly before the forest was cut down. If they moved camp, the palm trees would provide good shade. It would be cooler beneath them and also easier to forage.

But the women were reluctant to leave the Cessna's sheltering wings, and had no wish to get any nearer to the jungle than they already were. 'We're fine here,' insisted Anne. And Marjorie backed her up. 'It's cosy, and it won't be for long.'

In fact it was far from cosy: it was cramped and terribly hot. The metal fuselage still heated up even when covered with several layers of clothing, and they had to squash together like battery chickens to avoid the sun. It resembled if anything an overcrowded prison cell, while the Cessna's cabin stood at roasting temperature all day.

The sky next morning was a solid blue dome, but it stayed empty, and this time there was no sound, even at a distance. Once again Yves suggested a move to the oasis of palms, but again the women resisted: it was a waste of time, the plane's hold was useful for storage, and they wanted to be near their belongings.

'Looks like the mountain had better come to Muhammad,' drawled Salty, sucking a breakfast bantam bone; and, offering to build a lean-to near the plane, he went off after breakfast with the machete, Yves and Bill going along to help drag the materials back to camp.

Salty first cut a number of tall bamboo canes, then used the longest cane for a ladder to reach the palm fronds. Hacking the leafy lateral branches off to within a couple of inches, he lashed the cane to a palm trunk, tying it on bit by bit as he climbed, using the stubs of cut-off stalks for footholds. At the top he removed the machete slung on a cord over his shoulder, then hacked away at the huge fronds and at half a dozen coconuts, which Yves and Bill, who had stood clear during the operation, collected and took, in successive trips, back to camp.

'Tropical wells,' Yves described the coconuts to Bill, with a faint smile. 'Coconuts have, I suspect, saved quite a few lives in climates like this one.'

Impressed, Bill quickly counted the palm trees in the cluster (something Yves and Salty had already done). There were six in all.

That afternoon, despite the searing heat, Salty went to work.

Planting three bamboo canes upright in a line, about three feet apart, he lashed a long bamboo pole across the top to make a lintel. For lashing he had unravelled one of the aircraft's tethering ropes, using each strand separately as a cord. Next he propped a dozen tall canes up at regular intervals against the lintel and lashed them to it, tying others across these at right angles, for rafters. The result was a sort of grid. The lean-to's sides were trickier, being triangular. Salty cut half a dozen canes to different lengths, from long to short, and Anne and Marjorie, under Yves's direction, draped palm fronds over them, as if they were hanging clothes on a line. Then, splitting a long cane lengthwise, Salty made two triangular frames, sandwiched the palm-draped canes inside them and attached them to the lean-to's sides.

(This, said Yves approvingly, was traditional Khmer walling.) Finally, Salty covered the rafters with overlapping fronds secured at intervals with cords from the dismantled rope. (Traditional Khmer roofing, Yves affirmed.)

The finished shelter measured about nine feet in each direction. They could sit in a row at the entrance and, protected from the sun, gaze out at the view, such as it was. They could also stretch out comfortably inside it at night. The women need no longer sleep in the Cessna but could lie down properly, yet protected.

To spontaneous applause, Salty also produced an old mosquito net to hang across the lean-to's front. This made a fire unnecessary, except for cooking, he pointed out – a lucky thing, since most of the surrounding dead wood had already been gathered. There were few mosquitoes about – it was too dry – but more importantly, perhaps, the net would help to keep out snakes and creepy-crawlies.

The next day Salty's snares produced a guinea-pig-like rodent that he brought back to camp wrapped in his tablecloth-scarf, and hanging from the end of a pole. The scarf or *krama* was an essential Khmer possession, the women learned; useful for hats, towels, suitcases, sarongs, baby hammocks and, in emergencies, rice bowls.

Yves butchered the rodent, and Anne and Marjorie cooked it in the ashes of a fire Bill built inside a little circle of stones – something he'd learned to do as a Boy Scout. When dinner was ready, Salty pierced the coconuts and passed around plastic straws from his survival kit. The coconut juice was amazingly cool, and the colour of lemonade. The rodent tasted like veal. Sitting in a row at the lean-to entrance, shielded from the setting sun, they once again found good cause for celebration. Happy, convivial, replete, they counted themselves extremely lucky.

Increasingly impressed by Salty's practical skills, Anne told herself that had she been a pioneer, which mercifully she was not, his sort would have made a decent husband. Though not a man of words, Salty was handy, practical and unflappable. He was also surprisingly gentle, and sitting beside him Anne felt unusually relaxed and at her ease. Salty's no-nonsense, matter-of-fact style and general competence made her feel safe – and not much did – while the soft emerging cloud of ginger beard added a touch of gravitas, making him almost handsome beneath the cowboy hat that he apparently never took off, except to sleep.

Without any doubt, Salty was rapidly emerging as the most important member of the little group, and without him they would have been in serious trouble. Yves, who was neither active nor very handy, was, however, proving knowledgeable. He had grown up on a Cambodian rubber plantation, they learned. So, while Salty knew something about the wilderness and how to survive in it, Yves was familiar with Cambodia's flora and fauna. He knew what was good to eat and where they were likely to find it, as well as understanding something of the jungle's inherent, often invisible dangers. The two men complemented each other.

Food was now uppermost in everyone's mind. They looked forward avidly to the next meal and thought about food when they weren't eating. The men spent the day scavenging, setting snares, checking them repeatedly, and gathering firewood. The women cooked, tidied, talked and read. Although they were at ease with each other, their conversation was confined to the present and to practical things, tone of voice being of more significance than actual words. Water was a constant topic. They could boil it and purify it (they had purifying pills). But they couldn't find it. Mercifully, coconuts were able to quench their thirst, but without water washing was impossible. They scoured the dishes with leaves, but washing themselves or their belongings was out of the question. Rummaging through suitcases they came up with various lotions, however; and Bill, like the other men, began to grow a beard.

Aware that rescue was only a matter of time, Bill wasn't particularly worried. But he was angry and increasingly frustrated. The search party's incompetence infuriated him, and his own hands were tied. What was worse, or seemed to be, was the sense of having been pitched into a sort of psychological hell, of tumbling headlong to the bottom of a ridiculous and absurd hierarchy. William Bolton, a leader of men, a mover and shaker, creator of wealth and national prosperity, and head of one of America's most successful venture capital companies, had become a gatherer of firewood. In the primitive world where he now found himself, he wasn't even a hunter – he was a *gatherer* – by tradition, women's work (though Anne and Marjorie were afraid to do it, because of snakes). Even Yves Dumont, old, overweight, probably a drunk, and in no shape to survive wilderness life, knew what was edible. He could advise, suggest – administrate, should he choose to do so. While Salty Saltman, a Wild West hick out of some Hollywood B movie, had nimbly climbed to the very top of the greased pole of male superiority: the pole, in Bill's mental picture, being a palm tree any fool of a monkey could easily scamper up.

Increasingly, Salty's ginger ponytail swished in the camp like a provocative red rag.

'That guy is a draft-dodger,' Bill announced with conviction to Marjorie. They were strolling along the rutted logging road at sunset, the sun dropping into the jungle like a red-hot coal. 'Any guy his age should be in Vietnam. So why the hell isn't he?'

'But, darling, if he's draft-dodging surely he wouldn't be flying a plane for the American embassy, now would he?' Not that Marjorie cared whether he was a draft-dodger or not. She liked Salty and increasingly depended on him. Though she did not say this.

'He doesn't drink!' Bill thundered accusingly. 'Have you noticed that?'

Marjorie looked up in bemused bewilderment at her incandescent husband, then took his arm supportively.

'He smokes those goddamn cigarettes, grinning at the fire like some kind of cartoon show is going on. Honey, I think the guy's on dope. I think he's a pothead. Those cigarettes he smokes are marijuana.'

Convinced that Salty had strayed off the hippie trail and into Cambodia by mistake, Bill developed his scenario further. Salty was piloting one of the apparently *two* airplanes fucking Cambodia possessed, because everybody else was out there fighting the Viet Cong and protecting Southeast Asia from the Communists.

But Marjorie declared Salty a sweet and gentle soul. She liked him; indeed where would they be without him?

To which Bill replied emphatically: 'Thailand!'

But if Bill's opinion was skewed, his instincts in one respect were not. The women, sexual weathercocks, if inadvertent ones, were increasingly turning their attentions towards Salty. They solicited his advice, praised his contributions to the pot and urged upon him the choicest morsels of food. Now they began to admire his ginger beard.

Bill, fizzing with anger, was determined to turn the situation around. He was damned if he was going to end up like Francis McComber in that Hemingway story, where, on safari, when the white hunter outshines the husband, the wife shoots her husband, and not entirely by accident. Or so Bill remembered it.

That evening, the snares were empty and there was only jackfruit to eat. The resulting gloom was impossible to disguise. Observing the downcast faces as they sat in a row, hunched and silent, at the lean-to entrance, Bill saw opportunity knock. Casually, with a kind of offhand nonchalance, he volunteered to shoot something next day for the pot, provided Salty agreed to the loan of his pistol.

Salty didn't hesitate exactly, but in the silence that followed he was clearly turning the suggestion over carefully in his mind. And Bill, who didn't like being vetted by a doped-up hippie dropout, stubbornly refused to offer any credentials in reassurance. Salty could hardly refuse, Bill reasoned. And he reasoned rightly, because in the end Salty didn't.

6

IT WAS NOT QUITE DAWN, THE SKY A PALE BLUSH ABOVE the ragged savannah, when Bill headed towards the forest. He examined the pistol as he walked. Designed by Browning early in the century, the Colt had remained a favourite with American servicemen. The magazine held seven bullets, but on inspection Bill discovered only one was in it, plus another one in the chamber. Did Salty imagine he was some kind of city slicker who was going to waste his precious ammunition, or was Salty just plain scared of competition? He certainly ought to be. Or was ammunition really in such short supply? Bill doubted it. Salty never said much, but he would surely have said if he were short. No reason not to. True, the pistol's range, some twenty-five yards, made it extremely difficult to shoot wild animals. The Colt was best suited for a target that was coming towards you, or else standing still near by. There Salty had a point: success was highly unlikely. But Bill was strongly motivated: his self-respect depended on his bringing home some bacon.

Tucking the pistol into his belt, he entered the forest as the sun's first rays pierced the interior in a rush of radiant bayonets. Above the dense ground cover, vines and lianas wound like crazy plumbing beneath tall trees whose wood, Bill knew, must be worth a fortune. It was the first time he had been in the forest alone and he did not propose to venture very deep. It was too easy to get lost, since superficially everything looked the same.

Bill removed his denim hat and hung it on a branch as a signpost, regretting it wasn't brightly coloured. He had decided to go no deeper into the forest than where daylight could be seen coming horizontally through the trees, from the savannah. If he kept the sunlight on one side it would help to orient him.

Slowly and cautiously he picked his way through the undergrowth, alert and curious, a frisson of excitement, inspired by the presence of danger, infusing an extreme awareness. He was alone in a pristine world, surrounded by riotous nature: man at the very beginning of time, the planet entirely and exclusively his. And Bill loved it. But he was glad that he had a gun.

Soon enough he found what he was looking for: a log shielded by dense undergrowth, beside a small clearing. Checking underneath for snakes and vermin, Bill sat down and, taking the pistol from his belt, waited. It was a lot like waiting in a deer blind in America. But different, too, because, unlike New England's woods, the jungle was far from still. In the early morning it was full of noises, a continuous babel of languages carried on in the trees and undergrowth: screeches, exuberant bird-song, snarls, barks, mysterious sighs and whispers. The jungle was heavily populated and Bill was fascinated. The movement of leaves and branches high above, despite there being no breeze, suggested a vast if unseen trafficking. Bill wondered what monkey would taste like, and concluded he would probably find out.

Like himself, every creature in the forest was busy hunting. That was the jungle's mode of life, its only available career. But, unlike him, the others were also being hunted. Bill knew that tigers, leopards, elephants, even wild boar and rhinoceros inhabited Cambodia's jungles. But they were highly unlikely to attack a man, and it would be so marvellous to see one. At the thought gleeful anticipation coursed through his body. He began to imagine that bright eyes were peering at him, concealed in the thick foliage. He fancied he heard scurrying feet, the crash of trampled undergrowth and the dull thudding baritone of a growl or an empty stomach. As, pistol at the ready, he waited.

He sat for nearly two hours; alert, intent and very still. Whenever his mind strayed he willed it back to the present, scotching invading thoughts like the enemies they were. But he could not escape the knowledge that their predicament was serious – potentially it was very serious. Bill was tempted to blame Salty for being off course, but in truth the Boltons had requested the detour. The villains were Cambodian incompetence and Cambodian theft. But despite the search party's apparent ineptitude, it was impossible to believe that the search could be called off before any wreckage had been found. Cambodia was primitive, but hardly in the Stone Age. Moreover the embassy would be pressing the government, and Washington the embassy, being itself hard-pressed by the press. Added to which, a hundred thousand Americans were parked across the border, awaiting orders – and if the Boltons weren't found soon, Bill was convinced the troops would get them. It was a comforting thought.

But how long could they hold out? Only one palm tree remained untapped, after which they, too, would need to churn the milk ocean for something lifesaving to drink. And Bill recalled how long that took. Out of gas and out of water. The thought was no longer funny. Sooner or later rescue would, of course, arrive, but it had better be sooner. In the meantime some decisions must be made and Bill knew he was unqualified to make them: he didn't know enough. Was it possible, for instance, to walk out? The party had one knapsack between them, they had no provisions, and the women and Yves were hopelessly unsuited to a gruelling trek . . .

Bill pulled to quick attention. A small deer, no bigger than a hare, was standing in the clearing. The delicate nose, moist and pernickety, sniffed the air suspiciously. Lowering its head, the deer nibbled, then looked up, nibbled again, and again looked nervously up. When its head lowered for the third time, Bill pulled the trigger. Twice. To make sure.

Flapping, scurrying, shrieks and high-pitched cries filled the forest, as the jungle's invisible life, aroused by the shot, declared in a single desperate chorus its own strong-willed vitality. But the noise subsided quickly, like the Doppler effect of an oncoming train, building to sudden silence. Already the incident was forgotten. The jungle had no memory, and lacking conscious choice it had returned to its old ways – a routine unchanging till death: hunting, eating, mating and giving birth – the jungle's intractable law, and its avowed concomitant: survival of the fittest.

Smiling proudly, Bill approached the deer.

The animal had fallen instantly: a clean kill, probably through the heart. And hoisting the carcass on to his shoulders, like a shepherd carrying a lamb or, as Bill saw it, Hercules carrying a dead lion, he headed back to camp, suffused by a sense of accomplishment unequal to anything he could recollect. The sheer physicality of his achievement topped the more abstract satisfactions of pulling off a wizard financial deal or gluing failing companies back together; even of hunting back home, where invariably the larder was already full. Necessity made a big difference to fulfilment. Fulfilment. Bill pondered the word as he walked: full and fill; surely a tautology. Then, remembering to collect his hat, and following the line of sunlight shining forcefully through the trees on his right, he emerged from the forest, triumphant, and fifteen minutes later, his trophy draped around his neck, entered the camp a hero.

'I used both bullets,' he told Salty rather pointedly, returning the pistol.

'You got him through the heart with one of 'em,' answered Salty, examining the carcass with admiration.

Bill didn't admit – although he wanted to – that it had been with the first.

The prospect of a feast sent rapturous vibrations through the increasingly desperate camp, now frantically diverting itself with festal preparations. The fire built, Yves and Salty took up positions at each end of the spit (a pole mounted in the cleft of two forked stakes) and turned it patiently for two hours. The delicious smell wafting across the camp had everyone breathing deeply in and breathing deeply out, with 'mmms' of pleasure and anticipation, as the juices coated the meat in a luminous glaze, and the surfeit exploded grenade-like in the crackling fire beneath.

Yves, having collected romdul flowers in the forest, laid a sweet-smelling blossom beside each plate. When they sat down, Anne put hers in her hair.

Bill, as paterfamilias, carved the venison. 'Come and get it!' he called out, slicing off slabs with the machete, and praising in advance the jerky Salty had promised to make next day with what remained.

There were hardboiled eggs, from no one knew exactly what bird, and jackfruit for dessert, the rind decorated with an appealing saw-tooth design by Anne. All agreed it was the best meal they had ever eaten.

But with appetites sated and the fire's embers greying into ash, there emerged, like a groundhog from its winter burrow, a creeping suspicion that this was almost a last supper. No plane had been heard for five days, water was impossible to find, and the coconuts would not last much longer.

'Water's our real problem,' insisted Bill, purposefully nonchalant. 'Otherwise we're fine: we've got shelter, plenty of food, and good clear weather.'

'I suppose we could pray for it,' sighed Marjorie, attempting lightness, like her husband.

'Not me,' said Anne with a surprising intensity. 'I won't pray for it.'

The declaration caught everyone's attention, and polite digging revealed that Anne was the daughter of a cleric. In fact, as she reluctantly admitted, her father was a bishop.

'Hey, he's not the Bishop of Canterbury is he?' exclaimed Bill, who increasingly felt as if he was racketing around in some sort of Asian Canterbury Tale.

'He's Bishop of Bath and Wells,' Anne answered gloomily.

'Bath *and* wells. That's great, Anne. Just what we need. I hope to God he's praying for us!'

'I am sure he is,' she answered, with benign sarcasm.

Bill looked at her more closely. Maybe there was some fizz there after all.

Mention of home and family had brought to Marjorie's

mind again thoughts of her daughter, and how desperately worried she must be. Yves's daughter, everyone knew, was seriously ill, yet no one had mentioned it. They'd felt it better to pretend they didn't know. Best to keep the past tucked unobtrusively away, and concentrate on the present. In this there was an unspoken agreement.

But moods, having begun to shift, were tumbling fast. That they could have been so elated half an hour ago now seemed incredibly foolish and naive, even a kind of madness; because looked at straight, the search was evidently so off course that in the few days they could continue as they were, it was highly unlikely that they would be found. Yet they had put such faith in rescue, had been so sure they would be collected and wafted safely home – an idea that seemed as fantastic now as that of babes carried to the right address in the beaks of friendly storks. Yet what else could they have done?

It was Yves who mooted that their situation be openly addressed. 'We cannot go on as we now are,' he observed stonily.

Any one of them could have said as much: the point was what to say next; and there was silence.

'If a move is possible, I think it must be made,' he continued.

Bill agreed. He refused to stand there undecided, like Baalam's ass, he said, and die of thirst as a result. He was a man of action.

It was an attitude Salty shared. 'If we move we'll have to hide the Cessna. Tow it into the jungle, or else cover it up,' he pointed out.

Bill opposed this vehemently. The plane was proof they had survived, and spotting it a rescue party would begin to search on the ground.

But it could get broken into, even dismantled, insisted

Salty. The Cessna was his responsibility, and he had a duty to protect it.

'Broken into by whom?' Bill's heavy irony made his point. He understood Salty's duty to protect the plane, but in the unlikely event that it *was* vandalized, and the insurers refused to pay, he would pay the costs himself. Salty had his word on that.

'But if we find petrol and the plane is damaged we won't be able to take off,' reasoned Anne.

'We won't find any *petrol*.' Salty now informed them that Cambodia's only high-octane gasoline pump was at Phnom Penh airport. 'Yep, that's right: the gas has got to find us.'

This information was digested slowly in deepening dismay.

'Then we must find people,' Yves insisted.

The women looked at each other in alarm. The idea of a jungle trek was terrifying.

'Find them how?' demanded Anne. 'We can't just wander about, hoping. In that case we might as well stay here.'

Salty retrieved his charts from the plane, unrolled them and pointed to where he believed they were. Their best hope would be to find a dry riverbed and follow it towards the Tonle Sap. The rice fields – he indicated the area beyond the forest belt – were on the way.

But how could they get there without any water or provisions? They had one knapsack and two empty canteens. It was impossible.

In an effort perhaps to brighten the atmosphere, Yves, lighting a pipe and taking a few short puffs, recalled a tribe described by Herodotus. When the people wished to make an important decision, he said, they would get drunk and discuss the matter at length, then put it to a vote. The next day the issue was discussed again, at length and from every angle, but on this occasion everyone was sober. Another vote was taken, and if the verdict was the same, the tribesmen acted.

'Yeah, well we can't very well exercise that option, can we?' said Bill irritably. 'There'll have to be one vote: sober.'

Anne, her arms locked around her knees, was watching Salty lick the edges of his cigarette paper to make a bond.

'We could smoke pot,' she said.

Bill's 'I-told-you-so' was telegraphed in a rapid-fire look at his wife, who was staring at Anne in amazement.

Salty pushed his hat up slightly, scratching where the sweatband had been, and waited for the stem of dried grass he was holding over the embers to catch fire. When it did he lit up, inhaled deeply, then, frowning over the badly squashed ends, passed the cigarette to Anne.

Anne took a tiny puff and made a face, then took another puff and sat up straight, her head cocked thoughtfully, as if tasting claret in a London restaurant. With a perfunctory nod of approval she handed the cigarette to Marjorie, who was sitting beside her.

'Margie! Don't be ridiculous!'

But Bill was too late. A fat puff of smoke, as from an Indian peace pipe, floated up into the cicada-filled night air.

'You got to inhale first, before you let go of the smoke,' Salty allowed.

'Marjorie! For God's sake. Just cut it out, will you!'

'Oh, Bill!' Again an affectionate reproof, and, heeding

Salty's instructions instead of her husband's, Marjorie took a deep draw and then exhaled, one hand pressed to her chest, coughing, shaking her head and laughing ruefully.

Salty and Anne clapped in spontaneous approval, and Marjorie made a bow, a little Cambodian-like dip, before handing the cigarette back to Anne, who puffed it again, smiling broadly, before returning it to Salty.

For Bill chaos had descended. A serious insurrection was at hand. The women had gone haywire, like maenads at some Bacchanalian free-for-all, running amok to the pipes of Orpheus, who, Bill recalled with fleeting satisfaction, got cut to pieces by them in the end.

Yves could see that Bill had a rebellion on his hands – one the women were largely unconscious of – and was in grave danger of losing face. Retrieving the pipe he had been warming beside the fire, Yves didn't exactly offer it to Bill, rather he held it out, discreetly, in the neutral space between them. 'There is the possibility of opium,' he remarked pleasantly.

Bill was in battle mode, adrenalin and testosterone running high; had he received a bullet he would not have felt it. But he recognized a lifeline quickly enough, when it was offered.

'Why, thank you!' he answered warmly, as to a marked but unexpected courtesy; and, gritting his teeth on the pipe stem, gave several manly puffs. If you can't beat 'em, join 'em, he was thinking. Beat 'em at their own game.

'Well now,' observed Yves, a little later, filling two more pipes, 'shall we review our situation, prior to taking the first vote?'

'Sure!' the novice pot-smokers declared, grinning like

children; then, giggling, they fell silent, staring happily into the fire.

'I suggest we stay here till an aeroplane spots us,' Anne declared after a long pause, as if offering a new proposal. 'It's so nice here.'

'Or go on a coconut hunt,' chirped Marjorie, who was really thinking of Easter eggs. Coconuts were like big Easter eggs. 'Comb the beaches, shake the trees . . . But how will we carry them? That's the real problem, isn't it?'

'We will carry them on our heads,' declared Anne majestically. 'Like native women carry pots.'

'That is *so* brilliant!' Marjorie, hugely impressed, regarded her friend with wonder. Then, tilting her head from side to side like a metronome, she began to hum, 'I've got a lovely bunch of coconuts . . .' till, collapsing in laughter, she fell backwards on the groundsheet. 'It's all so funny!'

'Frightfully funny,' agreed Anne, with a determined nod. 'You know something?' She looked at them in surprise. 'Frightfully funny *is* frightfully funny. It really is, when you think about it.' Anne was a woman of intellect, and the two disparate words yoked together like that struck her as a potent revelation. 'It can't mean what it means. I mean, it shouldn't . . . and yet it does!' she marvelled.

Preachers' kids! thought Bill contemptuously. They were all alike: prim on the outside, tearaways underneath. He began to give up on the women and, having finished his second pipe, readily joined Yves in a third. Anger and irritation, even the desire to maintain order and impose supremacy, were fast draining away, becoming superfluous, a waste of valuable time and really not worth a nickel. In their place an unprecedented euphoria was mounting, a sense of well-being and tranquillity that was utterly new. Bill floated buoyant and serene upon its powerful and soothing tide, till the surging current, having entered his bloodstream, flowed unchecked through his arteries and, in a sudden and surprisingly ecstatic rush, penetrated the very marrow of his bones. He would gladly have spent the rest of his life in that moment, gloriously, serenely alive. Yet at the same time somehow seeming to be outside it, too.

'We have churned the milk ocean successfully,' he announced, to no one in particular. He was smiling. The thought struck him as poetic, even profound.

The pot-smokers screamed with laughter, literally fell about.

The opium-smokers smiled back, patient and uncaring; a pair of Buddhas whose knowledge and understanding had been perfected, and who, wandering in the neighbourhood of nirvana, had begun to knock expectantly on doors.

Their discussion forgotten, Bill was locked in contemplation of the new moon, thrilled by its sharp luminescence and the perfection of its crescent shape, when suddenly Salty began to sing, quietly and in a surprisingly beautiful tenor, of all things, 'Home on the Range': 'Where the deer and the antelope play. Where seldom is heard a discouraging word, and the skies are not cloudy all day.'

Anne and Marjorie joined, somewhat bayingly, in the chorus.

To Bill it sounded exquisite.

In Yves's mind another concert was being performed. The prelude to *La Traviata* had begun, the tender rhythms of the full orchestra, moving in a sedate waltz, threaded with occasional sombre undertones of mortality and impending death. Instantly the violins took over, full of sparkling gaiety, and the tempo grew, mounting and spiralling until the music, swaying back and forth between extremes, was harmoniously reunited, the opposing moods equal, elegantly balancing each other. At that moment a rush of dancers appeared, boys and girls full of youth and energy, spinning joyously around the floor, and the spirit of adolescent *joie de vivre*, of glorious life with all its promises and felicitous expectations, triumphantly prevailed.

'Cambodia is so beautiful. It makes me want to cry,' breathed Marjorie, wreathed in happy gloom.

Sitting as they were at the lean-to entrance, they had only to fall backwards, like a row of ninepins, to sleep; and eventually they did so, Anne and Salty falling together in a tangled huddle underneath Salty's cotton sheet.

Bill had his arm around Marjorie, who, snuggling close, instantly fell asleep. Bill continued to lie there on his back. His arm was numb but he felt no urge to move it, as through the veil of the mosquito net he continued to watch the moon, tracking its course with rapt attention, as the silver sickle, wielded by an invisible hand, cut with slow precision its exquisite arc across the velvet sky, the scythed stars tumbling in cascading showers in its path.

Yves sat up longest, a faint smile edged with sadness masking his own moon-like face. *La Traviata* was nearly over. The sedate waltz music of the prelude had returned, but the gaiety was gone, the earlier undertow of sadness now paramount, the unfolding tragedy irrevocable as, dressed in a silvery-blue gown, Maria Callas, in the role of Violetta, opened her incomparable throat. 'Goodbye to the past, with all its happy dreams,' she sang. '*Addio, del passato bei sogni ridenti.*' A beautiful woman in her prime, reluctantly bidding her life and love goodbye.

Such things happened.

7

BILL AWOKE, HIS EARS RINGING LIKE A GONG. IT WAS WELL past dawn and he couldn't think where on earth he was, till the evening's events sped like rushes from an uncut film across his brain. The venison he'd provided, their vague discussion, the women's ridiculous carryings-on; above all, the extraordinary tranquillity he had felt – truly a sort of heaven on earth – the moon's brilliance, and the simple clear beauty of that corny song. At which point reality delivered a vigorous thump to the left temporal lobe. The coconuts were nearly finished; they might or might not find more – but even if they did, trekking through the jungle was impossible. The truth, and it must be faced, was that they were well and truly stranded, pawns of fate, and there was nothing whatsoever he could do about it. Perhaps he would die there, the lingering death of a man lost in a desert, slowly collapsing like a plant without the benefit of rain. And what of Marjorie? Being unable to protect her was unbearable. Surely there must be a solution, something not yet thought of; he absolutely refused to give up hope. But any further reflection just then was blocked by the pressing need for a pee.

Standing beside the logging track, relieving himself,

Bill's real life – his American life – seemed about as real as a movie he had seen somewhere, and about as relevant, as gloomily he surveyed the now boringly familiar landscape. The logging track that stretched presumably to Thailand, but over mountains and through jungles, taunted provocatively. This morning it was curiously blurred, the horizon wobbling the way intense heat sometimes caused; although it was still very early.

The gong banged louder. Could his brain be permanently damaged? If so, it might not matter anyway.

Normally he would have judged something to be moving on the dusty unkempt track. Now he didn't know what to think: mist, heavy fog, a dust storm blowing up; a phalanx of ghosts wearing shrouds and beating a funereal gong, bong, bong, bong. Was he even awake? Perhaps he was having an opium dream, or hallucinating. But as he stood there, woozily fighting against a rising dread, the gong began to take on – or so it seemed – a fairly definite direction. The sound almost certainly was coming not from inside his brain, but from the direction of the logging track, where – Bill screwed up his eyes – unless he were truly hallucinating, a ghostly procession was marching in a tight phalanx eerily in his direction.

Rushing back to the lean-to, Bill woke up the others, shaking them, urging them to hurry.

'There's a fucking army coming,' he confided to Yves, as he pulled Marjorie to her feet. She smiled obligingly, imagining she'd been asked to dance. Bill hugged her close, more than faintly aware of Anne and Salty lazily untangling underneath the cotton sheet.

'Where's the pistol, for Christ's sake?'

To Bill's surprise, Salty groped under his anorak-pillow and wordlessly handed it over. Turning his back on the plaster cast of intertwined limbs, Bill tucked the Colt in his belt, covering it with his shirt tail so it would not be seen.

Minutes later, dazed, muzzy and dishevelled, the little group stood huddled together, rag-tail and dimly expectant, beside the overgrown track. The gong was getting louder, the phalanx advancing at a sombre military pace. Flutes or fifes, like the piping of shrill birds, sounded, and narrow pennants mounted on tall poles fluttered overhead, exactly as on the reliefs at Angkor Wat. Bill estimated about twenty in the procession. Far too many to fight.

'Lock the women in the plane!' he ordered.

But no one moved.

The procession halted a short distance away. A stocky man wearing baggy improvised-looking trousers, like a pirate, stepped forward and called out something in Khmer. It sounded aggressive.

'*John riab sua*,' Anne called back, and, hands clasped prayerfully, she bowed low.

Marjorie quickly followed suit.

Surprisingly, the war party bowed in return; and in a single motion moved, like a huge caterpillar, several steps closer. The man in baggy trousers spoke again, but this time Anne was out of her depth and could only bow again. However, Yves had now stepped forward, and in his deep and mesmerizing voice, answered with easy assurance.

More bowing followed on both sides. Even Bill dipped his head slightly, the hope of rescue alternating with suspicions of robbery and murder. Then he noticed a speck of colour. Like the impromptu dab of a painter's brush, it lit the sombre battalion with a patch of brilliant orange: a Buddhist robe. And at the back were standing several women.

An animated exchange was underway, Yves's fluent Khmer impressing and greatly reassuring his companions. At last treaty-making could take place, desires be made known, messages sent abroad. For almost certainly it was a party of peace. Indeed, several of the Khmers seemed to have lost interest in the Europeans and, peeling off, were now engrossed in a minute examination of the Cessna.

Salty watched them intently.

Yves said the Khmers had offered to take everyone back with them. They must get ready at once, in order to travel before it got too hot. At this, the rapture of being found was muddied by the practicalities of extensive preparation. There was a great deal of packing to do. How far was it, the women wanted to know? Salty was worried about the Cessna, which might be vulnerable now that its whereabouts were known. Anne and Marjorie insisted they couldn't pack in a few minutes; things were in such a mess. Could the Khmers possibly come back later? Now that they had been found, they could easily hold out for one more day; then everything would be ready. Salty said he would prefer that, too.

But Yves said no; today was an auspicious day and tomorrow might not be one. He told them the Khmers had seen the plane come down, but they had been waiting for an auspicious day.

'Shit, we could have died before one of those turned up,' declared Bill, shocked by the brutality of primitive superstition.

'It is certainly possible,' admitted Yves with a small shrug, adding that the Khmers were going to help them pack, and would also carry things. Already several *kramas* were being put at their disposal, and a flask of water appeared. But Yves said not to drink it; the water was untreated, and they must wait.

Frantically Anne and Marjorie began collecting clothes, while Bill threw whatever came to hand into the proffered *kramas*. *Kramas* – crammers. Could English and Khmer possibly be related, he wondered, and decided not. In just five minutes the Khmers' sense of purpose had evaporated, and the Cessna now consumed their full attention. They kicked the tyres, stroked the metal fuselage like an animal's flanks, tested with disappointment the propeller's blade, and ran about wildly flapping their arms to imitate flight. Then, discovering how to open the cockpit door, several piled inside and crawled excitedly about, Yves and Salty trying unsuccessfully to conduct an orderly tour.

Without any doubt the plane had excited far more interest than the unprepossessing Europeans – for the men, at any rate. The Khmer women were standing shyly at a distance, staring. They had never seen Caucasians before and were amazed how big they were. Their pale hair and bleached skin were very strange, best suited to creatures living under rocks who rarely saw sunlight. Were they a nocturnal species, perhaps? They didn't seem to be very wide awake. The load of belongings they were packing made no sense either.

Surreptitiously Bill stared back, fascinated by the bare-breasted yet totally unselfconscious women, a Tahitian idyll flitting optimistically across his mind.

When at last everything was ready, Salty locked the cockpit doors, and the Khmers, with smiles and gentle good-humoured laughter, loaded the suitcases on their heads, cushioning them with plinths of coiled *kramas*.

Gathering up the bundles, at a word from the burly baggy-trousered headman, whose name was Ty, they raised their banners, blew their flutes and, beating their insufferable gong, fell obligingly into line, the newcomers sandwiched somewhere in the middle.

The journey took about two hours. Leaving the logging track, they followed – as Salty had suggested – a dry riverbed winding through the forest. Occasional paths ran between the bends to make short cuts; and with the Cessna in mind Salty kept a careful mental record of the route. The forest was cool and welcoming, and the Khmers' easygoing manner within it tremendously reassuring.

Yves had joined Ty at the front of the column, and the two seemed to be enjoying an animated conversation, nodding, smiling, and from time to time gesturing with apparent enthusiasm at their surroundings. Yves's ability to throw a bridge between the two parties had catapulted him to the forefront of his own group, and when the procession paused so that undergrowth blocking the trail could be cleared, Bill, seizing the opportunity, thanked him warmly for his invaluable knowledge and assistance. Well, he was an old guy, so it was easy.

Anne and Marjorie, standing near by, handbags dangling from their arms as on a shopping trip, nodded approvingly, adding their own endorsement. Then, catching each other's eye, they grinned broadly, and unexpectedly began to laugh. It started almost noiselessly, but grew, bubbling up unrestrained and gushing forth in a cascade they were unable to contain. The tears came, they covered their faces with their hands, they bent double, they gasped for breath, they split their sides and shook their heads despairingly, but on they laughed.

The Khmers looked on, puzzled and polite at first, then, evidently judging it a desirable pastime, joined good-naturedly in the merrymaking. Soon everyone was laughing. Even those hacking at the undergrowth downed their hatchets to participate. A new sound, noisy, rippling, communal and infectious, reverberated across the intently listening jungle. Human laughter: but what did it really mean?

Bill, who found the whole thing pretty unfunny, put the women's outburst down to perfectly understandable hysterical relief. Anne and Marjorie had been under severe stress. They had borne uncertainty, danger and privation with surprising bravery and good humour, and without complaint: catharsis was only natural, and moved to sudden sympathy, Bill also felt immensely proud of them. They were both, he now perceived, highly remarkable women.

But Salty, transferring his canvas sack from one shoulder to the other before marching on, was smiling sagely to himself. He had recognized the delayed effects of marijuana.

They emerged from the forest into a landscape of extraordinary beauty. The green rice fields, nearly ready for harvest, had begun to turn pale gold. The sky, dotted with fluffy cotton clouds, was perfectly reproduced in patches of clear water that shimmered in shallow pools between the green rice paddies. Tall palms were scattered among the fields and, forming a solid fringe on the horizon, dipped and swayed like leggy, extravagantly plumed birds, flocks of them, ruffling their wings and preparing to rise in flight.

The village stood beside the riverbed, and the houses, built on stilts, were ranged along both sides of a dusty path, parallel to the riverbank and shaded by a canopy of palms, acacias, tamarisks and myriad fruit trees. The roofs were palm thatched, the walls made of sandwiched palm fronds, like Salty's lean-to. Carts, ploughs, hammocks, cooking pots, even buffaloes were parked haphazardly underneath, and simple wooden ladders gave access to the living quarters upstairs, as to chicken coops. The village was dusty and primitive but, as a staging post to the outside world, joyous to behold.

All the villagers had turned out, lining the path in front of their houses, and in spite of the dust and apparent domestic chaos in which they lived, everyone was immaculately dressed. The women wore printed pencil-slim *sampots*, and some, mostly the younger ones, wore blouses, though many did not. A few of the men had on shorts or culottes, but most wore baggy improvised trousers, like Ty's, the cloth wrapped round the waist, drawn between the legs and tucked into the waistband behind. Gaggles of children, the smaller ones naked as cherubs, clustered wide-eyed near their parents, who smiled and bowed as the pale, shabbily turned-out giants strode a little self-consciously down the village street. Anne longed to stop and pick a banana, but didn't dare.

Having passed through the village, the party, still led by Ty, left the main path and, turning down a narrow track to the left, seemed about to re-enter the jungle. A clearing loomed on one side and as they approached Ty stood aside, motioning that they should pass in, as into a corral.

Fearing a trap, everyone hesitated, and Bill, gripping the pistol hidden under his shirt tail, suddenly remembered that he had neglected to check the ammunition.

But instead of the feared ambush, the clearing, entered with so much apprehension, contained a house. Anne and Marjorie couldn't believe their eyes. It was a paradise of a house. Built on stilts in the traditional style, the square posts were smooth, with bevelled corners. Flat terracotta tiles covered the roof. The walls, made of horizontal planks, were painted cornflower blue; the open shutters, white. A loggia ornamented by a fretwork frieze ran the entire length of the upstairs façade, and instead of a ladder there was a proper staircase, with plank treads and a banister. At one corner of the house a gigantic bougainvillea, bursting with brilliant purple flowers, rose to the height of the loggia, and underneath the house were hammocks, and a broad bamboo platform about two feet high, the size of two double beds; there were also several baskets, a copper cauldron, firewood and a cement Ali Baba. The house was surrounded by palms and fruit trees: papaya, jackfruit, banana, mango, milk fruit. And wonder of wonders: in front of the house stood a well, with a bucket dangling from the pulley overhead.

'Pinch me,' whispered Marjorie, gazing up at the loggia. 'We're bewitched, aren't we?'

Ty indicated that they should go up the stairs, and Yves that they must first remove their shoes.

Upstairs the spacious interior was divided by a plank partition into two large rooms. The floor, a beautifully polished hardwood, was covered with woven mats. At the back, tacked on as an annex, was a sort of kitchen with a primitive terracotta stove. Crockery and utensils were neatly ranged on shelves above a wooden counter. And everything was spotless. The only other furnishings were some wooden chests and two bamboo platforms that Yves said were for sleeping on; mattresses and mosquito nets would almost certainly be stored inside the chests.

'It's simply enchanting!' cried Anne. 'I can't get over how lovely it is. And water! God, how I long for a drink of water and a bath!'

Salty, armed with purifying pills, was already carefully letting the bucket down into the well.

Two women appeared with trays and, smiling and bowing, left them on the platform under the house. There was tea in coconut cups and rice cakes wrapped in banana leaves. Frangipani blossoms adorned the bamboo trays. Yves said that when they had rested they would be formally welcomed: 'You can expect a feast. The Khmers love that sort of thing and jump at any opportunity.'

They took turns in the outhouse, which in addition to a lavatory – a sort of shower base with a hole in it that Anne said was very French – contained a concrete trough filled with water, a dipper alongside. This was a shower, Yves explained. You doused yourself – repeatedly.

Anne had discovered towels and sarongs in a chest, and after her shower she wrapped herself in a sarong and perched on the wellhead, smiling ecstatically, her eyes closed, her face raised to the sky, lifting her long corn-silk hair and spreading it out like sheaves to dry in the sun. She was, Bill saw for the first time, a very beautiful woman. How could he possibly have missed that fact before? He was incredulous.

Tasting the now purified water, Salty declared it 'as good as branch water back home'. They were gathered around the wellhead, an atmosphere of hilarity prevailing as, cups filled to the brim, they raised them in unison, toasted each other, and drank without stopping, breathing or thinking, eagerly holding the empty cups out for refills.

'It's a truism, I know,' observed Anne, resuming her seat on the wellhead, 'but water really *is* the most important thing in life. And yet we take it so for granted.'

'Have you ever noticed that it's invisible?' asked Marjorie, in earnest wonder.

The others gaped in bemused surprise.

'I mean, it's colourless. Isn't it strange that the most important thing in life is invisible? If water didn't ripple, you could fall into a pool by mistake and drown. So it's sort of treacherous, too.'

Everyone laughed, except for Yves, who saw Marjorie was struggling with something faintly akin to philosophy. 'So much that is important seems to be invisible,' he said kindly.

'Yes, doesn't it?' she rejoined, flushed and feeling very grateful.

Bill said that as far as he knew no one had ever got a monopoly, or corner, on water. 'Unlike coal or iron or anything else the earth produces.'

'Water is from the sky, Bill,' declared his mildly reproving wife.

The women decided to wear their best frocks in honour of the feast, and also because they were the only things that were clean.

The men shaved and dressed downstairs, where a small mirror was found nailed to a post. Bill had to stoop about a foot to use it. They assembled, rumpled but well scrubbed, in front of the house, and, as the women descended, burst into spontaneous applause, grinning and clapping; Bill produced an admiring off-key wolf whistle.

Delighted, Anne and Marjorie swung their hips and fluttered their arms a bit, waving the sandals they were carrying in their hands. Anne was pleased to see that Salty, unlike the other men, hadn't shaved; and taking his arm at the foot of the stairs, she gave him a rare and surprisingly brilliant smile.

Salty grinned back foolishly. 'You look great,' he said.

What on earth, wondered Bill, could a woman in her right mind possibly see in Salty?

Presently Ty reappeared, bringing with him an old man who, they were told, had reported an egret's departure, and should be thanked. For the past week, they now learned, an egret had been perching on the house's roof, and when this happened it was believed to be someone's ghost. Only when the bird departed, therefore, could a house be reoccupied, without causing serious harm to the occupants.

'You mean a fucking bird is what was holding up our rescue?' Bill demanded, as they followed Ty down a dusty path towards the pagoda.

'Other spirits will have had their say,' replied Yves wryly. 'The *neak ta* almost certainly will have been consulted.' The *neak ta* was the spirit of an ancestor or other dead person that protected the whole village. Yves nodded towards a small open pavilion erected beneath a broad-spreading acacia tree, beside the path. On the cement floor lay a piece of gnarled wood about a foot long. 'That's the *neak ta*.'

'What, that stick? Come on!' Guffawing, Bill looked closely at Yves to see if it was a joke, then looked back over his shoulder at the well-housed stick. 'A builder of Angkor Wat, I presume.'

* * *

The Boltons had never seen a Buddhist pagoda or *wat* before, and they were flabbergasted. The white stuccoed temple was the size of a big American church, but grander and a great deal more ornate. And rising as it did alongside a collection of palm-thatched huts, it awed in its way as much as had Angkor Wat. Tall square pillars – Bill counted twenty-six – surrounded the four sides, their capitals golden half-man, half-bird creatures that appeared to support, on upraised wings, the truly extraordinary roof. Terracotta-tiled, it was constructed in three layers, like three great tents, floating miraculously one above the other. The eaves of each layer were trimmed with a delicate fretwork frieze, and from every corner there flashed a sort of inverted sickle, like a raised scimitar. Anne said these were abstract *nagas*.

Within the temple precinct stood a wooden dwelling, not on stilts, and on the veranda lounged several young Buddhist monks. Newly washed robes, large rectangles of cloth in various shades of yellow, saffron and brown, were spread out on the veranda rail in front of them to dry. The monks regarded the visitors with a remarkable nonchalance, as though they routinely passed by every day or were part of the landscape; and they gave no sign of welcome.

Their destination was the building next door. Crowned by another spectacular multi-layered roof, it functioned as town hall and village school. Mounting the stairs, the party entered a vast shadow-laden hall, easily over a hundred feet long. There were three or four small open cubicles near the entrance, and in one or two of them candles were burning and a kneeling monk was quietly chanting his prayers. The hall was dark and cool and you could see through to the other end, which opened on to a large balcony, giving on to a sheltered garden beyond. On the floor at that end people were sitting in little groups. There was the smell of incense and a gentle wind-like chiming of bells and xylophones – the fairy-like tinkling of a traditional gamelon orchestra. As the newcomers approached, everyone rose and bowed, their hands held prayerfully against their hearts in a *sompeah*. Ty offered up words of formal welcome, and Yves made a short speech in reply. Then everyone sat down again on the floor, each family making its own circle.

A most excellent meal arrived. A delicious soup tasting of lemongrass was followed by rice, steamed crabs, dried salted fish, shrimps, mangoes, bananas and papayas. Everyone received a rice bowl and a spoon. Food was placed in the centre of each circle, and using your fingers you helped yourself.

Enthralled, Marjorie declared she could happily stay there for a week. It was all so beautiful and serene, and everyone so very nice, and so polite – so well turned out, too. 'You'd never guess they lived in huts!' she whispered to Anne.

When the meal was over, Ty joined them and, in response to eager questions, told them something of the history of their extraordinary house. It had been built by a Cambodian doctor and his wife, he said. The doctor was half French and the couple lived in Phnom Penh, but came to the village for two months every year, during the dry season. The doctor was writing a book. Ty didn't know what it was about. He said the doctor also wrote stories, and sometimes he read them to the villagers. He had cured many people who were ill, and his wife had taught the village women how to knit. Then, very sadly, on a trip to visit their son, a student in

Paris, the couple had died. No one knew the exact details, but the *neak ta* believed it was a road accident. What else could it be, said Ty, in an unexpected show of pragmatism. He said the house now belonged to the couple's son, and everything was kept in order, awaiting his return.

When did all this happen, they wanted to know.

Ty said about three years ago. No one knew exactly, because they only found out later, when the couple failed to appear and enquiries were made. Misreading their concern, he said it was most unlikely the son would return while they were there, so they shouldn't worry too much on that score.

'No,' said Bill, suppressing a smile; and seizing the opportunity, he politely broached, through Yves, the subject of their own imminent and necessary travels. They needed to get word to Siem Reap as soon as possible. Could Ty arrange that for them? It was a matter of some urgency, since people would, understandably, be very worried about them.

Hearing this, Ty smiled and nodded, as did others squatting near by, who were listening too. When Ty replied, Yves put one or two further questions to him, before translating, a process watched by the Khmers with rapt attention.

'Ty says there is no problem. When the rains come we can go to Siem Reap without any difficulty.' Yves didn't sound surprised.

'I don't think he understands,' said Bill shortly, irritated by Yves's own obtuseness. 'Please tell him we don't have to go there ourselves; we only need to get word, to notify people, and they'll come here. Say that if he'll arrange to send someone the man will be well paid; but that's all he has to do – send someone.' Bill had turned towards Ty. 'I have money. I can pay,' he said slowly, in English.

There was a further exchange among the Khmers, polite and affable; and again Yves translated: 'Ty says they are truly sorry, but it will not be possible before the rains, because the journey must be made by river. The river is their only road, and right now most of it is dry.'

'But that's crazy! We can't hang around here for four months. We need to get a move on.' Masking his annoyance and speaking through Yves, Bill kept his eye fixed on Ty, the better to judge the mood of his response. 'Please say that if the villagers will mount an expedition, cut their way through the jungle or do whatever it is they have to do, I will pay their costs, and they can take as many men with them as they need.'

Several others had gathered round, standing or squatting, and a further amicable exchange took place, some of the listeners voicing opinions among themselves, with sympathetic smiles being cast repeatedly at the foreigners.

'They say the rice harvest is about to begin,' said Yves, 'and all the men will be needed here.'

Instantly Bill recognized terra firma, and he relaxed. It was a bargaining stance, and Ty, smiling expectantly – a cat eyeing a defenceless canary – was waiting for Bill's next move. Bill judged his position to be relatively weak, on the face of it, but at least he now knew where he was, in what ball park; and the game was one that he was good at and could easily afford to play.

'Please say I fully appreciate their problem, and I don't want to cause them any loss or personal inconvenience. I'll not only pay the men well, but I'm prepared to compensate them in full for any rice lost as a result of the expedition.'

A short but animated discussion ensued amongst the intently listening but also smiling and chattering Khmers.

'They say that such an expedition would not only be difficult, but would consume the entire time needed for this year's harvest.'

'Greedy little bastards!' exclaimed Bill under his breath, a grudging admiration beginning to thread his growing impatience. They had him over a barrel and they knew it.

'OK, what the hell; I'll buy their fucking harvest, if necessary! Well, tone that down a bit if you can, but we've got to get out of here. Right now.'

When this proposal was communicated, the Khmers laughed with delight at their guest's charming sense of humour. 'If the gentleman buys our harvest, we shall have to eat his money,' they said, evidently highly entertained.

It was like butting against a rubber wall. It gave, and then you bounced back to where you'd started. 'These guys are either pretty wily or they're pretty thick,' said Bill, to no one in particular – he was just letting off steam. He didn't mind about the money – whatever they asked wouldn't be very much. It was a professional thing, a question of getting the best deal in the circumstances – a sort of poker game. And in poker, even if your hand was weak, with enough money and a straight face you could usually stay in the game and, biding your time, eventually get ahead. The ultimate trump card, of course, was money – also the ultimate shield. And in a tight corner such as this, Bill pitied the poor, who, unarmed, and therefore practically naked in the thick of battle, simply didn't stand a chance.

Folding his arms and exuding the confident nonchalance of a rich but prudent man, Bill delivered his familiar boardroom summing up: 'Please tell Mr Ty and his pals that I will compensate them for any loss to their harvest, and I will pay his men extremely well if he will send an expedition overland to Siem Reap as soon as possible. If they have to buy rice elsewhere, because they run short at home, I'll pay for that too. And the cost of transport. In addition, I will make a generous donation to the village, to be spent as they see fit.' He wondered if he should name a figure, but there was no time to consult Yves, and an evenly paced momentum was important.

More discussion, smiles, affabilities.

'They say that you will be very happy here. They are honoured to have you in their village, and while you are here they will help you in every way they can. Then, when the rains come they will escort you "and all your family" to Siem Reap with the greatest pleasure.'

'We don't need a fucking escort! Can't they get that straight? What we need is a courier!' Clearly he should have named a figure. Behind all the bowing and scraping, that was really what they wanted to know. How much? But Bill was also mildly alarmed. He had remembered Evelyn Waugh's *A Handful of Dust*, in which the hero, rescued in the jungle, ends up reading Dickens to his illiterate rescuer for the rest of his life. It was silly, of course. He knew that. They were simply waiting for his next move. And suddenly Bill recalled the Buddhist monks, their power, pervasive influence and ubiquitous begging bowls.

'OK. Let's get this over with, settle it once and for all,' he said, equanimity now fully restored. 'Tell them – and this is my last offer, so let's make that absolutely clear – that if they will get a message through to Siem Reap, in addition to the payments already mentioned, I will donate one hundred dollars to the village and another hundred dollars to the pagoda, whatever that is in riel.'

And turning to Ty and nodding – it was almost a *sompeah* – Bill produced a rictus of a grin, redolent if not of triumph exactly, then of equality – the sort produced by disputed draws, dead heats and pyrrhic victories: *primus inter pares*. Even Burt Lancaster at his most exuberant had never shown so many teeth. But he knew he had them. He could read it in the beaming faces when Yves delivered the good news in solid monetary terms.

8

SHANGRI LA, THEY CALLED THE HOUSE, AT MARJORIE'S suggestion; and all agreed that it was apt as, sitting on the loggia in chairs rigged up from hammocks cut in two and mounted by Salty on to bamboo frames, they sipped tea from little Chinese bowls and, with a dazed tranquillity, watched the sun rise in an opaline sky. In the evening they were there again, drinking rice wine and enjoying the same view, this time lit from behind, an alchemist-engineered projection that turned their world into twenty-four-carat gold.

The frustration of finding that they were truly stranded had been fierce at first, the necessary shifting of gears excruciating – particularly for Bill, for whom their hosts' intransigence had beggared belief. Sending a messenger to Siem Reap was certainly possible, and the couriers, well paid and spared the monotony of another harvest, would have come out better off. What then had gone wrong? Had something been left out of the offer, or was there perhaps a flaw in the translation? Yves, one way or another, was never very sober. But whatever it was, Bill had had to accept it.

'These folks sing from different hymn sheets, that's all,' Salty had obliged, in what was probably closest to the truth. 'The Orient's just real inscrutable, like they say.'

'They never had the Enlightenment, like we did, is why,' declared Bill, still smarting from his recent defeat. 'So they can't think straight. Their minds jump around like people's do in dreams. They can't reason, so you can't reason with them, or expect them to be reasonable. They leave all their thinking to gods or spirits, or whatever they are; just clue them in and sit around waiting for the answer, then do as they're told.'

'Gods are useful to the powerless,' observed Yves, with just the mildest shade of irony.

Which Bill missed. 'Well, these people will go on being powerless till they can stand on their own two feet and take some responsibility for their actions.'

Domrei Chlong meant 'elephant crossing', they learned. But the elephants had long since moved further west, into the Kulen hills. Bill, however, still seething from ignominious defeat, gleefully envisaged a large herd rampaging down the village street. He pictured himself astride a huge bull elephant, waving Salty's pistol, like one of the Rough Riders, and heading hell-for-leather towards Siem Reap, as the Khmers scurried frantically up their ladders and into their coops for safety.

But once the hand of fate, bad luck or rank incompetence had finally been accepted, the bitter pill digested, and the fact that they had no choice and were completely powerless had sunk in, they had with admirable alacrity settled down, addressing domestic details and beginning to make a place for themselves at Domrei Chlong.

To the Khmers they represented an extended family, and they had a surname: Barang. The word meant

'Westerner', said Yves, or more precisely 'French', which to Cambodians was the same thing.

'Possibilities for a soap opera,' suggested Anne, lying in a hammock, hands clasped behind her head, a small spiral-back notebook open on her lap. 'The Khmers and the Barangs. Like Montagues and Capulets, only more cheerful and banal.'

'Or cowboys and Indians,' offered Bill, returning from the bathhouse wrapped in a cotton sarong. And it was obvious who the Indians would be.

'Why go and turn it into a conflict?' protested Marjorie. 'Everyone's being so nice to us; and so helpful, too. It's a comedy if it's anything, and a perfectly charming one.' She gave the hammock she was sitting in an emphatic little push.

'*Une comédie humaine*,' Yves volunteered, stretched out on the platform, where he had been enjoying a post-prandial snooze.

'People love conflict,' continued Bill, answering his wife. 'And if there isn't any you can be sure they'll generate some, and then take sides. Like backing a football team. That's the secret of a good Western: them and us.'

'A good Eastern, too,' said Anne. 'The Pandavas and the Kauravas.'

'Yeah,' agreed Salty from the corner, where he was busy making a peg-board for hanging up their clothes. 'That's a real good story.'

Anne showed her surprise. 'You've read the *Mahabharata*, Salty?'

'Yep, sure have. It's in the plane somewhere. I ought to go and get it.' Salty was worried about the plane and had twice retraced his steps to check on it.

'There's this band of five brothers, the Pandavas,'

Anne told Marjo...
Kauravas, are their ...
famous battle. Mahabh...
which the Pandavas, who...
what's interesting is, they kn...
happen and that they're going ...
so they will destroy their ent...
The gods have told them and they ...
let it happen. That's the Eastern dim...
them.'

Salty pitched in. 'The narrator is tellin... ...ory to this elephant-headed god, who's writing i... down. He looks sort of like Babar. At one point the pen gives out, so Babar breaks off a tusk and goes on writing with that.'

'A wonderful touch!' agreed Anne.

'C'mon, it's kids' stuff. Fairy tales.' Sitting on the platform edge, Bill brushed the grass off his bare feet. 'They're children, like I said.'

'I'd like to read it, Salty; it sounds enchanting,' offered Marjorie.

But Salty was grinning at Anne and she at him, and balm was not required.

In the lean-to everyone had shared one room, but a house, even a two-roomed one, had revived respect for domestic conventions. Salty and Yves had volunteered to sleep on the platform under the house, and the Boltons without any hesitation had appropriated the inner room upstairs, being the more private of the two, leaving Anne the room that opened on to the loggia, which at least meant Salty could pay his nocturnal visits discreetly. But balcony scenes, even those without the benefit of Shakespeare, or a Cyrano in the wings, deserved a romantic line or two.

below in a soft whisper, me.'

t seem to mind.

alty so much,' Marjorie volunteered, as the women were picking papayas in the garden. It was her first attempt to broach the relationship.

'I like him, too,' Anne had replied. 'For the present it works very well.'

Marjorie was impressed if a little shocked by this casual, even buccaneering attitude, so typical of her daughter's generation, and part of a new, assertive independence. But she had quickly changed the subject.

They had inherited a gardener, Kieu, a wiry little man who wore wide-legged khaki shorts (cherished hand-me-downs from the doctor) and whose black hair, apparently unaffected by gravity, grew parallel to the earth, rather than pointing magnetically in its direction. Kieu had looked after the garden on and off for years. Each morning he watered, weeded, checked the ripening fruit and hoed the vegetable patch, muttering non-stop. Anne and Marjorie, eager apprentices, followed at a respectful distance at first, afraid to interrupt. But Kieu wasn't talking to himself, or even to the plants, exactly. Rather he was communing with the spirits that lived inside them: placating, encouraging, retailing local news and gossip, and generally chatting them up.

'They do look healthy,' Marjorie allowed, as she and Anne, anxious to get to know the garden, discreetly closed in on Kieu, grinning enthusiastic interest.

Kieu's wife, San, had taken charge of the cooking and cleaning. San was nut brown and surprisingly rotund for a Khmer. She had a typical Khmer nose, broad and flattish, and beautiful white teeth that gave her, in

Marjorie's Southern vocabulary, a watermelon smile. Marjorie liked her at once. San reminded her of Hattie: there was something solid and down-to-earth, practical and good-natured about her that calmed and reassured. San had cooked for the doctor and his wife, and knew some French recipes, she said – if she could remember them. 'So many monsoons ago.'

'Raw tattoo,' she announced, presenting them with an exotic Oriental ratatouille, the onions, aubergines and tomatoes spiced with hot peppers and garlic, and mixed with lotus seeds and water convolvulus.

'Konfutu.' San placed another dish before them, served separately Western-style, as a dessert.

'Tastes like jam,' said Bill. 'With pepper and stuff in it.'

Yves was smiling. 'Konfutu must be *confiture*. The Cambodians don't usually make preserves, unless it's fish.'

'With so much fruit around I suppose there's no need,' remarked Anne, wrinkling her nose. 'But let's steer San off French cuisine, shall we? I'd rather eat my jam on croissants.'

Marjorie disagreed. Sugar with peppery spices was an original touch. She was going to get the recipe, maybe even take a jar or two home. It would be wonderful with ice-cream, something really unusual.

In addition to rice, fish, soup and rice-noodle dishes, San made several 'desserts' using fresh fruit flavoured with coconut, palm sugar, ginger and cinnamon. She made little cakes from shredded coconut and others from sticky rice, wrapped in banana leaves. Bananas appeared almost as often as rice. They were fried, mashed, baked, eaten raw and used as garnishes, and their leaves were turned into plates, hats, fans, dusters and cooking foil.

But though food was plentiful, rarely it seemed were culinary possibilities rejected. Even red ants and termites were eaten. Yves said they were full of protein, a godsend in a country where meat was rarely consumed. Crispy and a little salty when fried, they were, once squeamishness was overcome, not too bad.

Anne began to make notes, ideas for articles flitting vaguely about in her head, like moths without the benefit of a candle: Khmer cuisine; Khmer domestic customs; religious beliefs and superstitions; legends and folklore, perhaps? Each morning, San put several rice grains on a leaf and placed it, as an offering, under the eaves. Was the spirit world supposed to eat, or, being a parallel world, did it eat symbolically? Or did spirits simply like a lot of attention? And did it really matter? Such beliefs were society's glue and to a degree its sense of security. Part of local culture. But what was culture exactly, and how important? This sort of speculation appealed to Anne. The cranial moths perceived the faintest flickering of light.

Marjorie's approach was different. Joining San in what Bill called a 'kitchen jamboree', she cut fruit into chunks, boiled palm sugar and stirred the thickening concoction to make a papaya konfutu. Marjorie had never thought about where jam came from, except a grocery store, and the miraculous transformation of nature's produce was a revelation to her. 'It's really amazing,' she told her husband with childish enthusiasm. 'And so simple. You boil fruit with a bit of sugar, and it thickens and stays like that. Maybe for ever, if you keep it sealed!'

Barang activities were followed with great interest in the village, especially by the children, who trailed about wide-eyed, with ready grins, becoming bashful and shy when noticed individually. Anne and Marjorie drew them like magnets. At first the children gathered on the path and stared; then, gaining courage, they invaded the garden on tiptoe and, advancing *en bloc* to the house, sat down outside it cross-legged on the ground, as other children might before a television set.

'You see, we *are* a soap opera,' whispered Marjorie.

The children were quick to repeat any English word that they could catch and would bounce it between themselves, then back to Anne and Marjorie, like a ball.

'Horrutoodai,' they cried out, grinning proudly.

'How. Are. You. Today,' enunciated Anne, carefully setting out each word, between long pauses.

The children were all ears. 'Hora utoo dai? Hara u too dai?' And the next time they got it. 'Har ar u too dai?'

Breaking down a phrase, Anne and Marjorie encouraged the children to test each word, polishing it carefully on the tongue. Then, like a necklace being carefully restrung, the sentence was, to great excitement, reassembled and the words repeated over and over, like a rosary. Rosary-making – they even called it that – became a game. The phrases grew longer, the words sometimes put together in a slightly different order, or strung with a mysterious new word that, fascinating in itself, when joined with others magically divulged a hidden meaning.

Till, almost without realizing it, the women found that they were running a school.

Essentially it was a school for girls. Boys went daily to the pagoda, where they learned to read and write and become good Buddhists. Girls stayed at home, looked after younger siblings and learned to be good housewives. Now, however, a dozen spindly-legged children with shoe-button-black eyes turned up at Shangri La each morning, evidently keen to speak English, and without any doubt keen to gaze in rapt enchantment at Anne and Marjorie, two great goddesses descended from on high, glamorous role models that the little girls, though keen to worship, were equally ambitious to emulate.

The girls sat cross-legged on the bamboo platform beneath the house, several holding younger siblings on their laps. They were exceptionally well behaved and could sit still for surprisingly long periods, the result perhaps of living together at close quarters. Anne and Marjorie stood before the platform or perched informally on its edge. There were no books or pencils or paper. Everything was done by rote, and the speed with which the children learned astonished the two women. Rhythm and repeated chanting were the key, instilling words with an extraordinary rapidity. But the children's accents and pronunciation were remarkably good as well.

Whenever an impasse arose, Yves was hauled in to translate. His deep voice seemed to mesmerize the little girls and his explanations, involving big theatrical gestures, riveted their attention. 'Sea' was '*sa-mot*', and '*sa-mot*', 'sea'. But as the children had never seen the sea, Yves described it to them. He made broad over-arm swimming motions, turning his head to one side, for breathing, in the classic Australian crawl. He made great circles with his arms to show enormity and little swirls of the hands, as if conducting an orchestra, to illustrate waves. Then, sprinkling salt into a cup of water, he passed it round for the children to taste. The little girls now had experience of the sea.

'He's an actor!' whispered Anne, delighted. 'A great ham of an actor!'

Yves was enjoying himself, and at the women's insistence he began to teach something more important than English: the Khmer alphabet, and how to write it. Climbing off the platform, the little girls squatted in the dust, inscribing letters in it with sticks. Anne joined this class as a pupil, sitting on the platform edge, writing her own letters on a foolscap pad.

Anne also taught mathematics, using dried beans. The children seemed to have an innate understanding of adding and subtracting beans, and Anne was reminded of Plato's belief that a slave, who had been asked several leading questions and had managed to solve a geometric calculation, had had the knowledge pulled out of him rather than put in. For it did seem like that. In two days the little girls were counting, singsong, to twenty in English, and not long afterwards Anne could do so in Khmer. Within the week everyone was into thousands.

Anne and Marjorie, putting their heads together, devised a primer. 'The cat sat on the mat' was adapted to 'The rat sat on the mat.' 'Tom and Jane go to the seaside' became 'San and Kieu go to the rice fields.' But 'San and Kieu ate dinner' caused a problem. In Khmer, 'to eat' also meant 'to eat rice'. Eating and rice were virtually indivisible: San and Kieu had to have rice for dinner. Language confined as well as expanded meaning, the women discovered with some surprise.

Soon a new sound could be heard throughout the village, a chirping lilting litany reminiscent of Mary Poppins: 'Hello Goodbye! Yes No! Thank You Please!' was chanted endlessly; and the girls being magpies as well as natural mimics, this was soon elaborated to include Bill's 'Hi ya doing?' a phrase that set Anne's British teeth on edge.

'How're *you* doing?' Bill would reply to gaggles of

infants who, finding themselves objects of direct address, hid their faces but nevertheless stood their ground, eagerly awaiting the next development.

The children also learned a proper song. 'You Are My Sunshine' was chosen because of the climate. 'You'll never no, deer, how much I love you, please don take my son shine away,' permeated the rice fields and reverberated along the spidery network of jungle paths from morning till night, adding yet another voice to the jungle's cacophonous and unorchestrated choir.

In practical matters, Salty, to Anne's smug satisfaction, still reigned supreme. Having rigged up hammock chairs, he constructed a new shower: a stoppered jug with a spout, which you tied upside-down in a tree. Showering naked surrounded by nature proved pure bliss. The caress of a breeze on bare skin, a sense of primal intimacy with nature or of unusual freedom – even abandonment; whatever it was, it smacked of paradise.

Soon Salty had branched out, if inadvertently, into diplomacy.

'His Excellency Our Serene Ambassador,' Anne pronounced with affection, when he volunteered to represent them at the rice harvest. No one else was interested. The women found the prospect of wading about in water-logged fields downright scary. What mightn't one step on? Bill had other, bigger fish to fry, if he could catch them, and Yves was too old and fat to be press-ganged into manual labour.

Wyoming's pastoral tradition lay deep in Salty's heart, but Cambodia's primitive agrarian world struck even deeper. Cutting sheaves with a sickle, threshing with water buffaloes, winnowing in shallow baskets held in arms outstretched to the wind, and husking by pounding with a mortar and pestle – activities unchanged for three thousand years or more – felt right, somehow. The sickle, once Salty had mastered it, was like an extension of his hand. Embracing a sheaf in its curve, pushing the sheaf against the blade and pulling the sickle towards him, he delivered up the sheaf and, laying it aside to be collected, moved forward in line with the other workers, their bodies bent at right angles in the muddy water, their tucked-up garments exposing bare brown legs, their heads wrapped in *kramas* or covered by the sort of hat that Chinese coolies wore.

Salty relished the laughing good humour of the people at their tasks, the improvised songs floating across the fields, the jokes and bonhomie, the spirit offerings stuck on split bamboo canes along the paddy edges, and the occasional scarecrows that, clothed in trousers, looked uncannily like Barangs, standing dazed and forlorn in the paddies, or their shades.

Returning home in the evening, Salty would stop to watch the buffaloes threshing the sheaves. They moved ponderously in a slow and steady circle under a tree, their hoofs separating grain from chaff as the dust swirled about them in a rosy cloud and the sun sank, round and red, on the horizon. It induced the serenity of an expensive drug.

Each day he brought home from the paddies crabs, snails, tiny shrimps and fish, which San cooked with coriander, water convolvulus, pepper and lemongrass, and which everyone ate with gusto, chasing mouthfuls with draughts of surprisingly cool palm beer. But they could not get used to eating sitting on the floor. So Salty volunteered to make a dining table.

Constructed from old planks found stored in the town hall, the table caused much talk in Domrei Chlong when word got out that the Barangs planned to eat off it. It was too high to sit around, and far too small for the oversized Barangs to sit upon. The village was unanimous in this view.

Given the near impossibility of making dining chairs, Salty opted for stools made from tree stumps. He had to use dead wood because green wood was sacred: there were spirits living inside, and to harm them would bring the villagers bad luck. It was hard work digging, prising, hacking and then sawing to make the stumps level, and in the end Salty made only three, placing the table beside the platform so two people could use it as a bench.

In the third week of residence, lunch was served al fresco and without leg cramps. San thought it a hilarious affair, and so did all the villagers, who regularly found excuses to trot past the clearing at mealtimes and witness the Barangs' extraordinary carry-on, sitting around their ridiculous-looking table on tree stumps.

'Don't fall off!' shouted little boys, who popped up out of nowhere, then ran off, yelping with laughter. And Yves overheard in the market, amidst much amusement – for the Khmers loved to laugh: 'The Barangs eat sitting in trees, like the monkeys do.'

Each morning a market was held near the pagoda. The Khmers called it a wax market, because, having begun at dawn, it melted away when it got hot, about mid-morning. The vendors, all women, sat on mats beside their baskets of vegetables, stacks of dried and salted fish, live fish swimming in tubs, rice (so many different kinds!), fruit, soybeans, peanuts, herbs, and Cambodia's drug of choice, betel nuts. But though people seemed to have these things already the market was always active, the commerce conducted for the most part by barter. Many of the customers came from nearby hamlets, and news and gossip were exchanged as well as goods; and on occasion land was sold and marriages cagily brokered.

But no meat was sold in the wax market. Buddhists believed in reincarnation and, as San pointed out, 'If you killed an animal it might be your grandmother, and who would want to do a thing like that?' Chickens, however, were sold for laying and sometimes cock-fighting, and, on occasion, sacrifice. Domesticated from jungle fowl, they were brightly coloured, with glossy black and red and yellow plumage. The Barangs bought them regularly, and when it was dark and San had gone home, Yves and Bill wrung their necks, Salty plucked them and Marjorie and Anne, having collected the feathers for pillows, tended the barbecue, basting the chickens with San's hot pepper and tomato sauce. They were delicious, the more so for being illicit.

Soon Salty was setting snares again and covert barbecues became a regular, much-looked-forward-to event, with loud whispering, smothered laughter and abundant refilling of cups with palm beer.

Every morning the monks or *bonzes* (Bill called them bonzos) toured the village with their begging bowls, and the villagers, no matter how poor, filled them willingly. Anne claimed this wasn't as generous as it looked: the Khmers wanted to earn as much merit as possible, in order to secure a favourable reincarnation.

'We did it for badges in the Boy Scouts,' boasted Bill. 'But this sounds like those medieval indulgences. When people catch on there'll be a Reformation, like there was in Europe – and with those god-kings over here.' Though privately Bill found that particular scam rather impressive.

Anne said that the peasants still believed in god-kings: they revered Prince Sihanouk as a god.

The *bonzes* stopped regularly at Shangri La, accepting alms with the same disinterested equanimity they had shown the Barangs on their arrival. Bill occasionally gave them money – they were useful as schoolteachers, maybe even as psychologists, if nothing else. But Anne and Marjorie always gave them food, laying it on little mats for collection, since women were literally untouchable.

'Poor things, they could do with some hugs and motherly affection,' Marjorie opined. 'Mind you, they don't look sad, just sort of pleasantly vague.'

'Stoned,' surmised Bill, regretting that Yves's opium supply had, with his help, run out. Happily, however, Salty had discovered marijuana on sale in the wax market, and now everyone smoked the occasional after-dinner joint. Anne claimed she slept better. She also believed it made for camaraderie, which extensive conversations in so disparate a group might have failed to do.

Although the wax market was mainly for food, fabricated goods were also sold: sickles (mostly after the harvest), cloth, kerosene, kerosene lamps, crockery, copperware, and the big cement jars that served as cisterns. But to purchase these required money, and money was perpetually in short supply. The peasants were forced to borrow from the Chinese, Cambodia's merchant class, at usurious rates. Yet families owned sufficient land to live on, not uncomfortably; they built their own houses from free materials, grew their food and made their own clothes. Despite this virtual self-sufficiency, however, the burden of debt weighed upon the people like millstones (the Khmers also loved to gamble).

Sitting on the town-hall steps with Yves and Ty, Bill, hearing of this, had instantly pinpointed the problem: it was balance of payments. The villagers bought very little, but even so they bought more than they sold, and this upset the balance of payments. 'If you want money you need something to sell. It's as simple as that. Export, and you're out of the woods.' (Later Bill thought this an unfortunate metaphor, but perhaps Yves had reworked it diplomatically in translation.) 'I'll give it some thought,' he promised. And he did.

Khmer agriculture was without any question archaic, but rice-growing, although spread out over several months, involved only some two months of actual labour each year. By early February the rice was stored and there was nothing further to do till May, when seeds saved from the previous harvest were sown in the newly ploughed nurseries. Why not use this free time to produce a commodity for export?

Bill thought they might grow rubber. Thailand wasn't far, and if timber made it there, so could rubber – straight to a tyre factory he happened to know about. Yves, as a former rubber planter, could get them started.

But Yves said rubber plantations were all in the southeast. Land in the west wasn't suited to rubber; it was suited to rice.

'Then they can grow a second rice crop,' suggested Bill. 'They've bags of time to do it in.'

The problem, it seemed, was water. Cambodia either had too much water or almost none at all. Yet Anne said the Angkoreans had produced two, even three rice crops a year. They did it, she said, by building reservoirs or *barays*, to irrigate the paddies. As a result Angkor had sustained a workforce big enough to build the temples, and in its day was probably the planet's largest city.

'Those guys had some get-up-and-go,' declared Bill, who found it unpardonable that a people who had got it so magnificently together should then go and lose it like that. Cambodia had immense natural wealth: rice, fruit, timber, resins, a fine climate and plenty of water. But the water was mismanaged and the people lacked motivation. Yet if they needed money, why not build a reservoir and produce a second rice crop?

Bill began to get excited. He talked to Marjorie about it and discussed the pros and cons with Yves and Salty. A few dollars could, if not exactly move mountains in Cambodia, easily dig a sizeable reservoir.

'We'd have spent a packet staying in fancy hotels over here and buying a lot of stuff we don't need,' he told Marjorie. 'Why not use that money to improve these people's lives?' Bill had plenty of riels and dollars, and if he ran short they would surely take his IOU.

'It's wrong to give people handouts. I'm dead against that. To value something people have got to work for it, and make their own investment.' But if the villagers would agree to dig a reservoir, he was prepared to buy the land and pay the diggers an hourly wage. 'Honey, I know it's charity to start with – I can probably even take it off my taxes – but these people are housing us, they're looking after us, and we ought to give them something in return. Leave our mark for the good, like that doctor did. There could even be some profit in it, for everyone.'

Marjorie needed no convincing; she was behind it a hundred per cent.

Anne was surprised and pleased, but none the less wondered aloud, to Bill's intense annoyance, if it wouldn't endanger the beauty of traditional life.

'Hogwash, Anne. We've got ahead in the West. Why

shouldn't these people have a chance? Would you want a child of yours brought up without any schools or medicine? Hell, no.'

Wisely Anne let the subject drop; while Salty, although sympathetic to Anne's viewpoint, on this occasion allowed his practical side to win, and offered Bill his assistance. He'd once helped to dig a reservoir back home. 'It's just a big pond,' he said. 'You got to dig some channels to take the water to the fields, and be able to open and close 'em. That's about it.'

Yves apparently had no opinion, or if he had he didn't voice it.

9

BILL BEGAN TO REGRET THAT THERE WAS SO LITTLE TIME. Impatient to get started, the venture capitalist was already leapfrogging over the well-intentioned philanthropist. The idea of a second rice crop, the removal of debt and the ability to buy a few kerosene lamps and lengths of cloth had expanded into thoughts of a thriving showcase economy. If the scheme was efficiently carried out and properly managed afterwards, Domrei Chlong could become a model village, setting an example for all Cambodia – even all Southeast Asia. And when they saw how small independent freeholders could enrich productivity and enjoy the profits, while being their own bosses, the Vietnamese would chuck Communism like the dud it was.

At a meeting in the town hall, Bill put his proposal to the assembled villagers. They saved rice every year for seed, he pointed out; but water could also be saved and put to use. With enough water in reserve, they could grow a second rice crop and sell it. A second crop would bounce them out of debt and it would keep them out of debt, as they would have something to sell on a regular basis. With extra money to hand they could buy better tools, and, if they worked hard, eventually agricultural machines. They could tile their roofs, import medicines, get a good education for their kids; they could have electricity, air-conditioning, radio and TV, take vacations and see the world. Others had achieved it and so could they. But the first step was a reservoir. It was a big step, said Bill, but he was prepared to help: he would buy the land and pay the workmen. He promised good wages. (Having learned from Yves how much rubber-tappers earned, this was easy.)

The Khmers looked surprised and pleased. They must consult the *neak ta*, they replied.

This sounded alarming, but drought and rain-making proved to be the *neak ta*'s special subjects. 'In that case the *neak ta* will be over the moon about a reservoir,' predicted Bill.

The village medium went to see the *neak ta*. The medium turned out to be San, who had seemed too down-to-earth to be speaking in tongues and conversing with an invisible spirit world. Bill had credited her with exceptionally good sense. But on second thoughts, mightn't this be another way of using it? After all, San was to the *neak ta* what a mahout was to his elephant, and vice versa. It was a powerful relationship. Bill urged the women to do some PR in the kitchen.

Neither medium nor *neak ta* needed coaxing, however. The *baray* was declared a good thing outright. People couldn't have too much water, so long as it wasn't on top of them, the *neak ta* had sagely observed.

'So it's on!' Bill pulled a hammock chair on to the loggia, poured himself a cup of rice wine, propped his feet on the balustrade and lit up a joint.

Then learned that the *bonzes* must be consulted.

'Well, hurry up; we haven't got all day; we need to get a move on.' And he gestured dismissively.

Discussions between the villagers and *bonzes* largely concerned where the reservoir might be built. It should not involve clearing the forest and should be able to reach the rice fields easily. The chosen land belonged to a peasant who had recently died. The family was poor and the children too young to work the land. If they sold now, when the children were older they could buy new land.

'We're off to the races,' cried Bill.

But this was not quite the case.

Spirits that might be incommoded by the upheaval must be appeased and their cooperation requested. Propitiating ceremonies must take place and a festival be held to mark the reservoir's inauguration and secure the spirit world's blessing overall, as well as that of the *bonzes*. Incense, scented rice, costumes, food and drink, dancing and gamelon music would be required. These needed thought and careful preparation. Moreover, a propitious day on which to begin the digging must be found.

San, in consultation with the *neak ta* and with encouragement from Anne and Marjorie in the kitchen, provided at short notice a propitious day.

'It's useful having a pythoness in the house,' observed Anne, pinning a little calendar to the wall. Using a valuable sheet from her writing pad, she had drawn three squares and divided them into grids big enough to tick off each day. With a flourish she now ticked off the first. 'We don't want to lose track, after all.'

Today was January twenty-eighth, all more or less agreed.

'A whole week's been wasted,' groaned Bill, who'd noticed that even the prospect of work was coated with a marzipan of meetings, incense, chanting and spirit offerings.

On the day of the festival, elegant white parasols, embroidered blouses, beautiful silk *sampots* and a surprising amount of gold jewellery appeared – even a few gemstones, sewn on to headdresses or set in necklaces and earrings. After the rains, gemstones sometimes got washed up in the fields, the Barangs learned, and you could pick them up at random. They were quite common a little further west.

Today, however, the number-one jewel was Bopha, a young woman whose engagement had recently been announced. Lithe and perfectly formed, when the dancing began, as Domrei Chlong's undisputed beauty queen she led it, her beautiful agate eyes focused on the ground.

'A pocket Venus,' Marjorie declared to Anne. 'I feel like a big truck beside her. Do you think we're growing too big in the West? Bigger clothes, bigger cars, enormous feet, and so on. Surely people don't need bigger bodies. We can hardly keep the ones we have in shape.'

Another week had passed without any real progress, and Bill was seething at the waste of valuable time. But Marjorie disagreed. The villagers lived their lives in a multi-textured way that had great appeal. They lived in several dimensions simultaneously, and the spirit world invested every nook and cranny. Everything was alive, nothing inanimate, and as a result even the simplest activity was enriched. Marjorie found it exciting, yet surprisingly restful, too.

At last, digging began. On the propitious day and to the sound of gongs and flutes, the entire village, led by the *bonzes*, marched in formal procession to the site, which had been pegged out and neatly cordoned off with string. Colourful paper flags fluttered on the string in an effort to appease the discommoded spirits and keep them happy. After a brief speech by Ty, Bill initiated the digging with a few ritual shoves of a borrowed shovel. The orchestra played, the *bonzes* prayed, bells jingled, gongs were bonged, children sang, women smiled, everyone chatted and laughed, and eventually the men picked up their shovels. It was more like joining in a waltz than digging a big hole.

At the end of the week Bill paid the workmen, who grinned, bowed and shook their heads, obviously highly pleased; apparently also highly entertained. The following week more diggers arrived from neighbouring hamlets. Women came too, carrying wicker baskets to help shift the soil. Baray Barang was up and running.

'It's a shame we'll never see it full of water,' said Bill, standing with Marjorie beside the hole that, if completed by the time the rains came, would, they had been told, take about a month to fill. 'Maybe someone will write, even in English by then, and give us a report.'

'Or we could come back later, and see for ourselves.'

Bill looked at his wife in surprise. 'We damn well could! We'll do that. We'll come right back in a year or two, and see everything for ourselves.' And they returned to the house, arm in arm, smiling and patting each other, as pleased as punch.

Bill told himself that in three months a fair start would have been made, but the Khmers were going to have to take it from there, and with this in mind he kept an eye out for someone who could reliably see the project through and, afterwards, develop its full potential. Efficiency was often a company's greatest asset.

Samnang, the beautiful Bopha's fiancé, appeared to be

the best bet. Samnang was from another village. He was small, muscular, hard working, and he appeared to have some ambition. Samnang had built a small house beside Bopha's. It was customary for prospective sons-in-law to live with or next door to their future in-laws for a time, helping them out and allowing everyone to get to know each other. A sort of all-round apprenticeship. Samnang had also helped to organize the *baray* construction team and plan the digging. Now Bill offered him the job of foreman.

Samnang listened carefully. He wished to know every detail of the work and he wanted everything to be precisely set out, all of which pleased and impressed Bill. Yet Samnang asked no questions about money. When Bill eventually made him an offer, he just stood there, evidently waiting for something more. So Bill promised a small rise in three weeks, provided all went well. Samnang bowed formally and Bill offered him his hand. As they shook, a broad grin spread across Samnang's face, and Bill wondered if he had promised him too much. In fact this was Samnang's first handshake, and he thought it an absurd carry-on between two grown men. But perhaps it was a final test, a covert trial of manly strength and endurance; so he pumped energetically away, like a man dying of thirst drawing up water from a very deep well.

'Hey, call him off!' Bill appealed, half-laughing, to Yves. The little fellow was indefatigable, and incredibly strong.

Over the following weeks, the raw red basin grew broader and deeper. A former rice paddy, the land was moist and comparatively easy to dig. The men shovelled the soil up in great clods and dumped it into large wicker baskets, which the women carried off on bamboo shoulder-boards, two buckets at a time, and emptied. Samnang seemed to be well in control. Bill's own contribution now largely accomplished, his visits became less frequent, his ever-resourceful mind turning towards new projects.

Guavas, mangoes, papayas, jackfruit and coconuts were there for the picking. If they were made into exotic chutneys and preserves and were properly marketed, they could become luxury items in the West. The villagers also made a delicious candy, simply pouring boiled palm sugar into tiny moulds and letting it cool. With the right advertising, attractive packaging and a tropical yet fashionable label – Palm Beach, for instance – these could rival expensive Belgian chocolates in the shops. Nuts, kapok, cotton and tobacco, all grown locally, had strong commercial possibilities. But the key was middle men: salesmen, administrators, advertisers and shippers – in short, a middle class – something that, apart from ethnic Chinese, Cambodia seemed to lack. But that could change. Khmers, too, could become entrepreneurs, and learn to ship and oversee production. Not everyone need grow rice. Pointed in the right direction, Domrei Chlong could begin to diversify, even to become a thriving town – and maybe one day a city, with hospitals, schools, shops, paved roads, motorbikes and cars, restaurants, movie theatres, and pleasure boats cruising on the river. Trade was the embryo, and the more diversification and specialization there was, the more productive, interesting and healthy society would be.

'This country is a goldmine,' Bill insisted over dinner. 'But only the Chinese are panning it.' They were sitting around the table, polishing off spit-roasted bantams caught in Salty's snares, picking at the bones and using coconut shells for fingerbowls. 'Raw materials, cheap labour, rivers for transport – you name it,' he went on. He thought cottage industries were the best way to start. They were easy to set up, and the investment was negligible. 'Stuff women can do at home: pots, baskets, exotic jams.'

'Beautiful silk is woven in Cambodia,' observed Yves.

'Hey, a silk industry! That's a great idea. Europe got rich by weaving cloth at home in the Middle Ages: France, the Netherlands.'

'You mean the country did, not the weavers.' Normally Anne kept her views to herself, in the interests of solidarity; but rice wine had weakened her judgement, awakening aggressive instincts that a stalwart defence of the underdog excused, indeed seemed to render imperative.

'Well, they didn't starve, and those were hard times,' answered Bill, with steady patience. Unable to use their fists, women tended when angry to buzz about like hungry mosquitoes, waiting for a chance to strike. Mosquitoes received a good sharp smack; but, a gentleman where women were concerned, Bill applied a gentlemanly tolerance and self-restraint.

'It's true middlemen tend to earn the most money,' he conceded. 'And some of them are pretty unscrupulous. But it's human nature to try and make the best out of any situation, and others will usually profit from the fallout. If cloth hadn't found a market back then, those weavers would probably have starved. Cambodia has plenty of food, mind, but a simple cottage industry like weaving could change everyone's life for the better – make people comfortably off – and, with a second rice crop, even well-to-do.'

'Well to do what?'

'To do whatever they want.'

'They may want to go on exactly as they are.' The buzzing mosquito was homing in.

'They may indeed, but frankly, Anne, I doubt it.'

Bill continued to pick meat off a chicken leg. 'Do you happen to know what life expectancy in Cambodia is?' he asked, off-hand, apparently intent on stripping the chicken bone.

'It's short,' she answered, aggressive and suddenly on her guard.

'Yes, it is short,' Bill agreed, with extreme gentleness, and laying the bone on his plate, he dunked his fingers in the coconut fingerbowl and wiped them carefully. 'But do you happen to know how short, Anne?'

'About forty-five or fifty. Like most of the Third World.'

A little piece of meat remained on the chicken leg. Bill picked it up again and, holding the tiny club, opined that the mosquito had settled within range.

'It's thirty, Anne. Exactly your age. Isn't that right?' And tearing the last morsel off the chicken leg, Bill popped it into his mouth, chewing with evident satisfaction. Then, grinning, he pointed the chicken bone at Anne. 'But great while it lasts, no doubt!'

10

INFANTS WERE AN INTEGRAL PART OF THE SCHOOLROOM, as the pupils were their nannies. Now two older girls arrived, holding hands, their eyes downcast, to ask if they, too, might learn English: Bopha and her friend Chandrea. Chandrea was a little older, a little more solemn, and rather less beautiful than her friend; but Chandrea's eyes were not downcast for very long. In fact, her gaze was surprisingly direct. Chandrea was ambitious. She wanted to learn English, she said, in order to go to Siem Reap, work in the hotel and find a suitable husband, a widower perhaps, who would take her to live in Phnom Penh.

In a society where husbands were carefully chosen by the family, this was an extraordinary plan. How had she come by it, they wondered? Chandrea knew almost nothing of the outside world.

Chandrea said she had figured it out for herself.

Bopha, timidly supportive of her friend, added that she and Samnang might go to Siem Reap, too, one day. 'Just to see it,' she whispered modestly.

'They want to see the bright lights,' Bill commented later, over dinner. 'There's electricity in Siem Reap!'

'That's so corny, Bill,' said Marjorie affectionately.

'There'll be some bright lights here pretty soon,' he continued, unfazed. 'As soon as we get to Bangkok I'm going to send the village a generator, as a present for looking after us so well.'

The plan was much applauded, and even Anne on this occasion saw no reason to object.

Each morning Chandrea and Bopha took their places on the bamboo platform as silently as two leaves dropping off a tree. As the tallest pupils, they sat at the back, their bare feet tucked neatly to one side, their voices lost in the declamatory singsong of the children, the youngest of whom they also helped to care for. But although Khmer women were deferential and demure, they also possessed considerable social power, as Anne and Marjorie were discovering. They owned property, managed the household purse and carried great authority in the home. They were responsible for transplanting the precious rice seedlings and at harvest time worked beside their husbands in the fields. Keeping in close touch with the spirit world further increased by association their power and importance.

'Little velvet gloves,' declared Bill, who found them enchanting. They also seemed to him steadier than the men, reinforcing his view that the home was the best place to start commercial enterprises.

But Chandrea, despite her ambition and determination, lasted in the schoolroom only two weeks. She was needed at home, they were told. Anne and Marjorie were surprised and angry that this intelligent and ambitious girl should be pressed forcibly back into the conventional mould. But parents must be obeyed, said Yves; respect for one's elders and betters was the basis of Khmer society –

that and keeping face. Chandrea's adventurous plans were the stuff of dreams.

Bopha had no such difficulties, however. Desirous of pleasing, she bent and curved instinctively to fit the world around her, and she did so with much elegance and grace.

'She'll make Samnang a fine wife, look after his home and back all his endeavours to the hilt,' declared Bill, who'd begun to take an avuncular interest in the pair and to see them as his heirs. 'In a few years those two will be the village big shots. Mark my words.'

Bopha rarely spoke, even in Khmer, and chanted her letters in a soft and sibilant way that could scarcely be heard. But she proved to have an ear for language, picking up English with incredible speed and needing to hear a word only once to remember it.

'What does Bopha mean?' Bill asked her one morning. He found it a strange and not particularly beautiful word.

Standing before him, Bopha examined her feet. 'Flower,' she whispered. 'Bopha, flower.' She remained like that, perfectly still, head bowed and eyes downcast, as though transfixed or else awaiting his congratulations or dismissal. This happened whenever Bill addressed her.

'Thank you, Bopha,' he would say, in order to re-animate her. And she would bow, then glide off, wafted by an imperceptible breeze. Bill had the impression of a delicate blossom, fragile and vulnerable, that could easily be trampled on.

'A flower born to blush unseen,' quoted Marjorie, when they were discussing it at lunch.

But even here Bill saw opportunities. 'Get some photographs of her, Margie, wearing one of those silk *sampots*, under a banana tree or something – sort of

Gauguin-like. You know, but a bit more glamorous. Maybe Sarah can get her into *Vogue*. It would make a great article – even start a Western fashion in *sampots*. You could write it, Anne.'

'Miss Bopha's stunning summer outfit was spun by industrious worms working in the mulberry trees of western Cambodia, and woven by the villagers of Domrei Chlong,' Anne teased. 'To buy your own genuine Cambodian silk *sampot*, fill in the coupon below and send us your cheque for one hundred and fifty dollars. Delivery within one year, almost guaranteed.'

But irritating as Anne found Bill's proposal, in truth she couldn't fault it, since everyone would benefit from such a scheme. It was Bill's optimism that so annoyed her, she decided. It was impossible to de-rail. The throttle wide open, the engine zoomed and tooted, full steam ahead, the track always assumed to be in perfect order and the destination the correct one.

Now Bill was discussing a jam industry with San. Fruit practically grew itself in Cambodia, he pointed out, and preserving it was easy – something that women could do in their spare time. If the village women would agree to make enough jam for a selling sample – about one hundred pounds, Bill estimated – he would underwrite the initial produce. Then if tropical preserves caught on abroad, becoming a new and sought-after taste, there would be big orders to fill.

San spoke to a cousin, who agreed to organize a team of women; and Bill let it be known that he would back other projects, provided each one was laid out for proper examination and approval first. All ideas were welcome.

The delighted villagers grinned and shook their heads.

Domrei Chlong began to buzz and bustle. Trays of fruit were carried through the village on the heads of swaying female bodies, as to a festival. Cauldrons boiled feverishly outside houses, and young men sprinted up sugar palms to place bottles over lacerated cat-tail-like fruit that oozed drop by drop its sugared broth, sprinting up again later on to collect them. Ox-carts loaded with bamboo for basket-weaving creaked along forest paths, and primitive looms, appearing from nowhere, were set up among the agricultural debris scattered underneath houses. Silk thread proved widely available. An extensive silkworm culture flourished near Siem Reap, and the villagers kept a supply to hand.

'Jayavarman!' the villagers began to call Bill, grinning and bowing whenever they saw him.

Anne told him they meant Jayavarman VII, the last of the great devarajas. Jayavarman VII had built the monumental city of Angkor Thom, as well as reservoirs, hospitals and Buddhist monasteries – even a chain of rest houses along the kingdom's principal thoroughfares. There was a rumour he had been a leper. 'After his death Cambodia was invaded and the country never really recovered.'

'Maybe folks were plumb worn out,' suggested Salty, propping up a table leg where the ground beneath it had eroded.

But Bill was delighted by the epithet. Furthermore, he could see how a clever, unscrupulous fellow might successfully set himself up as a god-king among such a trusting people, especially if he had a bit more learning than they did, which wasn't saying much. Unfortunately for them, perhaps, he was himself a dyed-in-the-wool Republican.

'When you go somewhere you should make a difference,' he now repeated, reviewing the nests of baskets accumulating in the pagoda, where they were being stored, together with jars of preserves – mango, papaya, jackfruit – and a length of azure silk that Marjorie was wild to buy outright. The reservoir was progressing, too: the overall shape was now carved out, the basin getting deeper every day, and the sluice gates under construction.

Bill was happy. The venture capitalist and developer of investment schemes had, he believed, discovered his rock-bottom self: he was a pioneer. The instinct that had driven his great-grandparents to seek their fortunes in the American West, carving out a place for themselves and helping to develop a wilderness, was in his genes. His parents and grandparents, though poor and at times destitute, had worked hard, and very slowly they had improved their lot, until good luck plus a shrewd investment had made Bill's father rich. Bill had built on his family's efforts and good luck, but his own success, though so much larger and on a greater stage, was considerably more abstract. Finance was largely paperwork, proposals, research and analysis; its weapons verbal, its innumerable battles masked as reasonable discussions.

Drawing a living from the land was literally hands on. It was man as he was made to be, as evolution answering early needs had made him. But it was also the past, and for Bill, therefore, ultimately an indulgence. The new worlds to conquer *were* abstract, involving brain not body work. Man in his eagerness for self-improvement was fast outstripping Nature's more leisurely timetable, and evolution falling behind because it was too slow.

Salty, too, was of pioneer stock, and as such was deeply attached to the American West. But what attracted him, Bill felt, wasn't the challenge of making a better living there, but of re-living the Western legend. Salty was a romantic. There had been plenty of Salties about when the West was being won. Essentially dreamers, they were mostly drunks by the end. The life itself didn't satisfy; only the idea of it. Which helped to explain Salty's cropping up on the other side of the globe and wandering down, or off, the goddamn hippie trail. Those kids were dreamers, too, new romantics, who in their search for soul food along the byways, like some kind of Holy Grail, had found it in psychedelic drugs and hare krishna gurus. Yet what wouldn't those who were dishing it out in places like India and Afghanistan not give for a slice of the big American pie! That was the irony of it.

'I may be a Republican,' Bill told Salty one evening, 'but you're the conservative, not me. I want change, progress, improvement. You want things to be not even like they are, but like they were.'

'Well, there's a lot to be said for how things were,' Marjorie piped up.

'I'm a conservative, economically speaking,' Bill went on. 'Free enterprise, minimum government interference, lowest possible taxes. But when it comes to how people live, I'm not just a progressive, I'm a radical progressive. Off the map, you could say.'

Anne smiled dubiously.

Bill noticed. 'OK, it's great to get these people on their feet and running with the modern world, put them in the big race. But the future's where the real excitement – the big challenges – are. Genetic engineering. That's the really big race. Genetic engineering is going to make man into whatever he wants or needs to be. Take the impurities out. That's where the world's headed. It's already helped to make me a wealthy man, and it's hardly started yet.'

'Is that right?' Salty was sitting on the platform edge, plaiting palm fibres to make a rope halter for Kieu's buffalo. 'Well now, that's real interesting. But this genetic stuff, I reckon it's a long way off.' Salty pulled and flattened out the braid as he talked. 'Seems to me folks over here live like folks were made to live. They use their bodies, they're crazy about their families, they're part of nature and not separated from it. Seems to me they live in the real world, and not some man-made contraption they can't bust out of till they can get their genes fixed up.'

'I agree with Salty,' said Marjorie, with surprising verve.

'Nobody's happy all the time,' continued Salty. 'But these people look real happy to me, in an everyday sort of way. They don't need new fixes all the time to make them feel better. Seems like they enjoy life and want to keep things as they are.'

It was a mouthful for Salty, and laying the rope aside, he patted his pockets in search of his tobacco pouch.

'They're not happy when their children die of malaria or dysentery; or when the rice crop fails.'

'The rice crop never fails in Cambodia, Bill,' said Marjorie. 'And the afterlife is so important here, the dead are sort of alive on earth. They're around. Don't look at me like that; they are! Families stay in touch. I think that's really wonderful.'

'Would you want your mother to come back as a chicken? You can bet your bottom dollar she'd rather stay dead and buried, I can tell you!'

This point was indisputable.

'Still, life and death aren't so separated over here as they are with us.'

Anne could not resist entering the fray. 'If you have

to have a religion, and some people – maybe most people – do, Buddhism is a good one. It's godless, but it's moral. All that thunderbolt-threatening stuff in the Old Testament and self-sacrificing stuff in the New is dreadful. And frankly, it's unhealthy.

'You're just getting at your father, Anne; you know that?'

'Whatever works,' interjected Yves soothingly from the hammock. 'Gods are useful to the powerless,' he added.

'Yeah, well America's the most powerful country there's ever been, so we don't need to invent a lot of imaginary protection – fairies flitting around, pieces of wood that can talk, grandmas pecking about in the garden. We have a stable government, comprehensive insurance policies and the strongest military in the world. Americans feel safe.'

'Religion is on the rise in America, Bill,' said Marjorie.

'OK, and if people want to believe in Jesus Saves, or Mickey Mouse, or Martians landing on Lake Michigan, they're free to do it. Nobody minds. It's live and let live. We're a very tolerant people.'

'Then why are you bombing the Vietnamese?' Anne's delivery was matter of fact and surprisingly calm, and for a second it brought Bill up short. Vietnam, so all-invasive in Connecticut, seemed almost on another planet.

Salty, who was busy rolling a joint, paused and, looking up, grinned almost aggressively, waiting for Bill's reply.

'We're bombing the Vietnamese because Communism is a virus and must be stamped out. For the good of everyone.'

'It does seem to be highly infectious,' remarked Anne drily.

'Yep. There's little messages tucked inside those bombs,' said Salty. '"This is for your own good. It's doctor's orders." But folks can't seem to read it right. Maybe it's because they don't speak English; or maybe it's something else.'

'Oh, for heaven's sake, don't let's get on to politics. Please!' Marjorie was steering hard, hoping to avoid an ominously rising wave, aware that their comfortable little boat might be severely rocked. And what would be the point?

Obligingly everyone acquiesced: the peace pipe had begun to go round and chemistry to perform its famously pacifying work. But not before Anne had pointed out that there were lots of old people in the village, so Bill's life-expectancy figures must be due to high infant mortality, something that modern medicines could put right. 'There's no need to change people's way of life to fix that,' she insisted.

'Not if a second rice crop brings in enough money for medicines,' answered Bill, giving a small toot to his own trumpet, and, taking a deep puff, produced two circles even Dante might have admired.

11

YVES SPENT SEVERAL HOURS ALONE EACH DAY, BUT HE WAS used to that. In the afternoon he normally went for a walk, his daily constitutional, as he said. Strolling into the village, he exchanged pleasantries with any villagers he met, and on occasion visited the pagoda, where he would sit down and talk at length with the *bonzes*.

He thought a good deal about his daughter. Her illness, if correctly diagnosed, was serious. Poor Esme had had no luck. She lacked beauty and her husband, whom she no longer loved, was a worthless fellow who drank too much. Now that she was ill he would drink more. Alcohol should be a tonic for old age and not wasted as an auxiliary and unnecessary fuel for youth. Once youth's exuberance was past and the battles that could be fought had been fought – except perhaps that most difficult battle of all: old age – then alcohol was beneficial as solace or as an elixir, for the tired and spent. Alcohol, mused Yves, wasn't called spirits for nothing.

Yves had lived in Cambodia all his life, except for six years as a student in France and the year when, during the war, the Japanese arrived and he had gone to Thailand. Being French in a French-ruled country inevitably bred false notions of superiority, but it also conveyed a sense of life's impermanence. Yves had witnessed the return of the French after the war, and their subsequent removal, spearheaded by Sihanouk and followed by fifteen years of precarious independence. Now Americans and Vietnamese were at the gates, the disruptions of that war seeping across the country's porous boundaries. The rubber plantations were virtually abandoned. The North Vietnamese used the region to track back and forth to South Vietnam – the Ho Chi Min trail, they called it – and Cambodia's plantation workers were mostly Vietnamese. The Khmers weren't interested in working for others, or in becoming traders or entrepreneurs, though Yves had seen no reason to point that out to Bill. Bill was keeping busy and doing no one any harm. Maybe some good would even come of it. But a Buddhist country, whatever its pluses, was unlikely to be sufficiently acquisitive or warlike to hold back ambitious, greedy or aggressive neighbours. Deference, keeping calm, keeping face and earning merit was the policy. Yet beneath the smiling, placid surface lay much repressed violence, Yves suspected. True to a degree in all men.

Marguerite had hated Cambodia, and had despised life on a rubber plantation. Probably she was right. It wasn't much of a life for a woman who wanted society and admiration, and could get it. She had gone off with the first opportunity. Yves couldn't really blame her. Their marriage, the result of a wild and passionate attraction, was a mistake from any practical viewpoint.

But Huoy, who had looked after the couple's house, had in her turn brought him something akin to peace; their two children had been a joy when they were young. Perhaps he should have sent them to school in France, but he had not. Huoy had believed that their best chance, being of mixed race, was in Cambodia. But now Sophatra was caught up in Phnom Penh's volatile student life, and Esme possibly dying of an illness that might conceivably have been cured in France or Australia. Huoy would be sitting on the couple's doorstep, silent for the most part, but doing what she could to help, waiting patiently and bravely. With equal patience she would be waiting for news of him. Huoy understood acceptance. In ways she was, he believed, the strongest person he had ever met, and able to give more as a result. The starting point was comprehending there was so little choice, that, despite so many illusions to the contrary, fate was largely (grotesquely so, in Yves's view) outside human control. Accepting it was another matter, however, and Yves sometimes wondered if imagination hadn't evolved as an antidote to consciousness, its marvellous powers of invention making reality possible to bear. Huoy, for her support, leaned on an invisible spirit world that, although benevolent, was quirky, bad-tempered, capricious and demanding. Yet for Huoy it worked. Yves had no such underpinning. For him belief simply refused to convert automatically into truth. He lacked faith, and that piece of blindness or transfiguring clarity was a necessary part of the package.

'Yves, look at this!' Anne was thrusting papers under his nose. 'What do you make of it?'

Reaching for his glasses, Yves shuffled quickly through several sheets covered in beautifully written Khmer script.

'It looks like a story,' he surmised, scanning a few pages.

Anne said she'd found the papers at the bottom of a linen chest. She had had no qualms about opening the sealed bamboo tube. The doctor and his wife were dead, and she was curious.

San, arriving from the garden with a load of tomatoes on her head, confirmed Yves's supposition. 'One of the doctor's stories,' she announced, with evident pride. 'The doctor used to read them to the whole village. Everybody liked them.'

'Oh Yves, you must read it to us! It would be such a treat,' said Anne. 'Besides, I'm curious about this doctor, aren't you? Let's see what he has to say.'

The following evening, when the fire had been covered and the supper things stored away, the Barangs carried their cups, together with a jug of rice wine, upstairs; and Salty, closing the shutters to keep out insects, lit the kerosene lamp. Shadows danced and fluttered about the room. Unbottled spirits, Marjorie chose to think.

Yves had written out a translation of the story. 'It's a fable, possibly a children's story,' he now warned, with a pointed look at Bill. 'Or it passes for one.' He lowered himself carefully into a hammock chair; Salty placed the lamp on an upended crate beside him, and the others pulled their own chairs nearer, to make a circle.

Yves filled his cup with palm wine; then, clearing his throat, he cast over his spectacles a quick but critical look at his audience, and began to read:

The Tale of Sala

When heroes walked on earth and all men believed in gods, a momentous event occurred in the remote and little-known kingdom of Botale. One day an enormous, brilliantly coloured bird appeared in the sky. Its plumage was emerald green, shot with gold and red and turquoise. Its head and claws were those of an eagle, but its eyes were round and gentle, even a little sad. On its back sat five young men, inhabitants of a faraway country. They had flown over forests and mountains, deserts and seas; and seeing below them a clear blue pool, a perfect circle, set like a glittering sapphire on the bosom of the earth, they desired to land.

'Let us get down and stretch our legs,' they declared, speaking as one; for they were brothers, and very united, as brothers go.

The enormous, brilliantly coloured bird landed smoothly on the water and, like a swan carrying cygnets to safety on her back, glided gracefully to shore. The young men clambered down, and in the manner of hitchhikers who have reached a desirable destination, they looked about, smiling and stamping their cramped feet, as they waved the departing bird goodbye. The bird, looking back under its wing, gave them a melancholy nod and flew on.

Beside the circular sapphire pond was sitting, all alone, a beautiful maiden. Her long hair, black as tar, was braided in a single plait, her eyes shone like cabochon emeralds and her skin was the colour of milk. She wore a dress of pale-green silk that draped to perfection the perfect shape of her slender body.

At once all the young men fell in love and wished to marry her. But after some discussion it was decided that Sala, as the eldest, should have this privilege, if it were possible.

Bowing low, Sala presented himself and introduced his brothers. Then, in a well-bred courteous fashion, he descended to one knee and without more ado asked the maiden for her hand in marriage.

'This is rather sudden,' she answered languidly,

though somewhat interested, adding after a thoughtful pause, 'But I have no wish to marry. I am happy as I am, sitting beside this pond. For it has my full attention, or what I see in it does.'

The young men were bewildered and rather vexed, also the narrator, for without love and a desire to marry there can be no stories, nor any events with which to interest and entertain the gods.

In fact the maiden was herself a goddess, but she did not know it, despite the young men's strong insistence on this point. She had known many men and marriages in her past, but in her present enchantment had forgotten them. Now she assessed the possibilities of this absorbing diversion anew.

'If you wish to marry me, you will have to court me, you know; for I must be persuaded,' she declared in a sweet bell-like tone that was also a trifle bossy.

'Most willingly, dear lady,' answered Sala. And opening both arms in a stylish theatrical flourish, he bowed again.

'You must perform feats of valour and daring that will impress me and cause me to fall in love and wish to marry.'

'Name any feat, dear lady, and I and my brothers will accomplish it,' declared Sala, for being young he was sure of his prowess and invincibility. And as the maiden was silent, thinking it over, he enumerated several possibilities: the slaying of a dragon or wild boar, saving the maiden from imprisonment in a tower or from enchantment by an evil sorcerer – the usual sorts of things.

'I'm sure I should like it if you saved my life. But from what exactly? Who are my enemies, pray?'

'Devils, evil men, wild beasts? You are all alone here, and unguarded.' It was obvious to Sala that the maiden, if not a goddess, must be at least a princess, even though no dragon lay at her feet waiting for prospective suitors to slay. 'Perhaps you are lost and I have found you and can restore you to your rightful home?'

'This is a very blue pond,' observed the maiden, changing the subject.

'That is evident,' replied Sala, and launching into courtship mode added, 'but as a mirror for your beauty it is far too small.'

His brothers nodded in confirmation and approval.

'When I see my face reflected in the water, I find I am very beautiful,' admitted the maiden, speaking in a soft and agreeable manner.

The rest is not bad either, thought Sala, but he refrained from saying so, though he was not sure why.

'Perhaps I am a little vain,' the maiden continued doubtfully, 'but gazing at my reflection in the water is what I like to do best.'

'Yes, but you must name your enemies, so that I may fight them and win your love, and also make the world a safer place!' For, being an honourable young man, Sala wished not only to do great deeds but to cause great happiness as well.

'Now you are talking,' said the maiden. She was, she told him, the prisoner of a sorcerer, and her father was dead. 'I am doomed to sit beside this pond, gazing at my beauty until the pond dries up.

When I can no longer admire my image in the water, I shall be free to fall in love and marry.'

'Then I will drain the pond, even if I have to drink all the water myself!' declared the gallant Sala, and, expanding on heroic opportunities, turned to matters of state. 'We have heard that your country is in the hands of an evil and oppressive ruler, who mistreats his subjects,' he confided to the maiden. 'When I have set you free, my brothers and I will endeavour to free these prisoners as well.'

'I had not noticed this oppressiveness,' answered the maiden vaguely. 'I suppose I have been too busy. But if things are as you say, then you must kill this evil oppressor first and dry the pond up afterwards. For that is the proper order of doing things.'

'It shall be so, dear lady,' promised Sala. 'The gods are on my side, and when I have accomplished both these feats, I shall carry you back to my country and we shall be married. It is the richest country in the world.' (Which was true as far as Sala, who was not much travelled, knew.) 'And my father is its ruler.'

'Of course, your own country is very beautiful, too,' he added, wishing to be polite. 'It is full of fruit and sunshine and as green as paradise. Yet it is very poor, because there is always warfare and dispute, and, all things being unequal, disruptive and full of unhappiness. Riches without peace are of little use in this world,' he declared, moving into a philosophical vein.

The maiden was much impressed. She also thought Sala the handsomest man that she had ever seen.

'Hurummm,' murmured Sala's brothers, clearing their throats to get their brother's attention. For he seemed to have forgotten their agreement.

'May I ask if you have any sisters at home whom my brothers might marry?' Sala asked the maiden. 'Since they too must risk their lives in this war, it is right they too should be rewarded.'

'As it happens,' said the maiden, 'we are quintuplets.'

'Then it will be in all respects a perfect match,' said Sala.

The brothers began to prepare for war. Their country was well advanced in the magical-scientifical field and had developed a new and powerful weapon: the capacity for replication. With a snap of Sala's fingers and the recitation of an obscure mathematical formula, his four brothers were multiplied five hundred times, and before the maiden now stood an army of two thousand well-armed and incredibly handsome young men.

'We are ready to slay the enemy,' they announced with great enthusiasm and in one voice.

'You will surely slay all the women,' answered the maiden, smiling, for she was not without wit. 'We shall have to see about their husbands.'

With a hurrah the army raised its banners, and beating drums and blowing golden trumpets, the young men marched off as one into the forest, with Sala in the lead. The noise they made was very great, as it was meant to be, and the forest creatures were filled with consternation. Green and red and yellow parrots flew frantically about gathering news of the invasion, and a conclave of forest creatures was rapidly assembled. The parrots repeated what they had learned: Sala, they said, was the son of a powerful demon who wished to conquer the kingdom.

This was nothing new, but till now no one had ever felt much concern, because the kingdom was so well guarded. A beautiful maiden, an enchanted creature sitting beside a sapphire pond, lured all potential invaders to their death by drowning, in their vain attempts to dry up the pond. Numerous aggressors had in the past been swallowed up by the water, but now, surprisingly, the maiden appeared to have slipped up.

The forest kingdom was politically and environmentally conservative, and so things rarely changed. Timber was never cut, trails were kept in good order by repeated usage, the undergrowth controlled by a continual nibbling of unruly plants. The kingdom was also hierarchical: all the inhabitants had their places and knew them.

Now, however, the parrots reported that the army intended to burn the forest down, in order to make a flat field, necessary for battle. 'What's more, they want to level more than just the forest,' squawked a green parrot apprehensively. 'They want to level the whole kingdom, and make everybody in it equal.'

'That is a silly idea, as well as impossible,' declared the tiger, mildly amused. 'It is obvious that I, for instance, am not the equal of a monkey, and never shall be.'

'Well,' teased a monkey who was sitting beside him, 'we swing in the tree-tops, so logically speaking, surely we are the higher up.'

But the tiger, who had no sense of humour and

did not brook insubordination, gobbled the monkey up in one bite, in order to prove his point.

'Well, no tiger is the equal of me,' trumpeted the elephant, irritated by this somewhat overstated performance. And to prove his point, he picked the tiger up with his trunk and gave him a resolute shake.

'You are really very thick-skinned, you know,' said the tiger, whose dignity was badly ruffled. 'You should be more sensitive and polite. Tigers and elephants go their separate ways. We have no need to discuss irrelevant issues like equality. We are chalk and cheese.'

'While we are on this subject,' growled the lion, 'remember it is I who am the king of beasts. That fact is known throughout the world, and never once has it been in dispute. What is more, the position is hereditary.'

A serpent, who had been snoozing beneath a tree, opened one eye. 'Though I am the very lowest of creatures,' he hissed ingratiatingly, 'I am among the wisest, and my advice should be listened to, you know, for I have my ear to the ground.'

'There's one in every garden,' yawned the parrot, who found the serpent a tiresome know-it-all, and was tempted to swoop down and carry him off to perdition.

The serpent was wise enough, however, to ignore this rude remark. 'We must ask the devaraja for help,' he continued, stretching out to his full length for emphasis; and he was not unimposing. 'We have no weapons or fortresses with which to protect ourselves, so the devaraja is our only hope. He is well connected in the very highest places, and we must beg him to speak to the gods on our behalf. Only the devaraja can save us from devastation.'

The debate continued for quite a while, with many different creatures having their say, taking turns in accordance with their standing in the established order. The rhinoceros wanted to attack the invading army at once. Unlike the other creatures, he was armour-plated, and being rather stupid would have made an excellent soldier had he not been too hot-headed to follow orders, crashing furiously about instead.

The tiger, however, was keen to make a meal of it, picking the soldiers off one at a time. 'Guerrilla warfare is the fashion just now,' he told them. 'And it is the ideal strategy in a forest.'

The lion supported this proposal, but others felt that it could not be accomplished before the forest was burnt down.

Near by some *bonzes* were meditating. Sitting in a circle in their saffron robes, they chanted their prayers.

'We are on a retreat,' they protested when the animals interrupted them. 'We must concentrate on emptying our minds, not putting new things in. That is the correct procedure in meditation.'

But the animals persisted, explaining that a powerful demon had sent an army to conquer the kingdom. The army had already entered the forest and was planning to burn it down.

Reluctantly the *bonzes* began to collect their thoughts.

'The demon wishes to make us equal, so that

everyone will work together to build we don't know what. A brave new world, some say.'

'Nothing is ever certain, or ever is,' answered the *bonzes* elliptically. 'But you have nothing to fear: if you die you will simply come back again as another animal.'

'Be that as it may, no one wishes to change his skin,' replied the animals. 'Except serpents, of course, and they are lowly creatures and always wanting to improve their miserable status.'

'Your thinking is gravely in error,' admonished the *bonzes*. 'It should make no difference to you, who you are.'

'Well,' said the animals, 'it does and we cannot help it. It is only natural. For it is the way things are.'

'Then you can forget about ever achieving nirvana,' replied the *bonzes* dismissively, and they returned to their enlightening meditations.

The devaraja lived in a great palace at the forest edge. He was enormously fat and also very lazy and complacent, for he had a fine life. He enjoyed the company of many beautiful wives, he dined on golden plates and drank the finest wines. The palace was always full of music and dancing, while the kingdom mostly looked after itself, for it was extremely well organized. The secret of its success was castes. With castes there were never any rebellions, for no caste would even dream of uniting with another one. That was the joy of it. At worst, members of each caste merely squabbled amongst themselves. So squabbles were the worst that ever happened.

Now, however, all the creatures had assembled to petition the devaraja's help, and he received them with a most gracious condescension.

'Invaders have arrived who want to level the forest and all the creatures in it, including, we imagine, your good self,' the animals announced.

'My god self,' corrected the devaraja, a trifle pompously. 'But do not worry.' He waved his hand, and his wrist jingled with many golden bracelets. 'No one can level the forest, I assure you, because they will not find any matches. It's as simple as that. Matches are forbidden. And no one will level all the creatures, because it's impossible. A cat may look at a king; that is well known. But he cannot be one, unless of course he has had a very lucky reincarnation. Otherwise his best prospect is to become a fat cat. For that is his nature, as the whole world knows.'

The vizier, fanning the devaraja with a magnificent peacock tail, now spoke. 'Man's talk of equality is arrogant and false,' he declared, between broad sweeps of the extravagant fan. 'Men don't want equality. On the contrary: they want to rise above the animal kingdom they are a part of.'

'Then they certainly have ideas above their station,' declared the king of beasts.

'They are well advanced in this magical-scientifical thing,' the devaraja allowed.

The vizier, folding his extravaganza of a fan, tapped it pointedly on the marble floor. 'Mankind is consumed by self-importance: not only does this specious species wish to tell us how to live, but they want to make damn sure we do it.'

'Well, I shall put them in their proper place, I promise you,' insisted the devaraja, and he agreed to take the matter to the highest authorities. 'Happily, my connections are the very best. They are tip-top. And that is what counts in the end: who you know.'

The army had advanced deep into the forest, and Sala, having worked out a plan of attack, presented it to his men. The plan included many clever flanking and outflanking manoeuvres and was much admired. 'But first we must level all this,' said Sala with a broad sweep of his hand, 'to prepare a battleground.'

'But what of the forest creatures?' his brothers asked.

Sala replied that in war there must of course be casualties. 'But once the kingdom is pacified and all things being equal, any sacrifices will have been worthwhile,' he told them. 'Besides, animals have a lot of feet, so they can run for it.' And Sala, who did possess a box of matches, struck one.

The forest burned for seven days and nights, and a most excellent battleground was produced.

'We must look sharp now,' said Sala, having approved the new terrain. 'The enemy will be ready and waiting for us.'

But as they advanced through the forest, which, always dark, was now very black indeed, everything was silent. The trees no longer rustled, no animals growled or chattered or cried out, and no birds sang. The forest was empty.

'If the cowardly enemy has fled it will be a grave disappointment,' declared the army, as one. 'But perhaps they are waiting in ambush.' And they marched hopefully on.

But no creature was to be seen.

'The enemy has turned tail!' declared the soldiers. And this did seem to be the case.

When they arrived at the forest edge, the devaraja's palace stood before them. It was made of marble, with many golden turrets, and the windows, framed in alabaster, had crystal panes. All the windows were open and music could be heard within.

Sala knocked firmly at the front door.

The devaraja, who had been too fat or else too indolent or unperturbed to flee, now received Sala with his gracious condescension.

'You have made an awful mess of my country,' he observed calmly, over a cup of jasmine tea scented with orange and mint and served in eggshell porcelain.

Sala apologized for the inconvenience and disruption. 'We will put everything to rights,' he promised. He was longing to complain of having had no one to fight, but thought it might not be polite. 'The setback to your economy is only temporary, and the new forest will be a huge improvement,' he assured the devaraja. 'Everyone in it will be equal and will work together for the common good, and live in peace. As things are, forgive me for mentioning it, but your subjects devour each other non-stop, which is not very patriotic, you know. It is the tribal stage, and more primitive than our developed demonocracy.'

'All creatures must eat,' observed the devaraja with a mild shrug. 'So, naturally, they eat each other. For what else is there? But hierarchy prevents reprisals. A caste system is very orderly and, what is more, it works. That is why the law of the jungle is so famous. And of course the fittest survive,' he added, not unaware of current magical-scientifical theories.

'But demonocracy is the modern system,' Sala explained. 'It is tried and true, and nowadays is to be found in all the very best places.'

'Is it indeed? And where would I be in such a system? I am a devaraja, a kinsman and a descendant of the gods. I have been put on earth to help out, generally speaking, and create some order, which, in my own way, I believe I have managed to do. But a god – even a demigod,' he added modestly, 'is not the equal of other creatures. He is indisputably on the top of any totem pole.'

Sala admitted this was so. 'It is a difficult question. But could you not settle down as a vicar or bishop – or even as the pope, given your impeccable connections?'

'The pope . . . ?' mused the devaraja, turning this new and rather attractive proposal over in his mind.

'You would live in an even greater palace,' said Sala persuasively. 'You would wear an embroidered silk cloak and a jewelled tiara and you would rule over the hearts and minds of millions.'

'There is something to be said for it,' agreed the devaraja.

'Of course you would have to dispose of all your wives,' added Sala. 'A harem would never be permitted inside the Vatican.'

'Well I could hardly do that!' declared the

devaraja. 'Who would look after them and give them the children that they crave? Shutting women up is permissible, sometimes even necessary, but shutting them out is a disgraceful thing. This popery is pure chauvinist-piggery!'

Sala, having with difficulty side-stepped this awkward point, left the devaraja to ponder his future, and, rejoining his army, the troops hotfooted it back across the smouldering forest, dissatisfied that there had been no battles nor any great deeds to perform. But the kingdom had been pacified, so that was something, insisted Sala. 'And besides, one great feat remains. We must drain the pond and win the maiden and her sisters' hands in marriage. We are going to need a lot of buckets, you know.'

'If we find one, we can replicate it,' declared his brothers.

But when they reached the pond, they had no need of buckets, because the pond was dry.

'This is very unfortunate,' declared Sala, again feeling much deprived. 'And where is the beautiful maiden whom I love and wish to marry?'

Beside the dried-up pond stood five gazelles.

'Have you seen a beautiful maiden?' Sala asked them. 'She who was waiting for me?' And he described her to the gazelles, who, crowding more closely together, kept backing nervously away.

'The forest creatures were so thirsty after the fire that they drank the pond dry,' explained one of the gazelles. It was the maiden herself, but even she did not know it. Nor did Sala and his brothers know that they had been transformed, in the gazelles' eyes, into woolly bears. Though the young men did find the gazelles the most delicious-looking creatures.

'Well,' said Sala to his brothers, 'I fear things have not gone as we hoped. No maidens to marry and no battles to fight. But there will be other battles and other maidens,' he added in his philosophical vein. 'And it will be nice to go home again.' And reciting the powerful mathematical formula, he divided the army by five hundred, so that only his four brothers remained.

'As soldiers, we have done our job, even if unrewarded,' maintained Sala. 'But it is our father who is the politician. And now that we have cleared the way, he can establish a demonocracy, and everyone will be better off, and live in peace and equality.'

Overhearing this, all those creatures who had survived the fire roared with pain and laughter.

Sala put down some corn and pretty soon the enormous and brilliantly coloured bird arrived. When it had pecked up the corn, the young men clambered on to its back and the enormous bird took off. As it flew over the blackened plain of burnt stumps and charred, ash-covered ground, the bird scanned the devastated landscape and looked sad, but that was its natural countenance; and as the young men began to sing and talk about the future, the bird caught the lively tune, and with a small sigh, flapped its emerald wings in a determined upbeat sort of way.

Yves laid the manuscript aside, and removed his glasses.

'Now that's a real cute story. I liked that big bird,'

declared Bill. 'Make a great Walt Disney movie: animals, forest fires; sort of like *Bambi.*'

'It isn't *remotely* Walt Disney,' retorted Anne indignantly. 'I should think a twelve-year-old could see that.' It was the rudest she had ever been to Bill and instantly she regretted it, because of Marjorie. Bill could, she knew, take care of himself – and did.

'Yeah, Anne. I got the propaganda angle. That swipe about "demonocracy". I'll bet you twenty dollars that doctor was a Communist, one of those 1930s do-gooder types; as naive and full of high-minded intentions as they come. Physician heal thyself, I say, and stick to things that you know something about.'

'I can see why the Khmers enjoyed it so much,' offered Marjorie diplomatically. 'It appeals so to the imagination, doesn't it?'

'Honey, it's subversive baloney.' And tossing back his rice wine, Bill stood up. 'Let's get some sleep, shall we?' He saluted the others with his empty cup, and Marjorie, gathering her things and saying her fond goodnights, with a special word of thanks to Yves, followed her husband dutifully next door.

Anne was livid. The man could be as thick as a post the way he blocked things out, simply refused to see them if they had no practical use or didn't fit into his narrow portfolio of beliefs. He was like a magpie, only retaining bits and pieces of information if he deemed them useful to enlarge and maintain his supremely comfortable nest. But outside this readiness for profitable exploitation, he was surprisingly indifferent; he took little notice. Challenges kept him busy, they excited and satisfied, but his soul never lit up. The thought inspired in Anne a remote compassion.

'It's going to rain soon; I can feel it in my bones,'

observed Yves, slowly prising himself out of the hammock chair.

Anne jumped up to help him, her thoughts returning to the present, and smiling conspiratorially over his shoulder, motioned for Salty to come back later – receiving a thumbs-up in reply.

12

AS THE HUMIDITY LEVEL APPROACHED THAT OF A STEAMY sauna, all unnecessary movement ceased. Blanketed in lethargy, the countryside watched and waited. Dark clouds, puffing and ballooning, had gathered in the southwest. Grey and heavy, they resembled nothing so much as soiled pads of cotton wool from which, given a cosmic squeeze, vast amounts of water might be wrung. As they lumbered forward, bearing their heavy load, the sky darkened to become a blue-black bruise. Then the fireworks began, the gods shaking golden sceptres in vainglorious exhibitions of celestial power, and the deep, low growl of approaching thunder rumbled in response.

Sheltering on the loggia, protected from the wind, the Barangs watched as from a theatre box, fascinated by the ferocious stabs of lightning and flabbergasted by the instant and dramatic change of scene. Till suddenly, with a sonic boom, the curtain was dropped, the stage obliterated. The rain gushed. It beat a tattoo on the roof tiles, turned banana leaves into tom toms, the bucket beside the well to a tin bell, pinging raucously. A percussion orchestra was in full swing, and the Barangs between the acts.

Inhaling the light fresh air, relishing the cooling drops

of moisture on their skin, they opened a jar of rice wine in celebration, and began to discuss with relish the details of their departure. Who should be courier, precisely what message should be sent, and to whom delivered?

The Grand Hotel, all agreed, should be the courier's destination. The manager spoke English and could telephone the American embassy, and explain fairly precisely where they were and that they needed gasoline. Bill thought Samnang the best man for the job, unless of course Ty could be persuaded. Ty had more clout, and it might well be needed.

Cries and shouting sounded on the path outside the garden, and gaggles of shrieking children, arms joyously outstretched in the downpour, ran skipping and frolicking along it. Marjorie was reminded of Harlem children, when fire hydrants were opened in New York on hot summer days. But these children were gleefully engaged in fleeing their parents, who followed in hot pursuit, as in a game of tag.

Yves said the first day of rain was believed to be dangerous: evil spirits were at large, so parents tried to keep their children home. A near-impossible task. 'Climate change *can* cause colds, so the practice is a good one, even if the reasoning behind it is dubious.'

'And who knows, really?' ventured Marjorie, braving her husband's impatient-looking glare.

Ty had said that if the rains continued heavy the river should be navigable in about two weeks; and Bill, bursting with curiosity about the reservoir, set off the next morning, keen to see what progress had been made. The digging was finished, more or less, the reservoir's sluice gate set in place. Now a damp stain was visible in the basin's centre, where the water had accumulated, then quickly seeped away.

'It will fill,' promised Yves, smiling kindly. 'It is only a matter of time.'

'The earth is thirsty,' offered Kieu, when appealed to, in the garden. 'It must drink, and then the plants must drink. After that the gods will give the people water, too.'

'Sounds about right,' murmured Salty, sitting on the platform, his normally busy hands hugging his knees. Salty had other things on his mind. Early that morning, en route to the wax market, he had encountered something odd. The village path, normally so dusty that every footfall produced a cloudy puff, had been turned to slush in the rain. But here, too, the water had seeped away, and the path, hardening in the morning sun, was an intaglio of footprints. Salty had been intrigued. As a boy in Wyoming, pretending to be an Indian, he had studied and sometimes followed animal tracks. He rarely saw the animals, but he'd learned quite a bit about them from their tracks. Now, idly picking out the prints of men, dogs, buffaloes, pigs and chickens, something unusual had caught his eye. In the path's centre were unmistakable tyre tracks. A number of dilapidated bicycles were about, but these tracks were wider, the tread marks sharply etched, as with new tyres; and instead of making a continuous line, they came in short, regular bursts.

Salty didn't need to speculate. He knew precisely what they were: Ho Chi Min sandals, they were called in Southeast Asia – sandals enterprisingly cut from rubber tyres.

After lunch, Salty retrieved his Stetson from the chest where it now resided, and set off, undaunted by the gathering rain clouds billowing again on the horizon. Local people paid no attention to rain, at most plucking a banana leaf for shelter. Rain was as natural to them as sunshine, and it was equally welcome. You got wet, you went on, you dried off, refreshed like any other forest creature. Salty liked that a lot.

Since the weather had changed, he had explained at lunch, he was anxious to check the Cessna's tethering ropes. And curbing his real concern, reducing it to a cool disinterested curiosity, he traversed the narrow forest belt with something like detachment. When the rain came, it was only a shower. Salty tilted the Stetson's brim forward and, pulling occasional leeches off his arms, marched purposefully on. When the sun came out again he could see the straggly savannah through the dripping trees, and the Cessna glittering brightly in the distance.

But closer up the picture substantially changed. Instead of the sleek, well-cared-for aircraft he had visited two weeks earlier, there stood the carcass of a half-eaten prehistoric beast. Salty's mind shut down. He moved robotically forward, his gait carefully controlled; he absolutely refused to rush. What would be the point?

Large slices of metal had been cut from the aircraft's fuselage, as from an animal's flanks. The propeller had disappeared, the cockpit doors were open and the seats removed, the gutted interior rain-soaked. The culprits hadn't managed to open the hold, however, and, surprisingly, the instrument panel was intact. But as Salty had foreseen, the tyres had been cut off the wheels, whose bare hubs were embedded in the rain-soaked earth.

The grim news, delivered in Salty's for once appropriately sepulchral monotone, and prefaced by 'We got ourselves a problem,' was received with better grace than he had expected. Predictably, the women looked shell-shocked, Anne's hand clasping her open mouth. But Yves, constitutionally unruffled, remained impassive; and Bill, whose reaction, Salty realized with some irritation, mattered most, was surprisingly unperturbed. Used to crises and enjoying the invigorating rush of adrenalin they produced, the alertness and gamesmanship required, Bill moved instinctively to take command.

Reiterating his promise about the plane's insurance, he paced the loggia for several minutes, and quickly came up with a new plan. 'Here's what we'll do. Instead of gas, we'll ask Rives to send an airplane straight to Domrei Chlong. In a way it's easier. No, wait a minute – here's a better idea. If we go out with the courier, the plane can meet us in Siem Reap. Best to be on the spot, as you never know with these guys. This way we can take everything out with us, and find a regular shipper in Siem Reap.' He grinned at Anne and Marjorie, whose faces were upturned like children listening to a lulling bedtime story. 'We'll make it a safari. If things are well packed, nothing will get wet; the boats have canopies. Hey, this could be a lot of fun, a real adventure. We can sail out of here in style, go straight to the Grand Hotel, and wait for rescue in comfort.'

Bill's resilience, his ability to step in and solve problems calmly, shrewdly and without a fuss, storing unwanted burdens neatly out of sight, impressed everyone. His good humour and enthusiasm were infectious. He would have made a good general, thought Anne, whose respect for army mentality ran pretty low. An avowed physical coward, Anne none the less loved adventure, provided there was, as now, the prospect of secure underpinning. 'Let's do it!' she cried enthusiastically.

'Dinner and a bed at the Grand – just think of it!' declared Marjorie, adding, 'I'll be sad to leave dear Shangri La, but oh so glad to see my daughter! I wonder if I can call her from Siem Reap. Surely I can send a telegram.'

'She'll read it in the newspaper first,' predicted Bill. 'Reuters will be on to it like a shot. They'll flash the story round the world – like that.' He snapped his fingers with an audible pop.

The Cessna's pillage, when reported to Ty, provoked commiseration but little surprise or indignation. Ty promised to investigate, but Yves said he doubted much would come of it. The Khmers held possessions lightly, and theft was not so seriously regarded as in the West, nor was it uncommon.

'What difference is it going to make now, anyway?' blurted Anne impatiently. 'It's too late.'

'It will make one helluva difference!' Bill retorted furiously. 'You can't start a business if people are going to steal things the minute you make them. And these people don't have locks on their doors; they don't even have policemen, for Chrissakes.'

'Maybe they won't want to steal anything,' suggested Anne, who on this occasion hadn't meant to be confrontational. 'I mean, if they need a basket or a *sampot*, they can always make one. That's a big difference, isn't it?'

'Yep. Self-sufficiency should help to keep folks honest,' Salty offered in support, though he intended to keep his eyes peeled on the villagers' feet.

It rained hard for the next three days, but Bill, busy arranging the details of their departure, found time at last to visit the reservoir again. A large puddle of cocoa-coloured water lay in the basin's centre: the water – or some of it – was holding, and each day now should show a visible increase. Encouraged, Bill decided to check one of the river pools for comparison. Fed by mountain streams, it would of course fill more quickly. But any pool right now, if it were full of water, would be quite a sight.

A narrow but steady stream of water flowed along the riverbed, and Bill, leaping across it to the opposite bank, followed the river's course as it meandered back into the jungle. A marvellous freshness filled the scented air. The new-washed trees had become a palette of myriad shades of green; the undergrowth seemed to have thickened almost overnight, and high up in the arching canopy, the forest denizens pursued with renewed energy their age-old occupations, travelling searchingly from tree to tree with the stealth of accomplished burglars.

The pool was in a clearing that through the trees took on a soft translucence in the filtered sunlight. As Bill came closer, his eye, scanning for the glimpse of a rare bird or animal, caught a sudden flash of scarlet. Or was it movement that had first snared his attention? The eye responded quicker to movement than to colour, so perhaps it was movement. Whatever the cause, Bill advanced more slowly, peering with new concentration through the tall columns of liana-festooned trees.

A woman stood in the pool. The water came up to her hips. A soaked red sarong clung to her glittering copper skin, and her hair, wet and shiny, fell in a heavy mantle down her back, almost to her waist. Above her head she held a calabash, from which the water streamed down over her body. Bill couldn't see her face as her back was to him, but he knew at once that it was Bopha.

He stood very still, a voyeur observing a seemingly mysterious and clandestine ritual. Later he remembered that a bird, hidden from sight, had been calling in a repeated high-pitched shriek. A peacock? He remembered, too, the rise and fall of the calabash, and the little waterfall pouring from it, the arch of Bopha's bare arm holding it above her head, her breasts veiled but perfectly moulded by the sarong, the shadowy cleft evident between, and her hips disappearing under the water, like a mermaid's. A moment of rare beauty and serenity, overlaid by eroticism, and coupled with a strange and melting tenderness. Bill stood, rapt, or perhaps he stepped forward and made a noise; because suddenly Bopha looked round, half turned, gazing back over her shoulder through the arc of her raised arm. Bill thought fleetingly of that deer, raising its head, graceful and nervous, in the forest. Bopha, too, was nervously alert, her gaze searching the direction of the sound, so that by accident their eyes met. Hers, dark and brilliant beams of unavoidable communication – and how frank they were. Yet she gave no sign of acknowledgement or recognition. Nor, Bill believed, had he. But a peculiar intimacy passed between them, an intimacy of the sort that strangers, meeting haphazardly, by the very fact of their unconnectedness occasionally create; a closeness, and sometimes an involvement, often denied to more deserving familiars.

It seemed a long moment; probably it was not, and Bopha was the first to break it. Turning away, swaying through the water, the silver-edged ripples ruffling in a train behind her, she climbed the low bank, stooped to collect something – it looked like a laundry basket – and was gone.

But the image remained razor sharp in Bill's mind, and

their not having spoken made its impact greater, giving to a mundane encounter an aura of mystery and pulsating sensuality.

Bill told himself he must be getting old if the sight of a pretty girl made him feel so dizzy and stupefied with pleasure – filled him with an absurd *joie de vivre*. But what the hell, he loved it; and that evening everyone noticed his exuberance and was glad.

'Reservoir filling up?' asked Salty.

'It sure is!' Bill was grinning, but not at Salty. He was grinning at the girl in the poster, holding a calabash and looking over her shoulder straight into his eyes, smiling a warm and beckoning welcome.

Due to meet Ty the next morning at the pagoda, Bill hung about waiting for Bopha to arrive in the schoolroom, but she didn't come. Perhaps she was right, he decided, although it showed an unnecessary exaggeration. But then he'd long suspected that Bopha had a crush on him. She was a naive and impressionable schoolgirl, to whom a foreigner would naturally appear immensely glamorous and important – eligible for hero-worship, even. It was up to him to behave responsibly. He had no intention of doing otherwise, however; and shaking his head like a wet hound drying off after a refreshing swim, he set his little fantasy aside and, revived and virtuous, marched off to meet Ty at the pagoda.

But when the next morning Bopha again did not appear, Bill became short-tempered and noticeably preoccupied; and by the following day, to his intense dismay, he was boiling in a stew of acute frustration and desire. He was rude to Salty, and openly irritated by Marjorie when, having accompanied San to see the *neak ta*, she cheerfully confessed to an interest in taking up spirit offerings.

Smoking a joint and humming 'Heartbreak Hotel', beating out the rhythm on his knee with a spoon, Bill drank a jar of rice wine, then opened another, his mood fluctuating wildly, like a broken compass. He wanted to fight, to dance, to kill, to murmur endearments – to perform some brilliant and valorous feat of daring. Above all, he wanted Bopha. How could such a thing have happened? He was no raw youth, and the sight of a woman bathing was hardly a big deal: he had hung around beaches and swimming pools all his life. Yet when he thought about it, mythology was full of bathing nymphs spied on by lecherous gods who, becoming obsessed, condescended into humans and fathered heroes. David, coming upon Bathsheba in a pool, was so consumed with desire that he sent her husband off to be killed in battle, so that he could have her; while poor Actaeon, spying the goddess Diana bathing, was changed by her into a stag in revenge, to be hunted and killed by his own hounds. The priapic hunter turned into quarry. A nasty trick, that: the sort so-called feminists would enjoy. And so unnecessary, when man was equally a victim of the proverbial cherub's dart.

'That little kid is some shot,' marvelled Bill, forcing himself to be upbeat and making up his mind then and there to pluck the poisonous arrow out. The hardest part, of course, was mustering the will to do it. But he *would* do it; he had the will, and no intention of succumbing to a toddler-inflicted wound on some silly metaphorical battlefield. He was the master of his destiny and, what was more, a happily married man, and he was going home.

So when finally Bopha did appear, things slotted

smoothly back into place, and Bill's perspective was rapidly restored. In truth, the real Bopha simply failed to match up. Compared with the smiling image of welcome in the poster, she seemed almost a stranger – at worst an impostor, and at best an understudy for the original role. But Bill was kind, his self-command admirable, and he was glad to see her, if mainly because it had freed him. Nor did their eyes meet. Bopha saw to that.

It was as if nothing had happened. But then nothing had, and Bill decided he was probably wrong about the crush. No fool like an old fool, he told himself, eating his breakfast and reviewing the day's agenda. Well, he was in his prime. He'd had a narrow escape, but the battle was won, the mischievous little archer had been defeated; Bill's heart was cauterized and on the mend. And with a yip of inner triumph, off he galloped at the head of a phantom cavalry to the next event.

By the end of the week the river had risen to become a strong current of muddy water, making for the Tonle Sap. The reservoir, too, was rising, and the Barangs' departure imminent, Marjorie on a sudden whim visited the pagoda. Inside the sanctuary, a gigantic statue of the reclining Buddha lay deep in meditation, the head propped up pensively on one arm. Villagers rubbed the Buddha's feet, the soles of which were engraved with symbols; then they rubbed their heads and faces, and said a prayer. With nobody around, Marjorie now did the same. Then, kneeling before the reclining statue, she lit a candle, and prayed for a smooth voyage and that all was well at home, Sarah bravely bearing up and Hattie patiently holding the fort. Performing this unorthodox little ritual in secret, Marjorie experienced a feeling of lightness that was magical and uplifting, and she left the sanctuary convinced that invisible powers had heard her prayers, and that they would be answered.

At Shangri La she found Yves and Ty walking about the garden, deep in talk. The others, fearing a hitch, were hovering in suspense, under the house. Bill strongly suspected a last-minute money squeeze, and Anne, who had caught the word '*jao*' – bandits – feared that they were in danger of being robbed en route.

'There is news from Siem Reap,' Yves announced solemnly, as he and Ty joined the others on the mat-strewn platform, and tea was served.

'Thank God! A boat must have got through; the river's navigable!' cried Anne.

Yves sipped his tea reflectively. 'The world goes about its business, and much has happened. Some of it rather serious, I'm afraid.'

'River full,' interjected Ty, smiling broadly.

'Prince Sihanouk, it seems, has been deposed.'

'Well now, that's too bad!' In fact, Bill wasn't so surprised. Mike Rives had said that the prince spent all his time making movies and the government more or less looked after itself. '*K'nyom s'dai*,' he managed in Khmer. 'I'm sorry.'

The others murmured in an appropriately funereal-sounding chorus, and Ty bowed in gratitude.

When had all this happened, they wanted to know?

'About six weeks ago, from what I can make out. Sihanouk is now in exile.'

'But this is serious!' exclaimed Anne. 'Sihanouk is like a god to these people; they worship him. They must be very upset.'

But Yves had moved on to the next point. 'It is said that American troops have entered Cambodia.'

'Yippee!' Bill shook both fists in triumph. At long last, troops were searching for them. He was vastly relieved, and also more than a little flattered.

Yves watched this display with owlish solemnity. 'Ty reports that American planes are bombing Cambodian villages near the border.'

'Well now, that's ridiculous.'

'Ridiculous or not, I'm afraid it affects our plans.'

'It sure does!' Bill, leaning sideways, was craning outwards in a strained examination of the sky. They must prepare a signal – build a big bonfire to attract attention. The bombing was a lot of nonsense, of course.

'The new government is headed by Sihanouk's former prime minister, Lon Nol,' continued Yves. 'Ty says there is a rumour that the CIA was behind the coup.'

'Well, it probably was!' Anne exploded, and instantly regretted it.

'Ty knows as much about the CIA as I do about Mount Meru,' retorted Bill, giving Ty a polite but cool little nod.

'The Vietcong have been using Cambodia as a safe house for some time,' Yves went on. 'But bombing their sanctuaries is pushing them further inland, away from the border.' He raised his eyebrows slightly – for Yves, an unusually expressive gesture. 'Ty says fighting has broken out in Siem Reap.'

'Siem Reap!' Bill was incredulous. It was pure Gilbert and Sullivan.

'The town is virtually surrounded. The Grand Hotel is army headquarters, apparently. The airport remains open and is supplying government troops. But it is of no use to us: we could not get through to Siem Reap unnoticed, and in my opinion it is too dangerous to try. Westerners, especially any Americans, caught by the Vietcong would almost certainly be branded CIA.' Yves did not elaborate on the outcome of such an encounter.

Salty, scribbling idly in the dust with the tip of a machete, looked up. 'What about here?'

'Here? We're Barangs,' Marjorie hurriedly broke in. 'English-speaking French.'

But already Bill was thinking ahead. 'OK, here's what we'll do. We'll send a courier as originally planned – someone who can sneak through to Siem Reap with a message telling the embassy to send a plane here.' He turned to Salty. 'A plane could land on the main dike, couldn't it?'

'Yep. If it's not too muddy and the pilot's good.'

'The boats will have to be unpacked, and what we can't take with us sent on later, when things have quietened down.'

Ty seemed about to say something, but changed his mind, so Yves broached the subject of a reliable courier, and Bill volunteered to pay him handsomely.

Ty said a boatman carrying dried fish to Siem Reap would be best, as he would not be noticed. It was agreed that the Grand Hotel should be his destination. Its being army headquarters could be useful, but the embassy must be the one to decide how useful.

'Old Ty's pretty well informed,' observed Bill a little later, still sitting cross-legged on the platform. 'Who told him all this, I wonder? Did you ask?'

Yves said it would have been impolitic, but the bush telegraph was a remarkably effective mode of communication, a first-class wireless, in fact.

'What's important is that Ty has chosen to warn us and to be of help; and I think he means it. Things have been going well for the village lately. Old Ty is an astute politician, and for the present at least we are a valuable as well as somewhat decorative asset.'

13

BY EVENING THE ENTIRE VILLAGE KNEW OF SIHANOUK'S downfall and the atmosphere was greatly changed. An air of mourning and insecurity had descended. The Khmers stood about in little groups, speaking with urgency and in hushed tones. The spirit houses outside family dwellings were being filled with offerings and the pagoda gong sounded non-stop, a steady bludgeoning thud, full of prescience, calling the monks to prayer. Their chanting could be heard outside as villagers came and went, lit candles and knelt in prayer before the smiling supine Buddha; then rubbed his feet and, afterwards, themselves.

Concentrated in prayer, whispers and spiritual communion, Domrei Chlong was drawing into itself, backing away from the threatening abyss of uncertainty and the unknown. Evil spirits had deposed the man through whom their lives were linked to the almighty powers, and only evil could come of it. A sense of foreboding had crept into the Khmers' normally cheerful faces, and the following afternoon, instead of rain, the sky was seen to weep.

The Barangs, equally if differently affected by the news, involving as it did another shift of gears, another delay, more frustration and uncertainty, put their own reserves of faith in Bill's new plan. They composed a short message to Mike Rives, setting out their needs and whereabouts, sealed it in a bamboo tube, and delivered it to Ty. Then Bill ordered the boats to be unpacked and went off to check the reservoir. The water level had risen visibly; the basin was about a quarter full. One thing at least appeared to be running on schedule.

The next morning, word of the Barangs' postponed departure having spread, half a dozen unusually subdued children turned up at Shangri La for lessons; and surprisingly, Bopha was among them. Bill greeted her kindly, a little taken aback that she had come.

'We'll be here a bit longer,' he told her, for want of something to say. 'I'm sorry about Prince Sihanouk.' His tone suited reference to a near and recently deceased relation.

'He is our king,' replied Bopha, addressing her feet and summarizing what, after much debate, had become the collective village response. The coup was deemed of no importance, the situation the same as when, years earlier, Sihanouk had stepped down as king, to become chief-of-state. Sihanouk, like the god Vishnu, had many avatars, but in his essence he could not be other than he was: their Royal Father; from that position he could never be deposed. Overnight, fact and faith had been smelted into a cleverly adjusted armour so that life could continue, protected from undue worries and without disruption.

'You stay at Domrei Chlong.' Bopha's polite Khmer monotone made it impossible to know if this was a question, a space-filler, or the result of verbal limitations.

'A little longer,' Bill repeated. And as Bopha continued to stand there, he wondered fleetingly if perhaps she had a crush on him after all; and he smiled benevolently.

Marjorie appeared with a basket of beans from the garden. 'Bopha, do come in. We'll begin in just a minute.'

And Bopha, released from her trance, glided smoothly off.

Without any doubt the Cambodian hive had received a substantial poke, but after much frantic buzzing, had concluded it was unnecessary to swarm. For one thing, there wasn't time. The seedbeds were being planted, and outside every house rice from the previous harvest was being soaked in pails, transferred to baskets and sown broadcast in the newly ploughed nurseries, the sower walking backwards, one arm flung out in a steady rhythmically repeated gesture, as a whirlwind of birds swooped and fluttered hungrily in the wake. Marjorie was reminded of St Francis scattering crumbs before a flock of sparrows. St Francis had talked to birds. It was said he had even preached to them. Like the Khmers, he, too, must have believed that they had souls.

Bill, pondering the rumours of American bombing, concluded that the US, currently reducing troop levels in South Vietnam, would understandably want to leave its Vietnamese allies in as strong a position as possible, which destroying Vietcong sanctuaries would help to do. And if bombing had been deemed necessary, Sihanouk might have got in the way. *Realpolitik.* They were themselves far enough from the fighting, however, that a plane coming from Phnom Penh should have no difficulties.

But when Ty showed up at dawn next morning, alarm bells began to ring. Invited up to the loggia, he sat down cross-legged on the floor, where the others reluctantly joined him.

Ty opened the conversation in his new-found English. 'Domrei Chlong good place,' he said.

'Very good place,' they answered in a nervous pidgin chorus.

Having cottoned on to the translation process, Ty was now in the habit of delivering one sentence at a time and waiting for its effect to register, before continuing. Yves, with only one sentence to work with, was obliged to translate more or less verbatim.

'The long-awaited visitor has arrived,' Ty announced portentously, gazing at his audience in order to read their reaction in their faces, something no Khmer, acutely attuned to face-saving and the importance of a politely impassive exterior, would have permitted. It was a form of nakedness, and public nakedness was a shameful and humiliating thing.

'There is no need to be afraid.'

The remark caused them to do just that.

'Narat is in the village.'

The Barangs relaxed. Having anticipated something dramatic, it was turning into local gossip and they began to lose interest.

Noting this, Ty came quickly to the point. 'Narat is the doctor's son,' he said.

His audience was back.

'Well, hey!' exclaimed Bill. And leaving Yves to translate that one, the others gaped in astonishment, which quickly congealed into open dismay. They would have to vacate Shangri La, and where on earth could they go? But donning masks of their own – putting on party faces – they expressed their delight at Ty's good news and volunteered to move at once. Did Ty know of a house that they might rent? It would only be for a few days.

Laughing good-naturedly, Ty said moving was unnecessary. Narat did not need a house. He would not be staying long, and he had found adequate lodging in the village.

Enormous relief was quickly succeeded by spiralling curiosity. Ty watched, fascinated. The Barangs were like children. There was no need to learn their language, because their faces gave so much away. Now they were happy again. How generous, they were insisting. They longed to meet Narat and to thank him for his hospitality. Surely he would want to visit his old home, if not live there?

'It is why I have come,' said Ty. 'In order to arrange a convenient time.'

'No time like the present,' declared Bill. '*Neak ta* permitting, of course.' Could Narat possibly come by after the wax market? (Sunrise, sunset and the wax market were the constants around which meetings could be fixed.)

Ty said this was exactly as Narat himself had wished.

'What a coincidence he's turned up now,' Marjorie observed, as Ty hurried off down the path.

'What a coincidence we're still here, you could say.'

14

NARAT DID NOT PAUSE TO TAKE IN EITHER THE HOUSE OR garden, but gave his surroundings a mere cursory scan as he advanced, as if he had been there recently, or was totally uninterested. The Barangs, not wishing to interrupt a heartfelt, possibly nostalgic homecoming, had waited discreetly upstairs; now they descended in a troupe, eyes glued on their mysterious host.

Narat was tall for a Khmer, long limbed and thin. His khaki slacks and shirt were meticulously pressed, his leather sandals in the European style. A red-checked *krama* hung towel-like around his neck, and over one shoulder was looped a canvas satchel. He moved leisurely with a loose-jointed ease, his eyes fixed on the path. And whether disinterest or deep reflection underlay his apparent inattention, something in his manner implied an intrinsic alertness, a readiness to react, even to spring or leap up high into the air, that was strikingly cat-like, and gave the impression of a man covertly on his guard.

But it was Narat's face that drew particular attention. The nose was straight and well proportioned, a nose of classical refinement; the cheekbones, round copper knobs, jutted out beneath tilted eyes that suggested

Mongol influence rather than that of recent French invaders. A shock of straight black hair fell forward over one eye, and, like a roof tile threatening to come unstuck, had to be pushed back repeatedly from what was indisputably an exotically handsome face. Apart from his nose, Narat's quarter-French inheritance showed not at all, unless it was in his height.

Anne and Yves, fluent French-speakers, took immediate diplomatic charge, and Narat, producing a formal yet surprisingly sweet smile, shook hands all round, bowing slightly, a vestigial *sompeah* that, when combined with his handshake, placed the gesture smack into European courtly tradition.

As they mounted to the loggia, Narat looked more keenly about, and Anne, trailing *politesse*, said how much they loved the house and how kind he was to let them stay; they were truly grateful.

It was assumed that he would sit in a chair, but he did not – probably never had in that house. So the Barangs were obliged to join him on the loggia floor, making a little circle. Anne was relieved that they hadn't asked him to lunch. '*Vous êtes très gentil de nous avoir laissé votre charmante maison*,' she repeated, for want of a further introductory remark.

'*Une très, très belle maison*,' chirped Marjorie, retrieving remnants of her schoolgirl French and beaming radiant goodwill.

'*Je suis heureux que vous êtes confortables ici*,' answered Narat, bowing again, this time more of a nod from the waist.

'Ask him about Siem Reap,' urged Bill, who was sitting opposite Anne. 'And find out what he's doing here, if you can.'

Narat looked across at Bill, seemed to study him, to be

considering. There was a short pause. 'I speak English,' he announced in a quiet voice.

Bill was totally unembarrassed. 'Hey, you do? That's great!' He wondered if it were true. People often made such claims, when in fact, having pocketed a few words, they lacked the grammatical thread with which to string them coherently together.

San, smiling broadly, had appeared with tea and rice cakes, and Narat's polite solemnity cracked into an open grin. The two spoke in a familiar and bantering fashion that seemed to indicate they had already met and talked. How long had Narat been in the village, the Barangs began to wonder.

But it was Narat who posed the first question, when San had gone downstairs. 'You are English?'

'Yes,' Anne piped up, hoping to let it go at that.

But Bill was undeterred. 'We're Americans – we three,' he proudly announced. 'Monsieur Dumont is French – French-Cambodian. Lived here all his life.'

Narat nodded briefly at Yves, and his eyes returned to the Americans. 'It is unusual that Americans are in Cambodia just now, unless on official business.'

'Mr and Mrs Bolton came here as tourists, to see Angkor Wat,' Anne explained, holding fast to her role of interpreter.

'Best time to travel, when others aren't,' Bill interjected lightly. 'We had the whole place to ourselves.'

'I was their guide,' continued Anne, trying now to guide them along a possibly thorny path. 'I have made a study of the temples' bas-reliefs. I'm writing a book about them.'

'A book, that is most impressive.' Narat seemed genuinely interested, and he looked at Anne with admiration.

It was becoming evident that the young man had some presence. There was a self-assured poise about him, and despite the spontaneity of his smile, a sense of things held in reserve. His English was excellent.

Bill explained that Salty was their pilot and that their fuel had been siphoned off at Siem Reap. He said the villagers had probably saved their lives. They were immensely grateful, and intended to return their kindness in some real way, as soon as they got home.

Narat, who appeared to accept all this as perfectly normal and to be expected, said how delicious San's rice cakes were. 'You wished to know why I am here,' he offered a moment later, looking steadily at Bill, then briefly at the others. 'I have come to see my family home.'

The Barangs, for their part, accepted it as perfectly normal and to be expected that a man returning to his country, even in troubled times, would wish to visit his boyhood home. But to relinquish it willingly to strangers showed a generosity and degree of hospitality well beyond Western standards, and they were humbled and filled with gratitude. That Narat did not intend to stay long in the village made sense too. Domrei Chlong had little to offer a young man who, comparatively speaking, was so evidently a man of the world.

'Your English is really wonderful. Did you study in England, as well as France?' Marjorie wanted to know.

'I have never been to England, but at the Sorbonne I studied Western languages. Communication is, I consider, a most important thing. Sometimes it is *the* most important thing. I have been in Cambodia for one month,' he added solemnly, and, shaking his head, produced another boyish grin. 'My God, it is in a mess!'

Everyone laughed and protested, insisting Cambodia was simply wonderful. They had loved every minute of their visit, and would be sad to leave. All of which helped to break the ice, so that the questions which followed became those of new acquaintances searching amicably for common ground.

But the Barangs were also eager for outside news, and in particular, news of Siem Reap.

Narat confirmed that the airport remained open; he had himself flown from Phnom Penh in a government plane carrying supplies.

'Maybe we could do that!' suggested Marjorie. Did Narat think a plane could be hired in Siem Reap to come to Domrei Chlong and take them to Phnom Penh? Would that be possible?

Narat said that with enough money anything was possible right now. Corruption was everywhere; the new government was deeply corrupt. He said there had been no difficulty on the river, but for non-Cambodians this would not be so.

At which point Marjorie remembered to say how sorry they were about Prince Sihanouk.

Narat replied that Sihanouk should have paid more attention to his work. He had let go of the reins, with inevitable results. 'Sihanouk is now in China. He is forming an opposition, and asking his people to rise up against the new government.' Narat paused before announcing quietly, 'There will soon, I think, be civil war in Cambodia.'

'Good heavens, I hope not!' cried Marjorie. 'That would be really awful.'

'But rural people are so removed from national politics,' protested Anne. 'Sihanouk's fall makes a big difference. I can see that. But it would be dreadful if they were pulled into a war that was really about a power struggle at the top.'

Pushing back the invasive shock of hair, Narat sat up straight. 'My country is very backward,' he said gently, almost impassively; yet the intensity of his gaze showed that considerable feeling inspired him. 'The peasants live as they have always lived. They know little of the outside world, and since everything must be ritually repeated to keep the spirit world happy and the universe in order, there can be no progress.'

'But the way they live is so delightful,' put in Marjorie. 'And everyone seems so happy.'

'Cambodia is one swell place,' Salty chimed in. 'You've only got to travel a bit to see how swell it is.'

Narat nodded politely. 'Yes, this is true. But unfortunately it is also true that what has worked in the past – yesterday, even today – will not do so tomorrow. The world shrinks and suddenly everyone is a next-door neighbour. But neighbours who live very differently from each other find it hard, sometimes impossible, to cohabit. Cambodia, with its ancient traditions, its lack of money and education, lags dangerously behind; and as neighbours we are increasingly undesirable.'

'But people all over the world long to come here,' insisted Marjorie. 'They want to see the temples and your beautiful ceremonies, and enjoy the peace and tranquillity, away from the bustle of big cities and connected so beautifully with nature.'

'This is so, and as a tourist attraction perhaps we might appease our uneasy neighbours. But to do so we must bend our lives to suit this future, and learn to give tourists the things they wish to see. "The customer comes first and he is always right." That is your saying, is it not?' The faintest hint of irony glittered suggestively in Narat's eye, then like a lamp went out.

'But to achieve this, our festivals and ceremonies, always deeply religious, and designed to give comfort and significance to people's lives, will take on a different meaning, and deliver a very different sort of comfort. They will be foremost a means of earning money. And that is prostitution, is it not? While we ourselves, dressed in our *sampots* and tiaras, our *kramas* and our Buddhist robes, will be picturesque curiosities, little dancing bears, relics of an idealized past that may never really have existed. This will happen before the people know that it is so, but when it already is too late.' Narat spoke calmly and softly, as from a great distance, like a man examining a city plan unrolled in front of him.

And then the roll sprang shut. 'But if this is not to happen, if Cambodia is not to become a zoo, it must change, and change very quickly.'

Bill was impressed. The young man had thought about a few things. He understood the importance – the absolute necessity, in fact – of progress. Cambodia could do with a few more Narats.

'But a lot of things work much better here than in America,' Marjorie pursued. 'Things to do with what's really important in life, and everyday things, too. Families seem happier. It just works, that's all.'

'The weak must adopt the gods of the more powerful, and imitate their ways,' said Narat solemnly. 'That is history, it is evolution; progress. And those who do not change can only survive in zoos, sustained by subsidies that, to those who hand them out, are always peanuts.'

'But how can things change if people don't want them to?'

'That is a very good question,' said Narat, and

Marjorie felt she had made a fine impression, even though Narat had no ready answer.

'You have built a reservoir,' he observed instead, to Bill. 'I have seen it. A second rice crop is a very good thing. When the people have had its benefits they will be grateful to you. And this house is now a school.' Again the boyish smile lit up Narat's face. And feeling themselves to be the cause of it, the Barangs found it was contagious. 'My house is well used. My mother and father would be happy to know that it is so. I thank you.'

'We found a story your father wrote. It's charming. Would you like to have it?' Anne enquired.

'My father wrote many stories. They were a little old-fashioned,' declared his Western-educated son with a benevolent smile. 'My father wished to be a writer, but he wished to help people even more; so he became a doctor. I, too, have wished to be a writer. It is why I have learned Western languages. Writers want to be heard where ears are largest – this is vanity, perhaps. But my father was right, I think. It is more important to help people.'

Bill, who found this sort of worthiness naive but youthful, returned the talk to their dilemma. They must get to Phnom Penh. A courier had been sent. Would he have trouble getting to Siem Reap?

'Ty is a careful man; he will have chosen someone reliable.'

Narat confirmed that the Grand Hotel was now government troop headquarters. He said the press were also staying there, news that pleased Bill almost as much as word of US soldiers in the vicinity would have done.

Yves asked about Phnom Penh and Narat said the

situation was getting worse. Refugees continued to pour in from the eastern and southern borders, and rice was becoming scarce. 'The government is selling it abroad, for money to buy arms, and the peasants are selling it to the Vietnamese, who pay high prices. People wish for money now even more than rice. They want to be able to travel light. But on arrival at their destination they may find that rice, always so plentiful in the past, no longer is. Hunger is something the Cambodian people do not know,' he added, smiling.

'I wouldn't follow Sihanouk if I was a Khmer,' said Salty, when Narat had gone.

'But if Lon Nol is an American stooge – nobody likes that,' replied Anne.

'Listen, a US-backed government is a helluva lot more likely to take Cambodia in the direction Narat wants than the comeback of some movie-making god-king – or a bunch of bald-headed bonzos, for that matter,' said Bill.

'I like Narat,' declared Anne, changing the subject. 'I like him very much. He thinks about things and he sincerely wants to help his country.'

'He's so handsome, too!' Marjorie chimed in. 'And his English is so good.'

'He seemed a nice enough young man,' pronounced Bill. 'Naive, but well intentioned.'

The women exchanged knowing and indulgent smiles. 'He must be about Sarah's age,' offered Marjorie placatingly. 'Just a boy, really.'

When Narat had got up to leave he had noticed the dining table underneath the house. 'A table. That is very good,' he had said. 'A table is a step forward for

Cambodia. In order to write it is necessary to have a table.'

'That was so sweet,' Marjorie now enthused. 'He must come to dinner, even if we do have to eat with our fingers and sit on top of the table. It's his house, after all.'

Salty promised to make an extra fork. 'He never said where we could find him, though.'

San, who was squatting outside, pushing rice dough through a sieve to make noodles, told them that Narat was staying at Chandrea's house, but he was leaving next morning for the Tonle Sap. It was a fishing trip. 'He will be back in a few days,' she added, seeing the women's disappointed faces.

'But we may be gone by then,' wailed Marjorie, 'and we won't have thanked him properly, or even said goodbye.'

'Besides, he's just arrived,' murmured Anne, frowning. Leaving immediately didn't make any sense.

San said Narat had been in the village for three days.

'Three days, before he visited his own house!' Marjorie turned to Anne in amazement, but the puzzle already seemed to be falling into place. 'So that's where Chandrea got her ideas from. Those two have been in correspondence, I'll bet you anything.'

'Chandrea can't write, can she, Yves?'

Though Yves said she could not, female intuition was not so easily derailed. Both women knew well that love's heavy shackles could be dragged in silence and without complaint to the farthest corners of the earth – especially if there had been a pledge.

'No wonder Narat braved a war zone to get here.' Marjorie's hands were firmly on her hips; she felt obscurely deceived. 'You remember how Chandrea wanted to get to Phnom Penh? Find a widower, indeed! She knew Narat was coming back, and very probably, when.'

'She's not beautiful,' observed Anne ruminatively, 'but she is intelligent. The gulf between them is enormous, though.'

The Barangs had seen little of Chandrea since she left the schoolroom, except at a distance. She always seemed to be with her family or sitting under her house engaged in some household task, eyes dutifully downcast, evidently under orders to avoid them. But if Narat and Chandrea loved each other, why had Chandrea's parents removed her from the school, unless they disapproved of Narat? And if they disapproved of him, why had they taken him into their house, like a fiancé?

'Maybe they don't want her to leave Domrei Chlong, and are playing for time till they know more about Narat's plans,' suggested Marjorie.

Anne agreed this would be wise, since the pair faced near insoluble problems if they were engaged. Narat could never settle in Domrei Chlong, while Chandrea, despite her intelligence, would be lost in a Western milieu. The furnishings in her head, fashioned in the local peasant tradition, instead of being viewed as quaintly charming antiques, would almost certainly be dismissed as junk. Education had separated the couple as ferociously as two opposing family clans. There was a hint of tragedy in it, if in fact they truly cared for one another. But the alternative, and in Anne's view the more unfortunate scenario, was the banal misery of an ill-suited and unhappy marriage.

'Why is Narat here, San?' Marjorie now pursued, through Yves, with a conspiratorial glance at Anne.

'He is here to help the village in troubled times,' replied San delphically, and, dropping the sieved noodles into boiling water, she gave them a vigorous stir.

'Does the *neak ta* say that's why he's here?' Anne enquired.

'The *neak ta* says that we should listen to Narat. There are evil spirits about who want to harm people, and everyone is afraid.' San stood up. 'I cannot come tomorrow. The spirits are angry and unhappy, and there is much to do. Trouble is coming and everyone must work hard to avert it. Last night many stars fell from the sky and the tamarind trees did not close their leaves, but stayed awake all night.'

'San's portents sounded like something out of *Macbeth*,' laughed Marjorie a little later, rocking gently back and forth in the hammock. 'People in Shakespeare's time must have believed such things, just like the Khmers.'

'They probably did, till the Church eradicated it as witchcraft and stuffed everybody full of their own superstitions.' Anne looked vexed. 'Narat is right. People adopt the dominant gods. That goes for culture, too, and I doubt there's ever been much choice.'

'Portents arise from seeing the world as interconnected,' observed Yves pleasantly, fanning himself as he sat on the platform edge. 'It's an appealing philosophy in ways, and perfectly logical, since if everything is connected the effects must always be knock-on. Like your famous domino theory.' He had turned to Bill, who was tiptoeing barefoot across the woven mat to the platform, carrying the empty shower jug.

'Einstein believed in that,' Bill cheerfully declared, sitting down beside Yves.

'Believed in Nixon's domino theory!' Anne blazed with indignation.

Bill leaned forward slightly, his hands gripping the platform edge, and regarded her with detached amusement. 'Uh-huh.' He wriggled his toes. 'Einstein believed everything was connected. He sat there at Princeton up to the minute he died, working on an equation to prove it. He wanted to pull Nature's forces into one. A theory of everything, he called it – TOE for short. "My big toe!" the younger physicists said. They thought it was rubbish. The old guy was pretty much sidelined by then. Uncertainty was all the rage – still is – flux, the impossibility of pinning anything down, what with light coming in waves and particles, and you can't predict which, or even where they're going to go. But Einstein couldn't let go. He believed there was a god, and God does not play dice, he told the uncertainty guys. But he could never prove it.'

'It's really about faith, isn't it?' said Marjorie. 'That's what it boils down to. Even things that eventually get proven start out as faith. And what science can't prove could still be true, only nobody's proved it yet.'

Bill gave a compliant little shrug. 'Belief, faith, hunch, whatever you want to call it – ideas; they're all great starting points. But they've got to be established as facts to be reliable. Otherwise they're just papering over cracks. But these people don't have facts even about stuff that was proven ages ago. They have no education; it's that simple. So they're stuck with what their forebears dreamed up as explanations hundreds of years back: evil spirits making you ill, bad actions in a previous life explaining bad luck now, people coming back as chickens, you name it.'

'Maybe people do come back as chickens, Bill.'

Marjorie's tone, as always, when she opposed her husband, was light and mildly teasing. 'Can you be sure they don't? Well now, think about it. Can you be really sure?'

'For God's sake, Margie, don't be ridiculous! If you believe stuff like that, you'll believe damn well anything!'

Anne, solidly in Bill's camp on this one, refused to join the fray.

But not Salty. 'I reckon you can't prove there isn't reincarnation any more than that there is,' he drawled, examining the piece of wood he was about to turn into a fork. 'If living things do have a spirit, that spirit has to move to some new place after death. Well, we can see a chicken, it's alive, so that's a possible address – a spirit could move in. While heaven is one hundred per cent guesswork, seems to me.'

Marjorie smiled fondly at her champion. Increasingly she and Salty found themselves united in sympathy for the Khmers' imaginative way of perceiving things. Recently they had visited the pagoda together, lit incense and rubbed the Buddha's feet. They had both enjoyed that a lot.

'Well, Einstein wanted proof,' said Bill, returning to the world of reason and common sense. 'He saw that without it the whole edifice was threatened, like leaving your flank exposed on the battlefield. And he was right. If something hasn't been scientifically proved then you're winging it.'

'When I was boy there were eighty-six elements, and that was a scientific fact,' said Yves, gazing across the garden to where Kieu was weeding at the base of a papaya tree. 'Now there are a hundred and three, and *that's* a scientific fact.' He smiled vaguely. 'Whatever works.'

Bill found the remark irritating, even faintly immoral.

'Yeah, well lunch would work a treat right now. How about it, folks? I, for one, am starving.'

They got up. Anne and Marjorie went to fetch the rice noodles and fruit salad, Yves saw to the water jug, and Bill and Salty moved the table into place beside the bamboo platform.

In the garden Kieu had also taken a break, and leaning comfortably on his hoe, chewing a betel nut and enjoying a respite from the sun, was amicably passing the time of day with the papaya tree.

15

THE COURIER'S BODY WAS BROUGHT BACK TO DOMREI Chlong the following evening, shot through the head. His body had been found beside his boat, some two miles from the Tonle Sap lake. His load of salted fish was gone and so was the bamboo tube. The men who brought the body home, passing acquaintances on the river, reported that the countryside was increasingly unsettled, with skirmishes occurring almost daily between Lon Nol's troops and the Vietcong, driven up-country by the bombing.

Stunned by the murder, the Barangs felt vulnerable for the first time since their arrival in the village, the women becoming nervous and dismayed. Anne wondered whether carrying their message might somehow be connected to the murder. But Ty dismissed this idea. The message had been a secret. And Bill, maintaining that no one would bother to steal a bamboo tube, kept up his energetic rallying: the message must have been delivered, and the boatman on his way home, when he was killed.

Encouraged by such confident assurance, the Barangs began, as four months earlier, to scan the skies and listen for the sound of an engine, a can of kerosene kept at the ready, beside a bonfire hatted with banana leaves to keep it dry.

For the villagers, however, the boatman's death, in addition to being a distressing personal event, had unnerved in a more general way. If Sihanouk hadn't been deposed, they now insisted, the boatman would still be alive, since no fighting would have broken out near Siem Reap. The conclusion, standing up to reason, underpinned a more arcane interpretation, as the first of to-be-expected knock-on effects.

Trouser-clad scarecrows now began to appear outside village houses, staring woozily. The eerie effigies weren't meant to scare off crows, but malevolent spirits (which might include crows, of course); while trifling occurrences like the loss of a comb or a tear in a *sampot* – even the shape of a rain cloud – were read as ominous signs, adding to the growing unease.

Yet people continued to smile and go about their daily business. Ploughing of the paddies was about to begin, and baskets of lotus blossoms, scented rice and water hyacinths were being carried on women's heads in a steady procession to the town hall, for the festival. Bamboo canes holding offerings again adorned the dikes, like garden torches waiting to be lit, and the spirit houses were daily stocked with titbits. The spirits' goodwill, so necessary for the success of any project, was of critical importance now.

On the morning of the festival a buffalo team appeared on the village path, yoked to a wooden plough. The plough was wreathed in garlands of shining leather-like vines and pastel multicoloured flowers that seemed to sprout miraculously from the plough shafts, as from Aaron's rod. The ploughman, bare-chested and wearing white bouffant trousers, carried in one hand a finely carved baton, which he waved vaguely at the bees and butterflies that hovered in a hazy cloud above the garlanded plough. Fairy-like gamelon music wafted across the village, and to the sound of drums and flutes, the villagers, wearing their best clothes, walked behind the buffalo team to the rice fields. The *bonzes* led the way – a saffron-clad choir, chanting their prayers as the morning sun refracted aureoles around their polished heads, like saints in a medieval painting.

Narat had returned the night before, and the Barangs signalled greetings from their modestly assumed position at the end of the procession.

In a highly symbolic act the sacred furrow was about to be ploughed, and as the buffaloes entered the rice paddy, the villagers, gathered along the dikes, fell silent. The ploughman lowered the metal-tipped ploughshare into position, and with a flick of his baton on the buffaloes' rumps the team moved ponderously forward. The blade, scraping the soil, sliced into the moist surface, gouging it up into a ridge and making a V-shaped cleft, as the earth opened in a display of readiness to receive the new year's seedlings.

Only one furrow was ploughed. The team was then unyoked and three bowls set down. One contained rice, another water, and the third was empty. The buffaloes, led by palm ropes strung through their noses, lumbered lazily towards the bowls. The ropes were then relaxed, but the buffaloes proved more interested in nearby stubble than the bowls, and as suspense grew among the onlookers, they had to be repeatedly coaxed and prodded in the right direction. At last one buffalo happened upon the bowl of water, and began to drink. Cries of delight rippled across the crowd. There would now be plenty of rain. But the second buffalo was nosing the empty bowl, and a murmured sigh followed upon the merriment like a wintry breeze. The buffalo moved on to investigate, not very enthusiastically, the bowl of rice, and the crowd exclaimed in joyous relief. The orchestra struck up, the monks chanted in unison their blessings; flutes piped, bells rang and drums sounded as, laughing and chattering, happy as larks, the villagers headed back to the pagoda for a feast. Rice and rain were now assured; the world, for the time being, was back on course.

Anne found this simple act of faith and its restorative power almost enviable. 'Innocence is marvellous,' she said to Marjorie, as they joined the procession back to the pagoda. Narat, she noted, was walking with Chandrea's family, near the front.

'You mean faith,' said Marjorie.

'Perennial childhood,' interposed Bill, from his Titanic position, head and shoulders above the chattering crowd.

'America might look childlike, too, to more sophisticated people, Bill.'

'Well, there aren't any.'

Anne, with great difficulty, managed to hold her European tongue.

'There could be in the future, though,' suggested Marjorie, sticking to her point.

'Then timing's everything. That and being on the top of the heap.'

During the festivities, the Barangs found time to ask Narat to dinner. He was, they noted, made much of as he moved among the men standing in little groups along the dikes. 'Sihanouk needs your help,' Yves had overheard. 'He is asking his children to defeat a corrupt and illegal government that has stolen our country and will do it harm.' A buzz of animated talk had erupted, but when Yves's proximity was noted it had fizzled out with equal rapidity, shifting seamlessly to the harvest and their belief that the spirit world had been propitiated; though most agreed that they still walked on eggs.

When Yves relayed what he had overheard, the others expressed surprise. Narat had been so dismissive of Sihanouk earlier.

Yves said Narat was probably using the prince to rally opposition to Lon Nol. Lon Nol was a foolish man, full of peasant superstitions, and as Sihanouk's prime minister had been violently repressive. He was responsible for the murder and imprisonment of many people and was much hated, especially by intellectuals and Phnom Penh's volatile student population, now passionately caught up in the intoxicating thrall of radical politics – Narat evidently no exception. 'Well, he *was* at the Sorbonne,' said Yves, by way of explanation.

Narat brought to dinner a jar of top-quality rice wine, and, sitting down cross-legged on the platform, admired the spitted barbeque and welcomed with enthusiasm the chance to eat red meat. It was well known that, despite their religion, the Khmers ate a little meat from time to time, but only if others killed it for them. Confirming this, Narat added mischievously that soldiers were a notable exception, because they sometimes ate their enemies' livers. The soldiers believed that in doing so they absorbed the enemy's strength, and since liver was full of protein, there was something to it.

'Don't they even cook it?' Marjorie exclaimed, dutifully wide-eyed.

'Tartare,' declared the ex-Parisian with cosmopolitan urbanity.

If the women were repelled by such a custom, they were none the less thoroughly enthralled by Narat, whose youthful swagger they had rightly perceived was meant for them, an instinctive gesture to amaze and shock, like a small boy suddenly pulling a toad from his pocket. The sheer boyishness of it, emanating from such a handsome young man, drew tenderness and, in a manner less explicit, obscurely excited.

During dinner, when questioned obliquely about Sihanouk, Narat announced to general astonishment that the prince had recently joined forces with Cambodia's Communist Party, allies of North Vietnam. Doubtless Sihanouk believed this desperate strategy was Cambodia's only hope – and perhaps his own. Sihanouk wanted to keep Cambodia independent, free from Vietnam and free from America.

'We do not wish for America's help,' observed Narat politely, addressing Bill.

Talk had turned a sharp and unexpected corner.

'Listen Narat, you sure don't want the Communists' help. Those guys are thugs. They want to turn men into machines, not individuals. They're trying to wreck a successful market economy that's taken centuries to build and has created undreamed-of prosperity. You can't even own your own land in a Communist country.'

Narat smiled. 'Before the French arrived, all Cambodian land was owned by the king. But the Cambodians did not mind. We are not so individual-minded as Westerners. Our unit is the family; our connection to our surroundings is intimate and real, but ownership is not so important, and arguably it is an illusion.'

'I think that's wonderful,' said Marjorie.

'I wish my country to be good and successful. Surely

this is every man's desire. But how can it best be done, and how much blood is that goal worth, how much disruption? These are difficult questions.'

To Bill they were student questions. Theories appealed to active young minds, they made the young feel involved and on top of things. But since they lacked much experience of life or human nature, its frailties got left out of their equations. Students should stick to chess, in Bill's view. And he rounded off the conversation with some advice: 'Take my word for it, Narat, the best government is one with low taxes and minimum government interference, and you only get that in a democracy.' He refrained from adding, 'and the Republican Party'.

'Democracy is a very good thing,' agreed Narat. 'But it will not work in Cambodia, because it cannot bring to Cambodia the changes that Cambodia needs. The peasants would never vote for them. With little knowledge of the world, they cannot judge what is in their best interests, and so they want things to continue as they are. There must be education before there can be change.' Though he spoke forcefully, Narat had maintained a lightness of tone that was non-confrontational, even rather cheerful. 'But first of all we must confront our enemies inside Cambodia.'

'But a civil war would wreck these poor people's lives,' protested Marjorie.

'War is a terrible thing,' Narat solemnly agreed. 'And in a revolution there is much civil violence – even when giving birth to a democracy. In the French Revolution,' he had turned to Yves, 'there were many massacres and executions. No one today would wish to have lived through that. Yet no one today wishes it had not happened. I find that interesting.'

'We managed to set up a democracy in America without too much trouble,' insisted Bill. 'There were some tough military encounters, but after that the British threw in the towel and things went along pretty smoothly for everybody.'

'Unless you were an Indian,' said Anne.

Bill looked at her in complete surprise. Clearly this thought had never occurred to him.

'America wishes for us to do what suits America's interests,' Narat continued, following his own thread, his voice dispassionate and polite, as though America was a sort of abstraction, removed from any of them. 'America helped Lon Nol to depose Prince Sihanouk, but the Cambodian people were not consulted. Democracy did not come into it. American democracy is, I think, a private club, and it wishes for no new members. What America wants is client states, who in return for American protection will do her bidding. And that is feudalism; it is feudalism on an international scale. The Cambodians have resisted this demand, and now America is bombing Cambodia.'

'Oh, come on!' said Bill. 'That's just a rumour. It probably comes from the *neak ta*.'

Narat might have been discussing the quality of mangoes in the wax market, his calm was so pronounced. 'The American people do not yet know of this, and perhaps they will not like it when they find out. But what can they do? Leaders can be the wrong choice, even in a democracy. But the wrong choice in America is bad for the whole world. Yet what can we do? We have no say. We must do as America says, or become her enemy.'

'Well now, I doubt that bombing story is really true,' repeated Bill. 'But if Cambodia *is* harbouring the

Vietcong, who are our enemies, then we have to stop it. That's *realpolitik*. And sometimes, well, war is plain unavoidable.'

'On that we seem to agree,' said Narat smoothly and with a quick smile. 'But if there must be war, then we, too, will need allies to protect us.'

'If you mean the North Vietnamese, believe me, Narat, stay away from that one. Sihanouk's got his strategy all wrong. He hasn't a hope in hell.'

'Sihanouk must look after Sihanouk. As for the Vietnamese, we can handle them; we have been doing so for centuries. But America is different, and if America truly wishes for our alliance, why does she not offer to us a vote? In this way the world can develop as a partnership.'

The idea was so preposterous that even Anne was speechless, suspended between a sense of fair play and an absurdity she couldn't immediately put her finger on.

Bill stepped smartly in. 'That's exactly what the UN is for, Narat. To give every country a chance to join in decision-making on world affairs.' Bill's expression showed he had settled the matter.

'I am sorry,' answered Narat with cool politeness, 'but the UN is not a democracy. It is like Europe's parliaments when kings were absolute rulers. The UN has five absolute rulers. When one of them disagrees with the UN's parliament, he vetoes it, and they veto each other, like warfaring kings. Europe's parliaments rebelled, and they beheaded the kings. Surely there is a lesson there.'

'Narat's right,' exclaimed Anne, visibly impressed.

'Damn it, Narat, I'm sorry to say this, but if you think Cambodia isn't ready for democracy, imagine what the

UN Security Council thinks about a lot of Third World countries having an equal say! The biggest problem isn't haves and have-nots, like people think; it's lack of education, as you yourself said only a minute ago.'

'Yes, but what is this education to be? I think it is Western education that is meant. Western science is a very good thing, and also Western democracy, if it can be made to work. But your history is not our history, and your gods are not our gods. Your culture will only make us feel more strongly that we are outsiders. Even our great temples cannot weigh sufficiently on the scales to balance this difference. We have no literature and our history, although visibly so impressive, is in its details largely unknown. Our animistic religion is deemed primitive and our Buddhist philosophy incompatible with capitalism.' Narat turned to Anne. 'I think we are like the American Indians you have spoken of. Those who survived did so in zoos – reservations, as America so ambiguously calls them.'

Yves, sitting quietly on the platform edge, morosely refilled his glass. Narat had perceived a sad reality. America, if unwittingly, was becoming a colonial power; its mode of colonization, American culture. World homogenization *à la américaine*: hamburgers, Coca-Cola, soap operas, loud music and the cult of making money, in return for medicine and modern technology. But no representation and very little choice. Societies could and did change, of course, but generations might be sacrificed in too sudden a transition. Angkor had collapsed five hundred years ago, and Yves wondered if Cambodia had recovered. If a successful culture was one that people believed in and where no one went hungry, then arguably it had. Now it must change again: good-neighbour policy would insist on it.

16

PLOUGHING OF THE PADDIES WAS WELL UNDERWAY, AND in the nurseries the tightly packed seedlings made a deep-piled carpet of brilliant and mesmeric green. There was no time now for gossip or speculation: everyone was too busy, and by evening, far too exhausted for talk. Looms stood empty, sugar cauldrons had ceased to boil, basket-making tools lay idle. In addition to ploughing, the water in the nurseries needed careful regulation, the excess repeatedly bailed out or a hole chopped in the dike and plugged when sufficient water had drained off. Yet an exceptionally heavy rain could still drown the tender seedlings. All eyes were on the nurseries, therefore, as the Khmers awaited uneasily the next knock-on effect.

Forced to conclude at last that their message had not got through to Siem Reap, the Barangs again took stock. As soon as the seedlings had been transplanted they would send another message, and this time they would send it to the press, who Ty assured them remained in residence at the Grand Hotel. Ty had kept it a secret that the boatman was carrying their message, and for this the Barangs were truly grateful. But the letter's fate was much discussed, for if it had been stolen they could be in serious danger.

Yves said the Vietnamese would have a hard time finding someone to decipher English. If Lon Nol's troops had found the message, however, translation would be more likely – and rescue too, if the new government was in fact American-backed. But the bamboo tube had probably been jettisoned; the boatman might even have done it himself, as a precaution, before he was killed.

Then something alarming happened.

Salty was setting snares in the forest when, stooping at the foot of an enormous tree, hiding the snare's loop with leaves, he heard a swishing noise in the thicket behind him. There was a short guttural cough and the undergrowth began to crash and shake. Tigers inhabited Cambodia's forests, and if one were near by, it would have no need to keep silent.

The tree was within easy reach, the branches low and spreading. Salty grasped a limb and hoisted himself up into the fork.

At that instant a man appeared. He was hacking through the thicket with a machete. Several others followed close behind, their eyes to the ground, slashing to left and right. The men wore black pyjamas; their heads were wrapped in red-checked *kramas*, and on their feet were Ho Chi Min sandals. One or two had guns, and all were strangers.

Although they wore no proper uniforms, Salty believed they must be North Vietnamese; and if so, knew that he, as a Westerner, would be desirable meat.

As the men reached the path alongside the tree, one of them stooped to examine the ground, then called out sharply. Salty became a stone, but inside he was jelly. He knew the man had seen his footprints and that leather soles would be highly suspicious. But the ground was hard and with luck the prints might look like rubber tyres worn smooth.

The soldiers began to poke in the undergrowth beside the path, making repeated stabbing motions with their machetes. Then one of them approached the tree. Walking carefully around the trunk, he examined the ground, kicking methodically at the undergrowth. He was nearly upon the snare; only seconds from havoc. Salty clutched tighter. As he did so the Stetson, pressed between his chest and the tree trunk, scraped against the bark, and the soldier looked up. He was hardly more than a boy, probably in his mid-teens. An amulet of the Buddha was strung around his neck to ensure invincibility, and his young face, serious and intent, looked confident and full of purpose.

Holding his breath, Salty closed his eyes. If captured, death would he knew be slow: they would want to eat his words, first. But as the boy peered up into the foliage, fingering his amulet, the troop's leader, evidently growing impatient, barked a command. Instantly, and without any sign, the young soldier turned robotically and quickly retreated the way that he had come. Yet Salty was almost certain he had been seen, and this confused him.

The soldiers, falling back into line, passed in single file down the track beside the tree. They were young and thin, their expressions grim and curiously intense. Their flip-flopping sandals made a squishing sound as they walked, and a hoarse cough broke from one or two, before they evaporated back into the thick and sheltering cover of the jungle. Salty counted fourteen.

* * *

Kieu, when pressed, admitted that North Vietnamese soldiers had recently visited the village. They had wanted food, but had paid for it and did not loot, even though they had guns. During the night they had returned to pick milk fruit, but had left money at the foot of the tree in payment. He said the soldiers were polite, and had treated the women with respect; the Vietnamese wanted to help the people, and they had promised local elections when Sihanouk was restored.

'Ty won't like that,' mused Yves with a wry smile. 'His job is hereditary.'

With soldiers in the vicinity, the Barangs began to fear they might become boxed in, and Salty suggested they consider trekking north, towards the Thai border. Once the seedlings had been transplanted, the village would almost certainly supply them with provisions and an armed escort.

Again the women baulked: the trip would be too arduous, and also dangerous, since no one knew where the Vietnamese were, and 'Barang' was becoming synonymous with 'enemy'.

Bill agreed. The Thai border was nowhere near Bangkok, and a few machetes hardly constituted an 'armed escort'. If they got boxed in, it would be in a safe box. The laws of hospitality ran deep in peasant societies. Moreover, the villagers were proud to have them there, and needed their help with the new enterprises.

A more pressing problem, for Bill at any rate, was how to fill the intervening days before another courier could be sent. The reservoir no longer needed his attention; it was filling steadily, each day now showing some improvement. Sitting idly on the dam, beside the new sluice gate, he imagined white water gushing out through the open gate into the canal, and spreading across the paddies to irrigate a second crop. The reservoir was small, but later on it could be enlarged. Much of its importance now was as a model.

Bill had also begun to set a few snares, to pass the time, and, leaving the reservoir, was on his way to check them when he spied Bopha, some distance in front of him, with a laundry basket on her head, evidently on her way to the river pool.

Reaching the forest edge, Bopha removed the basket, stooped down and placed a leaf holding a few rice grains on the path, before proceeding further. This was something all the villagers did; and for a moment Bill wondered how much rice was wasted on so silly and repetitive an operation.

'*Sue sdei*,' he called out in greeting, catching her up. 'We never see you these days.'

Bopha tinkled shyly, like a little bell, but whether she had understood him he had no idea.

Making a lifting gesture with his hands, Bill offered to take her basket, but Bopha wouldn't hear of it. A minute later, however, pretending he hadn't understood, he lifted the basket off Bopha's head and set it nimbly on his own, holding it in place with one hand. Bopha looked shocked but emitted another tinkle of shy laughter, glancing sideways in astonishment. Men did not carry laundry baskets.

'Zippity doo da!' Bill sang out, grinning, as they walked along the path together. One of his snares was near by and he wondered how Bopha would react if an animal was trapped in it, especially since he would be obliged to kill it. He decided to check the snares beyond the river first, and they continued in unselfconscious silence to the river pool, where, finding a grassy spot, Bill set the basket down on the bank.

'Thank you,' said Bopha to her feet. 'Is good.'

'My pleasure, dear lady.'

'You sit?' Pulling a *krama* from the laundry basket, Bopha spread it out on the bank, carefully smoothing out the wrinkles.

'Sure. For a minute.'

They sat down side by side, Bill clutching his knees and Bopha's little feet tucked neatly to one side. But no sooner had Bill sat down than he regretted it. Conversation, now a necessity, was impossible. How easy it was, when communication of a sort had taken place, to forget you didn't speak someone's language; how easily memory left this significant factor out. And aware that he must stick it out for a few minutes, out of politeness, Bill could think of nothing further to say.

But Bopha came to the rescue. Reaching inside the basket, she removed a banana-leaf parcel, and, opening it, produced slices of fresh pineapple.

'Your English is very good, Bopha,' Bill offered kindly, as he ate.

'I know a little words.' She smiled at the pineapple.

'You sure do. Quite a few, in fact.'

'Bopha and Bill sit on the mat.'

'Bopha and Bill eat pineapple.'

'Pineapul?'

He held it out.

'*N'noa-ah*,' said Bopha softly.

Bill repeated it as best he could. 'What other words do you know?'

Bopha, searching her schoolroom vocabulary, was silent for a moment, then smilingly announced, 'I love you.'

Bill grinned. For some reason this was always the first

foreign sentence people learned, despite being the most useless. *Je t'aime* was about the only French sentence he knew, and *ich liebe dich* the only German. Maybe it was because new languages, like new countries, inspired such fantastic hopes.

'Love, that's a big word,' said Bill.

'Big word,' agreed Bopha. 'Four letters.' She held up four fingers. 'I write four letters.'

'You do that,' laughed Bill, thinking he would like to receive four letters from Bopha, and wondering what they would contain. Cambodian weather was too predictable to be a newsworthy topic. They would, he decided, almost certainly be about the machinations of the spirit world.

Bopha stood up, dipped the edge of her *krama* in the pool and wiped her hands, then offered it to Bill, who had jumped up too, taking advantage of an opportunity to leave.

'I must be going, Bopha,' he said, wiping his own hands.

Bopha, standing beside him, was fiddling with one of the looped buttons on her blouse, and Bill began to hope she might be going for a swim; if so, he wondered if he could decently propose to join her. He wanted to very much, and decided to suggest it by making some corny swimming gestures to amuse her, keeping it light-hearted and innocent, which it was. But turning towards her, his arms slightly raised, about to begin his lunatic charade, he instantly gave it up. Bopha's dark eyes were gazing directly into his – eyes as black and shiny and opaque as mountain pools; and her little face, so still and serene, although lacking its perpetual smile, was not without expression. '*Saych-g'day s'ra-lul*,' she said softly, modestly, but with astonishing poise and self-possession, then repeated it carefully in translation, so that there could be no doubt or misunderstanding. 'I love you.'

'Hey . . .' answered Bill. But this time it was a deep male purr, as surging desire banished his amazement, and the consequences of their being seen, spinning at whirlwind velocity through his brain, only heightened his already intense excitement.

Bill dreamed of nymphs and dryads flitting about in short summer tunics, one breast bare, like the goddess Diana. Or could they have been *apsaras*? He was alone in a forest and encountered a young deer with brilliant wet eyes, caught in a snare. But when he approached, the snare was empty. There was a pool of clear water where animals came in pairs to drink: elephants, tigers, rhinos, rare wild oxen, even twin cobras, their heads raised and tongues flickering, like a pair of black-bonneted gossiping old women. A peaceful and colourful pageant that Bill, although unnoticed, was none the less part of, fitting in as neatly as a piece in a developing jigsaw puzzle.

He was surprised to be awoken by the angry squawk of parrots and shrill, malign outcries of unseen peacocks. Bopha and her laundry basket were gone. That, too, could have been a dream, it was so very extraordinary. But as he lay on his back, gazing up at the light falling in a shower of spinning silver coins through the thick-foliaged branches, he felt blissfully content. Bopha had taken all the responsibility upon her lovely shoulders. Collecting it like her laundry basket, she had carried it off, a graceful caryatid erect under a burden of potential difficulties. For it was clear from the *krama* on which he lay that she had been a virgin.

Bill took the cloth to the pool, washed it and then

washed himself. The air was close and sultry, a steaming sauna, the jungle uncannily silent as the piercing eye of the sun burned searchingly down. Then he put on his clothes and spread the *krama* out on the bank, sure that Bopha would return for it later. And holding fast to the shreds of his contentment, he went off to check the snares.

17

WEEDS FLOURISH ON FALLOW GROUND AND LOVE IN AN idle mind, the saying goes. But unlike weeds, love's vigorous vine requires support: a pillar or sturdy trellis to cling to in a fast embrace. And if the support is withdrawn, the vine, casting frantically about, shrivels and droops, dying a slow and anguished death.

But Bill's infatuation, well supplied with nourishment and support, had no need to put out searching roots or anxiously flailing tendrils. The vigorous vine spread easily in the sunshine, without impediment. The day after their meeting, he had gravitated back to the pool on the off-chance that Bopha would be there, which she was, spreading her laundry out on the bank to dry. She had taken his hand and led him deeper into the forest, along narrow animal trails winding through tall and shady stands of virgin timber, to a huge banyan tree, its trunk easily the width of a car. The tree's branches spread out in a massive umbrella, and in the fork of its outstretched limbs was perched a little house made of bamboo and thatch, with a ladder you could pull up when you were inside. If Bill understood correctly, the house must have been built as a blind, for trapping baby elephants to be tamed. But that was in the past, before the elephants had moved west, into the Kulen hills. Now the house was kept in good order simply to please the spirits, who were much attached to it, said Bopha.

On this point Bill declared his spiritual accord. He had entered a magical world: sensuous, thrilling, full of charm and playfulness, tenderness and soft laughter – his Tahitian fantasy come true – and he reeled about dizzily in its enchantment. Visits to the reservoir and the attention demanded by two or three snares provided him with cover for their meetings; while Bopha for her excuses relied on laundry and gathering *sdao* leaves, a malaria preventative her mother sold in the wax market. They managed an hour or so together each day – a little less when the transplanting of the seedlings began – but it was enough, and they were content.

Bopha's laundry basket proved a cornucopia of unexpected luxuries: bedding, cushions, delicious picnics, the coconut oil she rubbed on to Bill's body and the banana leaves with which she fanned him, singing little bird-like songs, sitting beside him as he lay on the cushions. Their need for words was minimal: touch, gaze, tone of voice and gesture expressed virtually everything they felt an urge to say. Little jokes developed, a word or gesture acquiring a meaning through some specific association that, repeated out of context, brought shared laughter and understanding. Bopha's adoration, her doll-like but sensuous beauty, her grace and unexpected ardour, wove a gossamer net of captivation. Her communings with the spirit world – repeated leaf offerings, the spirits continually invoked, their actions interpreted and their goodwill sought – were part of the enchantment. While with Marjorie, such things irritated in the extreme. But Bill didn't wonder at it; he didn't wonder much about anything. He felt no need. Suspended in a marvellous fairy tale, he abandoned himself to its fanciful and hedonistic pleasures, monitored by bevies of fluttering sprites and pixies, or their Asian equivalents.

Nor was he preoccupied when they were apart. Bopha simply retreated sedately into the recesses of his mind, where she reposed, a sacred goddess lodged serenely in her twilit niche, shielded from the common view. And Bill gave his conscious attention to his immediate surroundings. Merry, kind, humorous, considerate, he was pleasing to everyone – and he felt neither conflict nor guilt. A balancing element of unreality prevailed, of theatre, with its fixed beginning and end, its implicit understanding that when the curtain eventually came down, the actors, having taken their bows, would move on smoothly to the next production, or else go back home. But a double life was always there, and this was so emotionally as well. Bill loved his wife, but he had fallen in love with Bopha. And whatever else 'in love' meant – and it was highly variable – a defining characteristic was that you felt it for one person at a time; being like all madness a singular affair, and thus a thing apart.

It was Anne, not Bill, in whose mind the vigorous vine spread all-invasive roots, creeping into crevices and covering every thought with its thick and suffocating foliage. Anne lived actively in her mind; her imagination was strong, her powers of reason more than reasonably developed; her impressions, carefully filtered, were orderly arranged in useful categories. But if an idea or inclination broke free and took root in her imagination, a riot of growth could follow, to the point of total obsession, creating a wild and yet monotonous jungle, inhabited by a single plant whose very sameness made it almost impossible to navigate through.

The vine had been slow to root. Anne's haphazard liaison with Salty had dwindled more or less to extinction, without either of them much noticing, and Salty was spending more and more time with Marjorie, helping her with the cooking (San came less often now) and sharing her sympathetic interest in things traditionally Cambodian.

Both women also had a tender spot for Narat, whose youthfulness sparked affections that were largely maternal – or had seemed to be – and whose intelligence and considerable powers of articulation impressed everyone. Anne also admired Narat's dedication – his wish to pull his country forward into the modern world – and she sympathized with his political views. She was pretty sure he was a Communist, a philosophy with which Anne, like so many Europeans who despised hierarchical privileges of the past, was largely in sympathy.

But it was seeing Narat lying in the hammock at Shangri La, hands behind his head, one slender leg bare below the calf trailing the ground, the narrow elegant foot with the second toe longer, like a Greek god; he was so graceful and at ease, the epitome of an exotic prince, that Anne's fertile but fallow mind was suddenly seeded. Narat had smiled lazily up at her, and she could tell he liked her and found her attractive. When a little later he took her arm, quite unnecessarily, to help her down from the platform where she perched, she recognized a subtle pass, and was thrilled. She was, she guessed, six or seven years the elder. This consideration was quickly followed by the conclusion that, in the circumstances, age was beside the point. As for

Narat's supposed attachment to Chandrea, it was based on nothing more than the fact that he lodged in Chandrea's house, and there could be many reasons for that. In the three times Narat had come to dinner, Chandrea had never once been mentioned. But if there *was* any truth to it, extricating him would in the long run be a favour to them both.

Anne began to toy with the notion of a brief encounter. Well, why not? She had the time.

It was not until Narat failed to join them for dinner; however, that titillating erotic fantasy burst into riotous cerebral bloom, and Anne began to lose her mind.

Narat's messenger, a small boy – probably Chandrea's little brother – had no information other than his recited message, which he repeated, hands firmly pushed into the pockets of his wide-legged shorts. Narat was sorry. He had had to leave unexpectedly. The child knew nothing more.

'He must be coming back soon or he would have said goodbye,' Anne speculated aloud to Marjorie, the tension evident in her voice. 'Probably it's politics.'

Marjorie, who was kneeling on a mat, trying her hand at making rice noodles, agreed. 'Unless of course he's off fishing again.'

'He isn't some frivolous sportsman.'

But with the object of her infatuation removed from sight, Anne's imagination took off, unimpeded; and what had begun as a mildly intriguing and erotic musing metasticized overnight into a consuming fixation. Narat had sailed smoothly through a patrolled barrier of critical checkpoints into eligibility as a serious partner, and Anne was head over heels. She would, she told herself, willingly have followed him through the thickest jungle or down the Tonle Sap, chased by marauding

Vietcong and devoured by mosquitoes, if only he had asked her. She believed he would have asked her, had he known her feelings. If only she had known them soon enough herself, and spoken out: that was her great mistake. The vine, searching for nourishment, was pushing it roots into every crevice, the tendrils reaching blindly up for a trellis to cover with the abundant fruits of love.

When three days had passed, desperate for news and unable to bear the suspense (also getting suspicious), she decided to call on Chandrea.

Chandrea was sitting under her house, mending a yellow silk blouse. At Anne's approach she folded the blouse, set it aside and stood up. But instead of coming forward she stood quite still, waiting for Anne.

They exchanged greetings in Khmer, and Chandrea, to Anne's surprise, held out her hand. Then, calm and courteous, a teacher visiting her former pupil, Anne removed a terracotta jug from the basket she was carrying. The jug had contained the rice wine Narat had brought as a present to Shangri La. Anne assumed it belonged to Chandrea's family, and said she wanted to return it.

Chandrea set the jug down amidst a plethora of objects scattered about haphazardly under the house. Anne cringed inwardly at the appalling disorder. Khmer families lived amongst a chaotic jumble of tools, animals, looms, sleeping platforms, hammocks, crocks and utensils. Chandrea indicated the loom's bench, where Anne could sit comfortably, Western-style; she sat down herself on an upside-down cement jar near by.

How can people live in such disorder, Anne wondered? Does it reflect their mental state?

An elderly woman – Chandrea's grandmother, or

conceivably her mother – bowed and disappeared, returning with tea and setting the tray down, then evaporated.

Anne's Khmer had carried her smoothly through the formalities of greeting, but her inability to extemporize, and the ensuing silence, now brought her straight to the point, for which she was well prepared, having extracted from Yves particular words she believed she might require.

'Has Narat returned to Phnom Penh?' she asked Chandrea casually, sipping her tea, having said the rice wine was the best that they had had.

'I do not think so,' replied Chandrea simply; and she, too, sipped her tea.

'Then he'll be back soon, I expect,' reflected Anne, purposefully vague, her eyes fixed thoughtfully on the middle distance.

'It is his home,' replied Chandrea.

Presumably she meant Domrei Chlong.

'Perhaps he is in Siem Reap.'

'Siem Reap is very dangerous now.'

'Oh, then I hope Narat isn't there,' said Anne, and foolishly trying to make the remark sound unconnected to any particular pattern of thought, added, 'I hope everyone is well in Siem Reap.'

Chandrea either didn't understand, or she regarded this as the rhetorical remark it was, and gave no reply.

'He could be fishing,' Anne now suggested, grasping at straws. Her cup was empty, but there was nowhere to put it down except the ground, which seemed inappropriate, so, copying Chandrea, she held it in her lap. 'Isn't the Tonle Sap much nearer, since the rains?'

'Yes,' said Chandrea, equally thoughtful. 'He could be fishing.' And folding her hands around her own cup, unsettling a fly perched on the rim, she added faintly, 'I have never seen the Tonle Sap.'

Anne, amazed by the narrowness of such a life, was reminded of Chandrea's lost opportunity at Shangri La. 'We were sorry when you left the school, Chandrea. You were such a good pupil, and a little English could be useful in the future.'

'I am Khmer,' Chandrea answered softly. 'I do not wish for English.'

'But to read and write in Khmer? You could have learned that.'

Very fleetingly Chandrea looked sad. Then she rallied. 'We must work on the land,' she said. 'That comes first. To build up our country and to keep it free.'

It sounded like naive political jargon, but Anne suspected Chandrea was keeping her words few and simple out of consideration for Anne's own limitations, and she was grudgingly impressed. As well as being highly intelligent, Chandrea was tactful. And she appeared to have no idea they might or ever could be rivals – a view that cut two ways.

Casting about desperately, Anne attempted to thank her for making it possible for the Barangs to stay on in Narat's house. But the thought was too complex, and came out as a senseless muddle.

'You stay in his house,' repeated Chandrea, not understanding.

'Thanks to you.' Anne smiled, but Chandrea looked blank, her impassive detachment adding to her impressiveness.

Anne, at a loss and getting nowhere, now risked a bolder step: she became straightforward. 'Were your family and Narat's old friends, Chandrea? Is that why he stays in your house?'

'Yes, he is my friend.' The fly had moved to her bare arm, but Chandrea's hands still rested in her lap, holding the cup.

Defeated, Anne stood up. She should have known better than to try and breach the Khmers' curtain wall of *politesse*. The visit was a failure, and she was a fool to have come. Yet she wanted to say something complimentary, to show good will and, if possible, gloss over her evident failure. She was constructing a sentence in her head to this effect when Chandrea said quietly, as they emerged from under the house, 'You must go soon from Domrei Chlong.'

Anne, taken aback, wondered if this was an observation or advice, possibly even a command. Or had she simply misunderstood?

'We want to go, but it is difficult.' A safe response, either way.

'If I can help you, I will do it,' replied Chandrea, without the customary Khmer smile. But when they again shook hands, she did smile. A tired or else sad smile, the sort of smile Yves sometimes had.

Anne's feelings swung sharply round. 'Thank you, Chandrea!' She wanted to say how much she liked her, and that she was sorry she had been unable to teach her, especially since she believed Chandrea could go far in life, given the opportunity. But all of this was beyond her ability, and she simply said goodbye.

Chandrea again smiled her sad smile. Then, as they stood on the path, she lightly touched Anne's arm. 'Narat is in Battambang,' she confided softly. 'Across the lake.'

Anne was completely thrown, and showed it. Chandrea had seen right through her. To the Khmers such a thing was tantamount to losing face, but Chandrea had chosen to sympathize instead. Her sudden and unexpected generosity overwhelmed, and Anne, deeply touched, was also humbled.

'Will he come back soon?' she enquired, her pride erased in an unfamiliar rush of warm-hearted humility.

'Yes, I think so,' answered Chandrea, and she smiled a sisterly smile.

Anne took both Chandrea's hands in hers. 'Thank you, Chandrea. Thank you very much!'

'Have you really never seen the Tonle Sap?' she asked with quiet wonder.

'I will see it one day,' Chandrea answered a little coolly, having no wish to be patronized or pitied.

How little I understand these people, thought Anne as she came away. At times they seemed almost on another planet, at others like children existing in an innocent world of make-believe. And then suddenly they were full of wisdom, kindness and good sense. Another thing: what had struck her as such chaotic surroundings on arrival at Chandrea's house had, by the time she left, begun to seem rather cosy. Perhaps the eye refocused and adapted once you were part a place; the aesthetic or critical element disappeared, or else slotted in differently. There was much to reflect upon, but Anne's mind returned instead to Narat. Although it was impossible to know for certain, she decided that he and Chandrea were probably not engaged. Anne gave a little skip along the path. Then, remembering she was a teacher with pupils in the vicinity, and a Barang, pulled herself together and reverted to a fast-clipped walk. She must find out from Yves how far away Battambang was.

18

ALTHOUGH TRANSPLANTING THE SEEDLINGS WAS WOMEN'S work, men often pitched in; and again Salty had volunteered to help. Cradling a bundle of seedlings in one arm, he poked a hole in the earth with his thumb, set a plant in the hole and tamped the soil down with his forefinger. Time after time after time. It was back-breaking work being doubled over like a croquet hoop all day, even after he'd learned to do it properly. But Salty enjoyed it, and what was more, today was his birthday. He was thirty-two years old, and he had never felt more alive.

At breakfast little presents wrapped in banana leaves had surrounded his bowl of morning tea. Yves's was a packet of banana-leaf cigarettes, like those the Khmers smoked; and Bill's, his red silk Charvet necktie patterned with little yellow diamonds. Noting Salty's bemusement, Bill said it would make a great headband, and Salty, pleased, duly tied it in place.

'Wall Street on the warpath,' Anne declared, as everyone laughed and clapped, and sang 'Happy Birthday' for the second time.

But the gift that excited most attention was a joint effort. The previous day Marjorie had discovered a sheet of paper covered on both sides in Khmer writing, and wrapped scroll-like around a bamboo cane. She supposed it was one of the doctor's stories, and Yves, after a brief scan, confirmed this. 'It's a dialogue between a man and a cucumber plant,' he told her solemnly. Marjorie wondered whether Kieu had been the inspiration for it, and thought that, being agricultural, it would make a fine birthday present for Salty. So Yves had dictated a quick off-the-cuff translation, and Anne had written it down on a valuable, because limited, sheet of her notebook, declaring that it was 'right up Salty's street'.

Salty had brought the story with him to the paddies; and now, enjoying a mid-morning rest under the fanning shade of a sugar palm, he took out the sheet of paper, folded by Marjorie into a small origami butterfly. 'The title is my idea,' she had scribbled at the top, before printing in large capital letters: 'PLANTATION LIFE'.

'One morning a long time ago,' said the storyteller to her audience, sitting around the cook fire on a chilly evening, 'a man bought a cucumber plant in the wax market, to plant in his vegetable garden. He was a fair-minded, honest man, hardworking, also rather ambitious; and on the way home, seeking to strike a profitable relationship with the plant, the man explained his intentions.

'"I will water you, feed you, and protect you from invading weeds," he promised. "But in return you must give me all of your cucumbers."

'The cucumber plant was much surprised. "But that would mean parting with my relations, even parting with a part of myself; for ours is a close-knit family," exclaimed the plant, adding after a moment, "And what, pray, would become of the cucumbers?"

'The man, a keen gardener, saw no need to be delicate. "I will eat them," he said, not at all embarrassed.

'The cucumber plant shivered, and its leaves rose up like the hairs on a head. But noting this, the man sought to reassure the plant. "The cucumbers will help to nourish me, so I can look after you properly," he said. "And becoming part of me instead of you, will go on much as before, only reincarnated." Privately he thought it a fine opportunity for a lowly cucumber. "We shall be as brothers," he added diplomatically.

'The cucumber plant was mollified. Moreover, if it agreed to the man's proposal, life would be very pleasant indeed. But when they arrived at the vegetable garden the cucumber plant, having considered the matter further, added a special condition.

'"If you will promise to be buried in this garden when you die, then it is a deal," said the plant.

'"Why on earth must I do that?" demanded the gardener, whose funeral plans consisted of a flamboyant cremation, with prayers, incense, games and many festivities.

'"Because then you and I and all my family will be reunited."

'"As cucumbers," mused the man dubiously. He had worked hard and he regularly gave the *bonzes* alms. Soon he would be able to give them cucumbers, too, and by the time he died he hoped to have earned enough merit to come back as a rich man.

'But the cucumber plant, reading his thoughts, pointed out that the man's spirit would surely be given a new body: he would be tall and handsome and very attractive to women. "Put the old one to good use," admonished the plant. "It will earn you merit when word of our agreement gets around, as I will make sure it does."

'Won over by this argument, the man agreed. "If you will nourish me, I in turn will nourish you. That is only fair."

'"It is the way of the world," observed the cucumber plant.

'"It is economics, at any rate," said the man. "That is a science the gods well understand."

'"It is a circle, in fact," declared the cucumber plant.

'"You mean a cycle," corrected the gardener, though to disagree was not thought very polite.

'"A oneness, then," allowed the cucumber plant, waxing metaphysical. For, standing still all day, it was in its nature to reflect.

'"Well, not exactly that either, because a cucumber is not the same as a man. And even if a man eats only cucumbers he continues to be a man."

'"But if a cucumber plant eats a man, then that man will become a cucumber," replied the plant, ruffling its leaves a trifle smugly.

'A debate ensued. Were cucumbers therefore the dominant species and man put on the earth to cultivate gardens and take care of cucumbers? Was the good life the life of a man or the life of cucumber plants, or did it not make any difference, if eventually they became one?

'"They do not become 'one'," the gardener asserted. "It is always either or. Man and cucumbers are separate beings."

'"'Man' and 'cucumber' are only words," declared the cucumber plant, striving to maintain the upper hand and striking a sagacious-sounding tone. "And words can mislead, since they seek to separate what in fact is solidly joined together."

'"Well, separation is important for survival," insisted the man. "Good and evil, land and water, men and women. All are different and must be treated differently, or there will be trouble."

'"All is illusion," insisted the cucumber plant in a superior-sounding tone and with a triumphant note of finality.

'"Is it indeed?" exclaimed the man, who was becoming very angry. "We shall see about that." And he threw the cucumber plant into the bushes. "That is reality, and not illusion, as you will soon find out," he cried. "I shall plant tomatoes!" And, turning his back, he marched off.

'"Being and non-being are one!" cried the cucumber plant, a little weakly, from the bushes. "If I die here I shall become a weed; and if I become a weed, I shall marshall all the weeds to attack your garden. And the weeds will win."

'The man, although exasperated, was no fool. Why forgo a supply of delicious cucumbers and be forced to fight a battalion of upstart weeds, when it could be avoided? So he retrieved the cucumber plant, dusted it off, gave it some water and planted it in his garden. And so their pact was made.

'In the years that followed,' said the storyteller, 'the man ate many cucumbers and he gave many cucumbers to the *bonzes*. And when, finally, after a great many years, he died, he lived happily afterwards as a cucumber, and perhaps also as a very rich man. For who can tell whether all is one, or many things, or nothing, or indeed whether nothing is everything, or not, and all things possible?'

Savouring the story as he worked, Salty decided that when he died he wanted a tree to be planted on top of his Wyoming grave, and he began to think about what tree might suit him best, whether it should be evergreen or deciduous, fast or slow growing, native or imported. From time to time he scrutinized the nearby forest for ideas. But as the sun dropped and the long afternoon shadows emerged, a sense of foreboding descended. Salty half imagined he could see dark figures creeping along the jungle border, and could hear the soft but stealthy flip-flopping of myriad Ho Chi Min sandals. He thought of the young soldier with his life-preserving amulet, and envied him his faith and evident dedication. Because, for Salty, a gap of uncertainty loomed between the present and that as-yet-unselected tree. Since he was able to fly a plane, a blind eye had been turned to his irregular status in Cambodia. But the country was increasingly unsettled, and now that diplomatic relations had been re-established with America – Salty *was* draft dodging – his situation was becoming precarious. He must make a decision soon. And so far he could think of nothing.

But he made a decision about his immediate future that afternoon.

In the heat and sweltering humidity, his long hair, a long-vaunted emblem of dissent, had become a nuisance.

Even women tended to have short hair while working in the paddies. Added to which, Bill, out of indifference perhaps, was letting his own hair grow. Salty decided it was time to get a haircut.

The following evening, he sat patiently on a tree stump under the house, a *krama* draped barbershop style around his shoulders, as Anne sawed away with nail scissors, attempting to keep a straight line. 'Pure Vidal Sassoon,' she kept on insisting, as the uneven ear-length bob took ragged shape. And standing back to admire her progress – 'Only a rough cut, so far' – she saw Narat walking in his easy gait down the garden path towards the house.

'Ouch,' said Salty. 'You nicked me.'

Anne either didn't hear or else paid no attention. Her heart was pounding and the blood rushed to her face. Suddenly shy and self-conscious, only with the greatest effort did she manage to command a degree of poise, even a certain coolness, as they shook hands – the others expressing a warmth and enthusiasm she herself dared not show. The sheer reality of Narat had come as a pulsating shock to this cerebral woman, stumbling out of an obsessive dream and into life.

'We're cutting the sacred locks,' Marjorie grandiosely announced. 'It's a celebration, and you're just in time for the feast.'

But Yves and Bill, cutting through the frivolity, pressed for news.

'We heard you were across the lake,' Bill declared, almost accusingly, sitting down on the platform beside Narat.

Narat showed the faintest sign of surprise, before answering evasively that there was much work to be done in the countryside. His attention remained fixed on

Anne, now frantically trying to finish Salty's increasingly bizarre haircut.

'Salty saw Vietnamese soldiers,' Marjorie volunteered, as if these were a rare jungle species. 'They were sneaking around the forest in black pyjamas. It was pretty spooky.'

Narat, hearing this description, said the men were not Vietnamese, but the Resistance: Khmers fighting to restore Prince Sihanouk. Too poor for uniforms, they dressed like peasants in order to show equality with them. Cambodia needed more equality.

'Folks round here look mighty equal to me,' observed Salty from his stump, as Anne handed him the mirror to see how he looked.

'Their inequality is in status, not material things,' replied Narat, his gaze still fixed on Anne. *Bonzes* and elders demanded unfaltering respect, no matter what their individual merits, and their wishes had to be followed in everything.

Bill could see nothing wrong with respect, and said so. There should be more of it in Western society. 'It's face-saving, not respect, that's stopping progress here, if you ask me,' he said, though no one had. 'People are afraid to take chances. In America we expect a few blows to our dignity and prestige. People lose their jobs, their wives or husbands run off with other people, and everyone's always trying to outdo the other fellow. Face-saving is really a lack of humility. That's what it boils down to. "Turn the other cheek," the Bible says.' Not that Bill would ever have dreamed of doing so. 'The Khmers should stop worrying about what others think of them.'

'To want respect is in man's nature,' answered Narat, who did not seem much interested. He was unable to stay to dinner, he told them; he was expected elsewhere, having just returned to the village.

Anne removed the *krama* from Salty's shoulders and gave it a good shake. 'Come upstairs and see the new decorations before you go. Marjorie and I made a wall hanging from old *sampots*, sort of like a patchwork quilt. We think it's quite a success.

'You'll be staying for a while, won't you?' she asked casually, over her shoulder, as they went upstairs.

'Yes, I plan to. For a while.'

'I'm glad you're back . . . I've missed you.'

Anne had decided to take the initiative. She was the older and enjoyed, for whatever reasons, a superior status; it was up to her to pop the question. But her involvement was now so deep, and so much was at stake, that her confidence was badly shaken.

Narat admired the bright, multicoloured hanging. 'The walls were too bare,' he observed approvingly.

Anne hardly heard him. She was summoning up her courage.

'I want to see you,' she announced, quietly authoritative, still looking at the wall hanging. 'Alone.'

She could not have made it clearer.

Narat was silent for a moment. 'Things are difficult just now. My life is not what it seems. It is a dangerous time. It could be dangerous for you, too, by association.'

They were speaking almost in whispers.

'It doesn't matter. I know you're involved in politics, I know it's risky, and I admire you for it. I want to see you,' she repeated.

They had moved nearer to each other; but Marjorie was coming up the stairs. 'What do you think of our tapestry?' she called out.

'Then we shall meet,' whispered Narat.

'Is that a promise?'

'It is a promise.'

Though ready to decapitate Marjorie, whose head had surfaced above the veranda floor, Anne was sure now that things would go ahead – it was only a matter of timing – and was deliriously happy.

19

SALTY, HIS BROW ENCIRCLED BY THE CHARVET NECKTIE, pirate-style, was en route to the wax market the next morning for some kerosene when again he encountered soldiers. But instead of wielding machetes and creeping through the forest on rubber-tyre sandals, they were marching, heavily armed and in formation, down the village street. The soldiers wore khaki uniforms and their helmets resembled old-fashioned sola topi. Grenades dangled from their waists, and bandoliers stuffed with bullets criss-crossed their chests. They shouldered Russian Kalashnikovs. 'Sihanouk!' they shouted in greeting to any villagers they saw, stepping forward and offering them cigarettes. One of the soldiers was carrying a loudspeaker, and, as the street was virtually empty, began to address the peasants inside their houses.

'Join us, comrades! We are your friends! Help us to restore Prince Sihanouk and defeat the tyrant Lon Nol, a lackey of the American imperialists.'

Salty ran back fast to Shangri La, the kerosene can banging against the bushes like a gong. The loudspeaker could just be heard, blaring through the trees. Yves was sitting on the loggia, listening hard to what he said was very poor Khmer: the soldiers were North Vietnamese.

'Perhaps we should lie low for a few hours,' he calmly suggested. 'The Vietnamese are going from village to village seeking recruits, hoping the young men will join them as soon as the planting is over. They won't stay long in Domrei Chlong.'

Taking no chances, the Barangs set about removing all signs of foreign habitation from below stairs. They stored their belongings in the bedrooms, then carried the table into the bushes and turned it upside-down, masking the legs with improbable-looking stands of banana leaves.

Neither San nor Kieu had turned up, but around mid-morning Ty arrived, alone. 'Vietnamese soldiers are in the village,' he calmly announced, pleased to see the Barangs' presence already somewhat obscured. 'The soldiers have no reason to come here, but it is better, I think, if the house appears shut up. San is consulting the *neak ta*,' he added, an indication that help, should it be needed, was on the way.

'Ask him if the soldiers are getting any recruits,' urged Bill.

'The Khmers do not trust the Vietnamese,' answered Ty with a slight frown. 'But Sihanouk says we must do so right now. He has spoken from Peking, telling his people to join the Vietnamese in the fight against Lon Nol.' Beneath Ty's impeccable façade and carefully measured voice, small signs of tension could be divined. His eyes darted searchingly over the house and garden, and over the Barangs themselves; and behind his apparent calm he seemed to be in a hurry.

'Preoccupied,' was Anne's conclusion when he left.

Yves believed Ty had good reason to be. If the conflict persisted he might find it necessary to take sides.

'He will resist for as long as possible, I imagine; but with the Vietnamese promising to hold elections, he may find it is in his interest to back Lon Nol.'

Lunch was served upstairs. 'A picnic,' Marjorie declared, as she set down plates of chicken, chutney, tomatoes and bamboo shoots.

They ate in silence, sitting on the floor, feeling more suspended than in suspense, like waiting for forecasted bad weather to blow over. It was hot and stuffy with the shutters closed, though some air came in through a crack in the kitchen shutters at the back, which faced the jungle. The village was very quiet, but it was always quiet at this hour. Unrolling their kapok pallets, the Barangs stretched out for their own siestas; except for Salty, who sat up, his back against the wall-hanging, keeping a self-appointed watch.

The clank of metal and sound of shuffling feet broke all pretence of sleep. Salty leaped up and peered out through a hole in one of the shutters. Vietnamese soldiers were coming down the garden path; Ty was with them and he did not look happy.

When the soldiers reached the foot of the stairs, Yves opened the door and went down alone. Greeting Ty with a perfunctory *sompeah*, he raised his eyebrows questioningly; but although the sun was beating down and the humidity was ferocious, he did not suggest moving into the shade beneath the house.

'These men are our friends,' announced Ty inscrutably. 'They are the allies of Prince Sihanouk, and they wish to help us in our struggle against Lon Nol and the imperialist lackeys. We are honoured to have them in our village.' He tucked his thumbs into the waistline of his baggy trousers and continued smoothly.

'Our distinguished guests have seen the wreckage of your plane, and they were surprised and curious. I have explained to them your story and, being intrigued by your adventure, they have asked for the pleasure of meeting you.' Ty smiled ingratiatingly. 'Will you kindly ask the others to come down, please, and to bring their passports with them?'

When Yves returned upstairs to relay this, Bill wondered if they should say their passports had been lost. But Yves thought it would provoke a search, and possibly some unpleasantness. It was better to show that they had nothing to hide.

Anne rummaged in a chest and handed hers to Yves, and Bill produced his and Marjorie's. But Salty's passport was in Phnom Penh.

As they prepared to go down, Bill, sensing the women's trepidation, put his arms around their shoulders and squeezed hard. 'Heads up now, ladies. There's nothing to be scared of. We're going to turn this whole show to our advantage and use these guys to get us out of here. You wait and see.' And giving another firm squeeze, he led the way downstairs. Anne and Marjorie, heads raised but eyes fixed firmly on the ground, followed him, and Salty, having removed the Charvet necktie and thrown a *krama* around his neck, descended next. Yves, carrying the passports, brought up the rear. Yves had decided to say that Salty was English, in the employ of the British embassy, and must be respected as such. The fewer Americans the better. He knew Ty wouldn't contradict him. Lon Nol needed America, and increasingly Ty was going to need Lon Nol.

As they descended, Ty remained in conversation with one of the soldiers. The man wore a little Chinese cap and, unlike the others, was unarmed. As Ty talked, the man watched the Barangs impassively.

'Where are the passports?' he now demanded in Khmer.

Yves handed them over, explaining that Salty had no passport with him, as he had been on a day trip when the plane had crashed. But he was a British citizen. The young lady, too, was British. She was a scholar and had made a study of Angkorean sculpture, rendering a valuable service to Cambodia. The married couple were tourists. They had come to see Angkor Wat, and had been leaving for Thailand when the plane went down.

From the vacant expression on the other soldiers' faces, it was clear that only the man in the Chinese cap, evidently an officer, understood Khmer. Listening, as he examined the passports, checking each one against the owner's face, he seemed more interested in the passports being different colours than in what Yves was telling him.

When he stuffed them into his breast pocket, Bill loudly protested, but Ty insisted it was a formality; the passports would be returned. Bill had his word on that.

Two soldiers remained behind, posted as guards at the foot of the garden. But Bill was optimistic. If the Vietnamese intended to check passports, they must have a field telephone, or access to one; and any enquiry would be sure to attract outside attention. 'They'll end up helping to rescue us. And when they find out what a rumpus holding us is causing, they'll send us packing. Unless of course they want a ransom.' Bill didn't sound too concerned about that.

* * *

Next morning, having retrieved the table, they were at breakfast when Ty reappeared unexpectedly, accompanied once again by several Vietnamese.

Yves met them in front of the house; the others, at his request, stayed put.

A short exchange took place in Khmer, Yves pressing his points with some insistence before returning gravely to the Barangs to translate.

'Ty says you must go with them,' he informed Bill. 'They wish to ask you some questions.'

Bill stood up. 'How the hell can they ask me questions, when they don't speak any English? Tell them to ask them here, where we've got someone who can translate.' He wondered if a small donation would help, but decided it was probably too risky.

The officer in the Chinese cap responded sharply when Bill's suggestion, diplomatically translated, was put to him; and embedded in his aggressive-sounding reply the Barangs could make out, in a short staccato burst, 'CIA'.

Alarm now suffused the women's faces, but if Bill felt apprehensive he concealed it well; Ty, regarding him closely, was favourably impressed.

'I'll get my stuff,' Bill announced matter-of-factly, turning to go upstairs.

Salty believed he intended to fetch the pistol, but before Bill had reached the stairs two young soldiers stepped forward and grabbed him roughly from behind.

'Take your fucking hands off me!'

'It is military procedure, a mere formality,' insisted Ty helplessly.

Producing a roll of green plastic twine, the soldiers trussed Bill's arms together above the elbows, uncomfortably behind his back. Marjorie watched in horror, stunned and incapable of speech. Salty kept his hand reassuringly on her shoulder. 'We'll be out of all this in no time,' he told her, scowling at the soldiers, who glanced briefly at him but didn't bother to respond. Salty was fairly certain one of them was the soldier he had seen in the forest. Yet the young man paid him no attention whatever.

Bill was not paraded through the village. Ty, sensitive to face-saving, chose a path that ran roughly parallel to the village, leading eventually to a little clearing in the forest. In the centre of the clearing was a hut. It sat on the ground, in the fashion of Cambodian municipal buildings. The hut had one room and at the far end stood an improvised table made of planks laid across two sawhorses. Three upright wooden chairs were ranged haphazardly around it. The slats were missing in one, another lacked a seat, but a *krama* had been wrapped around the frame to make one. Against the wall beside the door were a couple of low-slung bucket seats, the upholstery badly torn, and instantly Bill recognized them as the Cessna's. The heat was stifling, and some barking dogs were creating a rumpus outside. Ty had not come in.

The officer in the Chinese cap blurted a sharp command, pointing to one of the chairs. Bill stood firm, insisting that he be untied. But a soldier stepped quickly forward and pushed him into the chair, and another one began to bind him to it, wrapping the plastic twine around his chest, even though his forearms were already pinioned behind his back.

The door slammed shut and there was silence.

From the corner of his eye, Bill could see a soldier sprawled in front of one of the bucket seats, his gun held casually upright between his legs. Bill's mouth was bone dry, and even though he had been drinking tea fifteen minutes earlier, he put it down to thirst: the room was an oven with the door closed.

Bill was too outraged to be really frightened; officers' training had prepared him well, and he set about reviewing the situation. He was an American citizen in a neutral country, and an innocent man. The Vietnamese wouldn't want an international incident – a possible war crime – on their plate; they had enough problems. And Ty had plenty of clout – the village was almost a personal fief. He told himself he must be patient, and he tried to clear his mind and think of something prosaic. It would rain soon. The sooner the better. It would be cooler then. And with a kind of infinite trust, he sat there, suspended in a sort of limbo, waiting for rain.

After what seemed like hours, the door behind him opened. Bill gave a powerful jump, managing to turn the chair halfway round in order brazenly to confront the enemy.

Three men had entered. They wore black pyjamas, and had *kramas* looped bandana-style around their necks. They were unarmed – and one of them was Narat.

Hugely relieved, Bill knew better than to react. He must let Narat take the lead, until he could more safely determine how best to proceed.

Narat, however, seemed to defer to the older man who was with him, and who now gave the Vietnamese soldier a quiet but firm order. The soldier began sullenly to untie Bill's cords.

Rubbing his arms to get the circulation going, Bill faced his liberators in haughty silence, the indignation on his face unmissable.

'You have been rudely treated,' Narat, evidently much embarrassed, offered in apology; and he introduced the older man: 'Comrade Tak'.

Comrade Tak smiled and held out his hand. 'The Vietnamese mean well, but on occasion they can be *un peu sauvage*,' he observed genially, showing a familiarity with English as well as French. Bill estimated him to be about fifty. Though small, he was robust, and surprisingly muscular for a man who, having received a proper education, would presumably have worked indoors most of his adult life. Tak's face was intelligent and sensitive looking, its roundness and narrow eyes suggesting traces of Chinese blood.

Bill complimented him on his English.

'I do not speak such fine English as Comrade Narat,' Tak rejoined with a broad grin. 'I have learned my English in Australia. "Billybong!"'

Everyone laughed, relief spreading in a cooling balm across the stuffy room.

'Comrade Tak is being modest,' said Narat. 'He was a teacher of history in Phnom Penh, but he criticized the government and his life was threatened. Many teachers have been imprisoned and some assassinated, but others, acting swiftly, have managed to escape. And they have joined the maquis,' he announced with evident pride.

'Jungle life has a remarkable simplicity,' observed the urbane Comrade Tak; indicating they should sit down, he chose for himself the *krama*-wrapped seat, before speaking briefly to the young aide-de-camp who was with them.

Tea soon appeared and the pleasantries continued; Tak, like Narat earlier, remarked how unusual it was to find Americans in Cambodia just now.

'Naturally our leaders are curious, and naturally their curiosity must be satisfied.'

'Well, I sure as hell didn't mean to be here, I can tell you. And I'm certainly not CIA, if that's what you're thinking. I'm a businessman. I run a successful investment company.'

Bill explained why he had been going to Thailand and that he'd brought his wife to Cambodia for her birthday. 'It should be easy to check all this out in Phnom Penh,' he rounded off.

'It is not always easy for the maquis to "check things out in Phnom Penh",' laughed Comrade Tak. 'But it is not impossible. We must be very careful, however. We do not wish the backfire, especially now that we are at war with America.'

'You *are*?' The idiots, Bill was thinking.

'If your presence here is as you say, then we will see to it that your party returns in safety to Phnom Penh. You have my word for that. So do not worry, please. But it is important that everything is done properly and in the right order, with attention paid to all the relevant details. First of all, therefore, I must ask you to kindly write for us your biography. That is our system. It will be studied and the details carefully checked at our headquarters.'

Narat had opened his canvas shoulder bag and was removing several sheets of lined paper. 'Here is paper, also a Biro.' He smiled encouragingly.

'When your biography is finished,' continued Tak, 'Comrade Narat will take it to Angka – our headquarters – to be checked. Everything must be done properly,' he repeated. 'Every inquiry is always thoroughly conducted.'

'Won't Angka have trouble, too, checking things out?'

'Angka has as many eyes as a pineapple,' answered

Comrade Tak confidently. 'But these are difficult times. Many lives are at stake – also the future of Kampuchea. We must take no chances.'

'Who's Kampuchea?'

'Kampuchea will be the name of our country,' said Narat. 'Cambodia represents the colonial phase.'

'OK, let's get going!' Bill reached out for the sheets of paper. 'Listen, I'd be really grateful if someone could let my wife know I'm all right. She'll be worried sick.' Bill didn't like to ask Narat directly. Their staying in his house might already have compromised him. He wondered whether word had reached Bopha, whom he had failed to meet that morning, and he decided that it must have done. The whole village must know by now, and they must know, too, that he'd been trussed up like a chicken. He would lose face. And for a moment, unaccountably, he felt ashamed.

In curriculum-vitae style, Bill wrote down where he had been born and educated, that he was married, lived in Connecticut and had a grown-up daughter. He did not mention the summer house in Maine or his training in the United States army, but noted that his family had been poor, and that a good investment had changed their lives for the better. Enjoying the chance for a polemic, he even ventured briefly into venture capitalism, pointing out that backing sound ideas benefited not only those who invested and those who found employment, but national prosperity as well. There was always the risk of losing face, he wrote: schemes sometimes failed; money, even reputations, were lost. But success when it came was well rewarded, and those who took the chance were never too proud to fail. If they did fail, they usually tried again.

Bill finished off with a description of his Thai plan. It would use Cambodian rubber, he decided to say, and he gave the company's name and its Bangkok address, so it could be contacted for confirmation. Doing so would be bound to create a leak as to their whereabouts, or at the very least indicate that they were still alive.

When Narat returned to the hut, Bill had written three or four thousand words, and fancied himself a not indifferent pamphleteer.

'You have had a full life,' observed Narat with an admiring smile, holding up the sheets and turning them over.

'I *have* had a full life. But c'mon, Narat, you know I'm not CIA. I'm a businessman – a successful businessman. You know that.'

'I know what you have told me.'

This cautious response Bill recognized as probably necessary, for form's sake. He could tell that Narat believed him.

'So what happens now? Is that it?'

'I must ask for your cooperation a little longer, until we have received Angka's response.'

'Angka sounds sort of like Angkor.'

'Angka is Khmer for "organization",' answered Narat flatly; and, putting Bill's manuscript into his canvas satchel, he held out his hand.

Bill was sitting at the table eating supper, the rice accompanied this time by fish paste, a Khmer staple, when Comrade Tak returned. He had a jug of palm wine with him, and taking a rice bowl from the tray beside the guard, sent the boy off to find some cups.

'I have read your biography,' Comrade Tak

announced, sitting down and helping himself to rice. He regarded Bill shrewdly, but with a smile. 'I expect all will be well, but we cannot be too careful now that we have become the *résistance*.' And noting Bill's incomprehension: 'You could say that Cambodia resembles wartime France, and that Lon Nol has taken the role of Marshall Pétain, while America chooses to play the part of Germany. So history repeats itself, as is so often said.'

'Comrade Tak, America is not Cambodia's enemy. It's unfortunate what's happened on the border, if there really has been bombing, like people say. But our fight is with Vietnam.'

'And what has Vietnam done to deserve this close attention from America? We in Asia cannot understand that.'

'Well, it's pretty straightforward. South Vietnam is our ally and North Vietnam tried to overrun it. It's our duty to help our ally. And if Cambodia knowingly shelters the enemy, then it's no longer neutral, is it?'

'To bomb Cambodia makes it no longer neutral,' replied Tak. 'But tell me, do you think it is right to help depose an elected chief of state, as the United States has done?'

'Listen, I'm not a politician, but international politics can be pretty rough. We both know that. There aren't many rules, and the lack of them has turned plenty of decent governments into common thugs. America is above all that, but when others are gangsters, then *realpolitik* – doing what you have to do – is sometimes necessary.'

'You are an important man,' observed Comrade Tak approvingly. 'Your views would be listened to in America. The young there, who protest against the war, are discredited because they are young; and since they do not wish to lose their lives, are thought too prejudiced for their opinions to be of value. But if a man like you tells Americans of their government's wrongdoing, surely they will listen.'

'If I'm convinced wrong's being done – and so far, with respect, Comrade Tak, it's all hearsay – then I sure will speak out. In America people can say what they think.' Bill was rather flattered that Tak had attributed to him far more influence than in fact he had.

'Would you be willing to tell your government they should not meddle in our affairs, that we have a right to live as we see fit?'

'Sure, but listen, I don't have a lot of political pull. As I said, I'm a businessman. I steer clear of politics.'

'You surprise me very much.' And Comrade Tak did look genuinely surprised. 'In a democracy there is much responsibility in the hands of citizens.' Then, to Bill's amazement, Comrade Tak quoted from Pericles' famous speech to the Athenians. '"We do not say here that a man who has no interest in politics minds his own business; we say here that a man who has no interest in politics has no business here." That is democracy!' Comrade Tak, visibly moved, declared.

The soldier had returned with tin cups that looked suspiciously like US army issue. Tak poured palm beer into them. 'America is far away,' he continued lightly. 'So, although she has bombed us – and you must take my word that this is true – we find ourselves unable to return her visit. What then ought we to do? Normally we would match our armies against our enemy's armies. We have always done this. You have seen it depicted in much detail at Angkor Wat. Armies in the field are like a duel, and there are formalities to decrease barbarity and maintain a sense of honour. The rules make it sporting, and of course more civilized.'

'A fair fight's always the best kind,' agreed Bill, having missed Tak's irony.

'But when our country is attacked and there is no enemy in the field, what should we do? I would welcome your view. You have run large enterprises and found solutions to many difficult problems. What would you do in this situation? I am serious. I wish very much to know what is your opinion.'

Tak was appealing to skills Bill valued in himself. The development of useful strategies was central to his profession, and the strategies of war had for him, as for most men, a primal appeal. Yet Bill hesitated. To argue for the little guy on this occasion felt a little like turncoating.

Tak appeared to sense this. 'Let us put our own countries aside,' he suggested affably, 'and take two abstract countries, one very big, the other very small; and each country thinks that it is right. You are the big country, and the little country has become a nuisance. It is a buzzing mosquito, and although the mosquito is far away, you believe this buzzing must be stopped, because malaria could result. Malaria is contagious, and it can spread. So potentially the little country is a threat. What would you do?'

Bill grinned. Tak was a shrewd yet highly congenial fellow, and something of a character. Bill was beginning to enjoy himself.

'Well, first of all I'd steer clear of invasion. Getting bogged down in a guerrilla-led war on foreign soil is always a mistake. It's how the British got beat in America. They had the better army, but they couldn't use it in America's forests, and they were sitting ducks.

So if diplomatic efforts failed and the dangers persisted, I'd bomb any strategic assets – and their army, if they have one and I can find it. And along the way I'd look for a puppet ruler to install.'

'Even if the country is a democracy?'

'Even if the country is a democracy.'

The two men grinned knowingly at each other.

'Now let us turn the table around, and this time you are the country on the receiving end, the "mosquito", or the "little guy", as you say. What would you do then?'

'Sue for peace!'

Both men laughed and Tak poured some more palm wine into the tin cups.

'But what if you have access to the big country, through infiltration, or some of your own citizens live there?'

'Well, in that case I might try to sabotage their installations. But it's not so easy.'

'This must be true. What about their leaders?'

'What about them?' Bill sipped his palm mine. 'Ah, you mean assassination. That's even harder. Besides, a country usually grows a new head, so it's pretty pointless, unless you can start a civil war or something. But assassination can cause quite a swarm. You're a historian: Archduke Ferdinand's, for instance. No, I wouldn't do that.'

'Why not disrupt day-to-day living? Blow up their trains, the market place, their banks and churches. Hit them where it hurts, as you Americans say.'

'I'd draw the line there, Comrade Tak,' said Bill soberly, setting down his cup. 'I wouldn't kill innocent people.'

'How can people be innocent in a democracy? They

are not children; they have a vote and they are responsible for their country's actions. If they support a war or back a war leader, then they, too, are the enemy. This seems obvious to me.'

'But women and children . . .'

'Women have the vote!' Comrade Tak sounded mildly outraged, as well as surprised by so faulty a piece of reasoning. 'Children, of course, must be protected; though sadly there are always unfortunate casualties in war.'

'Well, I don't buy terrorism,' insisted Bill. 'I draw the line there.'

'Oh, the hive might buzz, maybe swarm furiously, even foolishly, for a while. But in the end . . .' Comrade Tak smiled his sunny smile. 'Terrorism – or freedom fighting, depending on your point of view – is economical, in money spent and number of lives lost – or saved. It works.'

He peered more closely at Bill, whose thoughts seemed to have wandered. 'But I see you find this tactic uncongenial,' he added amiably. 'Frankly, that surprises me. Vietnam villages are napalmed every day, and now Cambodian villages are being bombed. That is terrorism on a massive scale.'

Bill suddenly felt very tired. He had never followed the war in any great detail, but he had wholly accepted the premise on which it was based. Communism was the enemy of capitalism. It had to be stamped out. And that was that.

'America is doing this because it has to,' he responded flatly. 'Not because we want to. We're doing it for the best. Americans are not terrorists, and never could be. We are a good people.'

Raising his virtually non-existent eyebrows, Tak

regarded Bill with a kind of paternal benevolence. 'Americans have hearts of gold,' he slyly posited. 'But let us keep to the abstract, shall we?' he added, politely redirecting an awkward conversation and moving it on. 'There is also hostage-taking.'

Downing his palm wine, Bill pulled himself together. 'Good for money-making,' he shrugged, lightly dismissive. 'Or exchange and barter.'

'And sometimes highly symbolic – even cathartic,' added Tak. 'A single prisoner can represent an entire nation. He can be killed in effigy, like the burning of a national flag.' Tak laughed his jolly laugh, and he, too, shrugged. 'With no access to the enemy, you must do what you can.'

Bill's mind had snapped to full attention, and he peered hard at Tak, suddenly aware that he did not know this man at all.

But Tak seemed not to notice. 'Like you, I am an optimist,' he went on affably, and he, too, finished his wine. 'Goliath was killed by a slingshot, and David became a hero. It can happen, since for many people, as you will have noticed, the underdog is a favourite pet.'

There was a noise outside, and Tak looked at his watch. 'But it is late and I expect you wish to go home. Here is Comrade Narat to escort you.'

They stood up; Bill felt dazed and utterly exhausted.

'I have enjoyed our little chat,' continued Comrade Tak, 'and I hope there will be others. We must learn all we can of the American point of view, and the precise meaning of your "*realpolitik*". It is a German word, is it not?'

* * *

Unbelievably, miraculously, it was over. Bill was strolling with Narat through the village and everyone in it was behaving normally, smiling and bowing as the two men passed. Despite Bill's vague sense of an elusive, dangling thread, the nightmare had evaporated in single puff. He felt like a schoolboy granted an unexpected holiday, and, obscurely grateful, tried to show it by offering Narat some avuncular advice.

'Frankly, Narat, I don't know what America's up to over here, and your friend Comrade Tak made some interesting points. But one thing's sure: Communism isn't the solution.'

'In my opinion, Bill,' confided Narat, 'Communism is useful as a transitional stage. Communist countries have good schools. There is order and security, and there is equality. There will be men with too much power, yes; but they will represent the people's interests, and not the nobility or the rich. Then, when the changes needed to give Cambodia a foothold in the modern world are in place, democracy can follow, since perhaps by that time the people will be ready to vote for it.'

They had reached the garden path, and ecstatic cries of welcome and relief burst forth as Marjorie rushed down the path, closely followed by the others. Narat received almost as much affectionate attention and goodwill as Bill, particularly from Anne, who, taking advantage of French custom, kissed him twice on both cheeks, delivering a telling look in which dewy-eyed admiration was coupled with unmistakable dewy-eyed adoration and desire.

'I must go away again, after all,' he told her glumly, lingering behind as the others headed upstairs to celebrate and they were finally alone.

'You don't mean *now*?'

'Tomorrow morning – in order to secure Bill's formal release. These are uncertain times, as I have said; and everyone walks the tightrope. We must be very careful. But I think quite soon you will be able to go home.'

Nothing at that moment was further from Anne's mind, and she felt obscurely rebuffed. The whole night was before them. Why didn't Narat suggest something?

'Is it Chandrea, Narat?'

Narat took her hand, playing with it gently. 'For now I must be as a monk. I am pledged to a cause, and a known connection between us could endanger your life, and perhaps your friends' lives as well.'

'*Is it Chandrea?*'

'Like me, Chandrea wishes for Cambodia to be a modern country. In that wish we are closely bound.'

'She's a very nice and very intelligent woman, and I like her a lot. But Narat, you could never be happy here. You're too well educated, too Westernized. Cambodia would be too narrow an existence.'

'A man who has a little education can sometimes accomplish much in a backward country.' Narat placed his hands on her shoulders.

'Is it far? Will you be gone long?'

'Only a few days, I think. It is across the Tonle Sap; but that's a secret.'

'Ah, Battambang!'

'What makes you say that?'

'Oh, only because it's the only town I've heard of across the lake.' And removing his arms from her shoulders, she put her own around his neck and, drawing him easily to her, kissed him hard. Why shouldn't she stay on at Domrei Chlong? There would be articles to write, and if civil war came she could join the Resistance and do something actively worthwhile with her life. With Narat beside her, she would be safe. The book could wait; there was no real hurry. Angkor Wat wasn't going anywhere.

20

BILL WAS NAPPING, STRETCHED OUT COMFORTABLY ON A kapok mattress, a silk cushion underneath his head. Bopha sat alongside, her little feet tucked to one side, fanning him with a couple of banana leaves while he slept. Bill was dreaming of *apsaras*, or at any rate miniature women. They were dancing like colourful butterflies above a milk-white Tonle Sap. Bill was in an open boat, together with others whom he knew and loved but could not readily identify. Nor did he know where they were headed, only that he was happy.

'Bill.'

Opening his eyes dreamily, realizing he had been asleep, Bill glanced quickly at his watch. They must part soon, as Bopha's wake-up call was meant to indicate. Bopha, having laid the banana-leaf fan aside, was busily searching in the laundry basket on the floor beside her. 'I bring baby, Bill.'

Bill's head turned expectantly towards the basket, always full of little surprises. But Bopha, somewhat to his relief, lifted out a fresh pineapple, together with a wooden plate and a knife.

'Bopha and Bill eat pineapul.'

They both laughed, and Bopha, setting the pineapple down on the plate, began to cut it in two.

'Where's the baby?'

The pineapple halved, Bopha laid down her knife, and with an affectionate sweep of her hand lovingly traced Bill's profile with the tips of her fingers, delivering a hypnotic frisson of pleasure. Then, taking his hand in hers, she guided it a little shyly to her stomach.

Bill sat bolt upright.

Gently Bopha pushed him down again. 'Soon you go; it must be so. But I bring baby, Bill.'

Flabbergasted, Bill knew that in truth he should hardly be surprised. From the beginning he had let Bopha bear all responsibility – simply left everything to her. But contraception would have been a difficult, perhaps impossible, matter to discuss. 'Listen, Bopha . . .'

Bopha covered his mouth with a light kiss. 'I marry to Samnang soon.' She told him the *bonzes* were already looking for an auspicious date. The present month, being a female month, was highly suitable. Weddings did not take place in male months. Bopha smiled serenely – calm, happy, matter of fact – as if the whole thing was perfectly normal and natural, the details well taken care of. But that was the Khmers all over again; and how much of it was good manners, how much face-saving, and how much on this occasion an act designed to spare him any anxiety? Bill felt a twinge of guilt.

She would have plenty of money, he now declared, rising unsteadily to the occasion. Enough for all her needs. And he would send more, regularly, later on.

But Bopha said this would not be suitable, and though Bill could understand how the sudden evidence of money might look suspicious, so too would the baby when it was born, he wanted to say.

'He will be our son,' said Bopha, who, having consulted the spirits, knew that it would be a boy. The 'our' was generously inclusive.

Despite his concern, Bill experienced a happy pang. He had always wanted a son. His daughter's difficult delivery had made it impossible. Now, amazingly, it was going to happen. 'Little Jayavarman,' he declared, grinning his pleasure.

Bopha laughed and shook her head; returning her attention to the pineapple, she began slicing a series of little yellow halos. 'People say America bad place, Bill. Barangs bad people. It not right.'

'Do they? Listen, Bopha, about the baby . . .'

'Bopha bring baby,' she repeated sweetly and with finality, arranging the pineapple in neat overlapping circles on the wooden plate.

Bill was expected to put in a daily appearance at the hut, to show he was still there, improbable though any alternative was. The real reason for it, he suspected, was that Tak, bored stiff in Domrei Chlong, welcomed an opportunity for some conversation. Invariably tea was served, and Tak's round face lit up in anticipation when Bill arrived, reminding Bill once again of Evelyn Waugh's hero, who, providing such desirable company, is never in fact set free.

'To get to the top of the mountain it is necessary to start at the bottom,' Tak observed with sagacious-sounding solemnity. And Bill suspected they were off to the races. 'Change, too, I think, should be a steady climb. Comrade Narat thinks differently, but he is young. Most of the maquis are young; some very young – fifteen, sixteen years old.'

'Well, Comrade Tak, you're Narat's superior, so you

can influence what happens,' said Bill, who wasn't much interested and, given Bopha's recent news, had other things on his mind.

Comrade Tak laughed his jolly laugh. 'In the hierarchy of age – a matter of great importance in Cambodia – you are correct. I am his superior and I must be deferred to. But in the hierarchy of the *résistance* – the Khmer Rouge, as Prince Sihanouk has named us – it is Comrade Narat who enjoys the higher position, and I who must defer to him. As you have seen, Comrade Narat reports directly to Angka.'

Although surprised, Bill said nothing in response. Narat was hardly more than a teenager himself. He had little experience of life and only the thinnest veneer of Western education. He couldn't begin to guess how much he didn't know – something that gave young men their often dangerous self-confidence.

'Order and security can be forcibly imposed,' continued Tak, 'and sometimes this is necessary. But if the old traditions are suppressed, and new ones fail to root, the people's souls will starve. And when the seeds are imported . . .' Comrade Tak shrugged despairingly, his Oriental eyes looking piercingly into Bill's. 'Narat and his Paris-educated comrades are impatient for their new Eden. They have come home, their pockets bulging with packets of foreign seeds – French, Russian, many of them Chinese.' Tak's hands were folded around his tin cup, and he gazed into it reflectively, sticking out his lips. 'Change must come. I do not quarrel with that. I, too, wish for change. But grafting, although slower, would be a safer method. Yet the world wishes for us to hurry and catch up. We are becoming an embarrassment, even to egalitarians, who find we are too quaint to be considered equals, and dislike us for putting them in this immoral position.'

Bopha's wedding was set for two weeks' time, and there was much to prepare. Weddings were elaborate affairs. The bride changed costume three times in one day, she had informed Bill proudly; the *bonzes* would be present and a great many guests. There would be music, food, dancing, drink, prayers and blessings – three full days of celebration. It was a serious business.

Bill was glad he would be gone by then. Disenchantment was setting in and losing Bopha would complete it. At least the reservoir was full. That was something. But although transplantation of the seedlings was finished, none of the village industries had so far been revived. Drinking, gambling, cockfighting, party-going, pagoda-going and general lounging about occupied everyone's day.

The people were recuperating, said Kieu. It was only natural.

'They lack a work ethic; that's the real problem,' Bill complained to Marjorie, who, standing on tiptoe, was tucking a leaf offering under the eaves for San, who had failed to show up that morning.

'No they don't, Bill. The Khmers work in order to eat, and when there's enough food, they stop working and enjoy life. That's a work ethic, too.'

'OK, then they need motivation – some get up and go, like their ancestors had.'

'Sticks or carrots?' enquired Anne drily, from the hammock, where she lay re-reading *Mrs Dalloway*, who seemed to inhabit an increasingly vague and unreal world.

* * *

The missing motivation, when it materialized, was fear; and as with the Khmers' Angkorean forebears, its resolution was sought almost exclusively through religion.

Three unnerving events had occurred in quick succession.

First, a white crocodile was sighted on the Tonle Sap. Several fishermen had seen it, so there could be no doubt as to its presence. And when a white crocodile appeared, as everyone knew well, dreadful things were about to happen.

This alarming news had coincided with rumours of elephants in the vicinity. Bombs had fallen in the sacred Kulen hills, it was reported; and the elephants were coming home. As yet none had been seen, but in a nearby hamlet trees had been uprooted and two fields of melons trampled to smithereens. The young rice could be in serious danger.

Then two young men went missing. The *neak ta*, when consulted, declared them dead or 'as good as', whatever that meant; many thought it meant the crocodile had eaten them. But Ty, level-headed as usual, strongly suspected that the young men had joined the insurgency. There had been much talk of doing so once the planting was finished. Normally youths would spend a month or two with the *bonzes* in the pagoda at this time, but restoring Prince Sihanouk would earn them far more merit, and provide excitement of a kind notably absent in the pagoda's syllabus.

Unnerved by so many portentous signs, the Khmers once again examined their world for tell-tale signs of flaws and misdemeanours. What spirits had been slighted or insufficiently propitiated, what rituals imperfectly performed or ominous signs foolishly ignored or overlooked? In addition to consultations with the *neak ta*, prayers were offered up non-stop by the *bonzes*, whose chants floated out mellifluously over the pagoda's walls. And in the village a chicken was sacrificed, its entrails studied and discussed at length. If the error could be quickly unearthed, there might still be time to appease angry or neglected spirits and restore the status quo.

Marjorie was the first to hear of Narat's return. She was kneeling before the Buddha, burning incense. An old woman was kneeling beside her, and the two of them left the temple together. The old woman, adjusting the *krama* on her head with a quick twist of her arm as they descended the steps, told Marjorie she had seen Narat lying in a hammock at Chandrea's house.

Marjorie rushed home with the good news. Freedom was on the way; they must prepare a feast and get ready to travel. Narat was back, and they would be going home!

But by evening, when Narat had not appeared, the Barangs realized how self-centred they were being. Narat would have a lot to do, including consulting with Ty and Comrade Tak. (When Bill had gone to the hut that morning, it had been empty.) Narat might even be arranging for their departure. They went to bed chastened but full of anticipation, and the next morning sat idly about, waiting, as the heat thickened into a stultifying haze and dark clouds gathered overhead that Salty said resembled starved black sheep.

They were finishing lunch, Marjorie ladling out coconut and orange ambrosia mixed with honey, when, before anyone had noticed, half a dozen black-pyjama-clad youths were halfway down the garden path. Lean and grim, they looked like a tough adolescent street gang.

There were no *sompeahs* or handshakes, and no smiles. Yves, napkin in hand, came forward from beneath the house, demanding in a surprisingly formidable voice what this was about.

A youth, his unkempt hair secured by a black cloth strip, answered briefly in a harsh staccato. The tall American was under arrest. Those were his orders, he curtly declared.

Gravely Yves demanded more information. Orders from whom, he wanted to know?

But the youth only stubbornly repeated his words.

Bill, a scowling Gulliver towering above the Lilliputians, had joined Yves. 'Ask where the fuck Tak and Narat are,' he insisted.

Yves spoke at greater length.

'They will only say that you must come with them. Their orders are to arrest you.'

'We must find Ty!' cried Marjorie, clinging desperately to her husband. 'Yves, tell them to get Ty. For God's sake, *tell them*!'

'Where is Comrade Narat?' Anne demanded majestically in Khmer.

The youth didn't even look at her.

'We could take 'em on,' whispered Salty, 'and break out of here. Three against five. They don't have any guns. We can hijack a boat.'

'I think you had better go, Bill,' said Yves. 'There has clearly been some mistake, but violence will only make things worse. I will go to see Ty at once, and also have a word with the *bonzes*. We'll get this sorted out.' Though Yves did not say so, he had volunteered to accompany Bill and been refused.

Bill was gently detaching himself from Marjorie. 'Honey, it's just a bunch of kids playing silly war games. Tak and Narat will fix everything. Don't *worry*! It's looney tunes. It's Cambodia, for Chrissakes!'

Bill sat on the platform edge and put on his sandals. He was uneasy, but not afraid. He found it impossible to take these people seriously. They were pygmies, in all respects.

This time there was no trussing up. Placed at the centre of a tiny, primitively armed phalanx, Bill was marched off in the direction of the village.

'You mustn't worry!' insisted Anne, attempting to comfort a distraught Marjorie. 'It's going to be all right. There's been a mistake, that's all. Narat will fix it. He'll sort everything out.' Eagerness to see Narat had stifled Anne's own apprehensions – or most of them – for she had begun to wonder if the old woman had been right about Narat's return, or had Marjorie misunderstood? It was a chilling thought.

The village street down which the little platoon marched was empty. Behind the houses a few women were squatting beside cook fires, but they did not look up, and Bill decided this was probably a good sign. At the end of the street, farthest from the pagoda and where the poorest huts were built, the soldiers threaded behind the shabby dwellings, taking a path that Bill had never noticed. It led to an isolated clearing, and in the clearing stood a dilapidated hut, mounted on crude pole stilts and evidently unoccupied. The garden was overgrown, the ground outside the house bare and untended.

'Lie down!' the young cadre with the headband ordered, pointing at the ground.

'Comrade Tak!' Bill demanded imperiously in return. 'Get Comrade Tak.'

'Down!' the youth repeated.

Bill refused to budge. They hardly came up to his chest. 'Comrade Narat and Comrade Tak!' he shouted – and stunned, fell forward on his knees before the teenage soldier. He had been hit hard from behind at the knee joints.

Two youths pushed him backwards on to the ground and stood over him with knives, while two others disappeared under the hut, re-emerging with what looked like a short beam mounted on a low frame. The youths grabbed Bill's ankles and, opening the beam, which was on a hinge, placed his feet in two holes in the centre, then closed the beam and padlocked it.

Bill lay on his back, his feet raised several inches higher than his body. The soldiers had disappeared and he was staring at the sky, which had begun to clear. Soon he would be in direct sunlight. His skin itched with real and imagined bites, his legs were aching from the knock-down blow and from the pressure of the wood against his ankles, which were too large for the holes. Where the devil was Narat, and why hadn't Tak been in the hut that morning? Where was Ty? Where were Kieu and San? It began to dawn on him that some kind of coup might have occurred. Yet to be at the mercy of this gang of surly adolescents was a prospect too ugly to contemplate.

Bill lay there all afternoon, thirsty, sunburned, aching, itching, and trying hard not to panic. At dusk a clutch of children gathered a short distance away, wide-eyed and silent. Greeting them familiarly, Bill asked for Ty, but the children only stared, aghast no doubt to see so god-like a creature now so miserably reduced. Bill longed to ask for water but knew that even if they brought it, it would be undrinkable. Attempts at conversation and to persuade the children to take a message to Shangri La failed: they remained frozen in wonder.

Finally a little boy stepped forth, his arms held rigid at his sides. Coming up very close, and with no expression whatsoever, he prodded Bill in the hip with his bare foot, the way one did an animal to find out if it was still alive.

With a roar Bill reared up on his elbows.

The little boy ran off and the clutch of children drew back several steps. One or two girls giggled nervously, another began to whimper.

Presently a boy wearing the remnants of a red T-shirt tiptoed forward, and, acting as if he were invisible, circled round and came to a halt just above Bill's head. The children's eyes grew large with surprise and fear. Bill knew this was a grave insult: the top of the head was sacred. The child might as well have been standing triumphantly on his chest. But Bill was unfazed: the custom was for him a piece of nonsense.

When eventually two little girls stepped shyly towards him, holding hands, Bill thought he vaguely recollected their faces from the school.

'Hey,' he said kindly. '*Sue sdei.*'

The little girls looked at him solemnly; then they, too, came up very close, and still clutching each other's hands, spat in unison.

At this, like a flock of startled birds, all the children fled.

Hungry, thirsty, desperate and in increasing pain, Bill lay there all night, bitten by insects and uneasy at the thought of spiders and snakes. It was also very cold. The entire village must know where he was, yet apart from the children, no one had come; nor, he felt sure, had anyone informed the Barangs. They were outsiders. Bill knew Marjorie would be in a dreadful state, imagining all sorts of horrible things, and he longed to comfort her. But at bottom he was thankful, too, that she and the others couldn't see him, pent up in stocks like a village thief.

At daybreak two young soldiers appeared, and one of them was carrying a rifle. Without a word, and without looking at Bill, they unlocked the stocks. Bill had trouble getting to his feet, but no effort was made to help him. Nor would he have allowed it, he told himself. The soldiers waited while he relieved himself, the rifle trained on his back, then frog-marched him down the path that continued into the forest. Since Vietnam, rumours of Communist atrocities had stretched to America, and Bill tried hard to suppress these recollections. More alarming was a recent remark of Yves's, that assassination was becoming commonplace in Cambodia. The insurgency did not waste bullets – could not afford to. Its victims were beaten to death.

'Marxist economics,' Bill had joked. Now he gleaned a modicum of reassurance from the rifle's presence.

What he feared above everything was a coup.

When the municipal-style hut appeared through the forest undergrowth, it looked almost like home. Bill was shoved inside, a bowl of rice and a large pot of tea were put on the table, and again the door was slammed shut.

Scalding himself, he downed the tea, then attacked the rice with both hands, cramming it ravenously into his mouth. His mind had no other thought. His entire being was concentrated on the pure animal pleasure of filling his stomach, and in relatively familiar, therefore seemingly secure, surroundings.

The youth with the rifle had settled on the floor, his back against one of the Cessna's seats, evidently in another world. But Bill decided things were looking up and, feeling encouraged, asked for some more tea.

The soldier did not respond. When the door opened a little later, however, he quickly jumped to his feet – as did Bill, pride and indignation overcoming the ache reverberating painfully through his legs.

Narat entered the room, accompanied by a young aide-de-camp.

'Narat, thank God!' Bill's voice, though showing relief, was edged with self-righteous anger.

'Please sit.' Narat gestured towards the chair that, as before, put Bill's back to the door; and going around the table he took the opposite place for himself, sitting down formally, as at a desk.

'Narat, what the hell is going on?' Though neither of the young recruits would have understood a word, Bill, leaning across the table, had lowered his voice.

Narat, sitting up very straight, fixed Bill with a solemn and disappointed look. 'You have lied to me, Bill.'

'Narat,' said Bill patiently, as to a child, 'I haven't lied to you. Now what the fuck is going on? I've spent the night in goddamned stocks, being eaten alive by mosquitoes and spat on by a bunch of unruly kids. For God's sake call off the black pyjamas, will you, and tell me what this is all about? Couldn't Angka check anything out? Is that it?'

'I am sorry, Bill, but there is nothing I can do for you.'

'You can tell me what the hell is going on!'

'You are CIA, Bill.'

Incredulity was swamped by a spontaneous burst of hilarity, and Bill laughed out loud. 'C'mon Narat, somebody's setting you up. I'm no more CIA than you are! You know who I am, and I know you know it. So out with it. What's all this about?' He leaned back in the chair and, balancing it on its back legs, scrutinized Narat with almost benevolent amusement.

'I wished to speak to you first, because of the gravity of the charges,' Narat continued quietly.

'Narat, my friend, you're being bamboozled – misled. I appreciate there could be some trouble checking facts, in the circumstances. But the story will have been in all the newspapers – America, Europe, Cambodia, you name it. "Read all about me!"'

'You are an important man, Bill,' acknowledged Narat solemnly. He pulled a folded paper from his shirt pocket, opened it, smoothed it out and handed it across the table.

Bill read:

Dear Mr Rives,

My wife and I will be arriving in Phnom Penh on January 2nd. Our flight arrives from Bangkok at eight a.m., and I gather the embassy has kindly offered to send a car and driver to meet us.

I'm enormously grateful to you and your staff for setting things up for us, especially as I know that there are difficulties right now and you must have a lot on your plate. For what it's worth, I promised State to report to you any signs in the countryside that might indicate the presence of North Vietnamese, or indeed the presence of Communist activities of any kind. But my visit is short and I fear I shall be of little use.

I look forward to meeting you and will come by the embassy at noon on the 2nd.

Yours sincerely,

William F Bolton.

The telex was headed 'Bolton Venture Capital'.

Narat held out his hand for the paper.

'Oh for Christ's sake!' Bill was wild with frustration and amazement. 'This is just a formality! People always get asked to do that – keep their eyes open – if they visit an inaccessible country. It doesn't mean a thing. I'd forgotten all about it. Believe me, Narat, I've no intention of reporting anything to anybody. Shit, man! I've absolutely nothing to report. I just want to get my wife and myself safely out of here.'

But the telex would, he knew, be damning evidence. Narat and his cronies were far too unworldly to put it into proper perspective, and guerrilla movements, by their very nature, were inevitably paranoid.

'You have lied to me, Bill,' Narat repeated, visibly disappointed. He sounded sad.

'Narat, you're a man of the world; you know how these things work. The State Department did me a big favour getting me a permit. I pulled a few strings; it paid off and I wanted to thank them. But that letter doesn't mean anything. It never occurred to me there were any Communists in Cambodia. How would I recognize one if there was?'

But underneath Bill's steady, doggedly defensive line ran the unnerving realization that, for Narat to have obtained a copy of that telex, there must be a Communist spy in the embassy in Phnom Penh. And if so, then everything coming through it was being passed on to the insurgency – now the allies of North Vietnam.

How could he possibly keep quiet about that when, unheeded, it could lead to serious, even disastrous consequences for American troops?

He could not. And Narat must know this.

Suddenly Bill was well and truly scared. He realized his hands were shaking, and he clasped them tightly together under the table as he stubbornly persisted in his defence. 'Look, Narat, I was only going to be here for forty-eight hours, traipsing around some temple to please my wife. There was no war going on then; the war was in Vietnam. I'd no idea Cambodia would become involved. I didn't know anything about Cambodia, or the Communists – the Khmer Rouge.'

'But now you do know.'

For the first time, Bill glimpsed, behind the poised, boyishly smiling yet intense young man, a determined, guerrilla-trained young Communist.

'Do I? Listen, I don't know anything the whole world doesn't know by now. And I can forget about you showing me that telex.'

'I am sorry, Bill.' And Narat did indeed look sorry as, folding the paper, he returned it to his pocket.

Both men stood up, Bill's hands now clasped hard behind his back. His voice suddenly hoarse, he asked, 'What about the others?'

'I think we will not meet again,' answered Narat, looking beyond Bill to the door in indication that the interview was over. And without another word he left the room, his teenage aide-de-camp following, quick-step, behind.

Bill stared at the door; but seeing the guard was watching him, sat down again. He had to think; to figure things out and come up with a plan. He could tell that Narat felt personally wounded, possibly even betrayed, and by a man he had believed to be his friend. Moreover, in vouching for him, Narat might have raised suspicions about his own loyalty. The Boltons were living in his house. Narat, too, could be in boiling water; and if so he would want to convince his superiors that he was a hundred per cent behind them.

In a chilling moment of revelation, Bill perceived, in its entirety, what had just occurred, the logic of it sweeping in a numbing blizzard across his stunned but no longer befuddled brain. By showing him that telex, Narat had verified beyond any doubt what Angka, on such meagre evidence, must have declared necessary. In giving Bill information he would be obliged to pass on, no matter what he promised, there could be no doubt now about the need for his elimination.

And the others' fates were tied to his. The Khmer Rouge would not waste time on moral or legal quibbles. They had no courts or prisons, but lived a brutal existence in the forest, sustained like anchorites by an implacable faith in the future and their own messianic role within it. Dispatching the Barangs would be easy and without diplomatic repercussion, since most people probably believed they were already dead. They would simply disappear.

The guard sat dreamily on the floor. Bill was pretty sure he could overpower him and get hold of the rifle. But then what?

In the early afternoon, after eating a bowl of boiled rice, washed down with tea, Bill was returned to the stocks; and a little later it began to rain. A blessing at first, he opened his mouth wide, savouring each drop like the elixir it now was. But before long he was lying in mud, and by evening the mosquitoes were launching their attacks in squadrons. Bill flailed his arms about, slapping and cursing. At least the children had not returned, he told himself. But still he had no plan; and the situation was serious, deathly serious. He must not panic. He must think clearly and cogently, and come up with a plan. Things always came out right in the end.

Convincing Narat of his innocence was pointless, now that Bill had seen the telex. But what about Tak? Tak might help him. Tak was worldly-wise, and he distrusted the extreme politics of the young. He might not know about the telex. But to find him Bill must escape, and quickly.

The two guards were hunkered under the hut, sheltering from the rain, tossing pebbles into a hole and betting on their success. Bill had heard that the recruits, although dedicated Communists, longed for three material possessions: a bicycle, a wristwatch and a transistor radio. If he gave the guards his wristwatch, they could compete for it in their game and he might be allowed to slip off when he went for a pee. He knew that the soldiers would never take the watch by force. They had their own high code of morals, so bribery too was probably out of the question. He *must* come up with a plan!

Bill didn't know whether he had slept or not. Cicadas were shrieking like the high-pitched, non-stop ringing of a dozen doorbells. There must be a nest of them near by, and if he had been asleep, they must have woken him up. As he lay there in the dark, the full import of his situation again took hold, like the waking nightmare it now was.

He had never taken his promise to the State Department seriously. In fact, he had forgotten all about it – although the presence of North Vietnamese troops and, later on, the discovery of an indigenous Communist movement, had briefly reminded him; and fleetingly he had been pleased at having something to report, in return for the favour he had received.

Now, however, the desire for information was dramatically reversed. For if the Khmer Rouge really believed that he was CIA, they would want to know a great deal more, before . . .

Bill blocked it out.

He must have fallen asleep again, because when something brushed against his arm he flinched in horror, opening his eyes wide.

Bopha was kneeling beside him, her little face bent over his. She held a finger to her lips.

Looking into her solicitous eyes, Bill felt tears on his face, and realized that they were his own.

'I have key,' whispered Bopha, holding it up; and without pausing further, she set about opening the padlock. Carefully removing it from the clasp, she slowly raised the hinged beam a little at a time. Miraculously, it did not creak.

'We go quickly. The others wait for you.'

Getting to his feet with her help, Bill found that he could barely walk. He had to lean on Bopha's shoulder, limping and bent over until his circulation was restored. Once again, this gentle, self-effacing creature had risked everything, and as soon as they were away from the hut Bill took her in his arms. 'Darling Bopha! I'm *so* sorry.'

'Bopha and Bill eat pineapple,' she whispered singsong, recalling almost elegiacally an idyllic past. But already she was pulling away, and taking his arm to give him her support, she urged him forward. 'We hurry, Bill.'

'How did you get the key?' he whispered, as they ran,

arms interlocked around each other's waist, heads bent forward, along the dark, foliage-tunnelled path.

'Chandrea. She will put back.'

'Won't they guess?'

'*Neak ta* say, "Spirits free Bill."'

Despite everything, Bill grinned. A leaf offering certainly seemed to be in order.

'Samnang take you. Hide in forest.'

'Samnang?' Bill's mind swirled, a turmoil of worries, gratitude, affection and guilt.

At the entrance to the garden, Bopha kissed him. Then, still holding him fast, she laid her head briefly against his chest. 'I come back soon,' she whispered, and stepping back, gazing at him with solemn tenderness but giving him no time to respond, she melted, ghostlike, into the darkness. It was the last time Bill would see her.

The others were gathered below stairs, huddled on the platform, clutching *krama*-wrapped bundles. Bill was enveloped in hugs, with joyful whispers of relief and welcome – Marjorie desperate to learn if he was hurt.

'Bruised is all.

'Samnang!' Bill exclaimed with feeling, shaking his hand.

'We go,' whispered Samnang urgently.

'Yves isn't coming, darling.'

Yves, moving forward out of the shadows, spoke quietly, his deep voice resonating reassurance. 'You are going to a safe place,' he told Bill. 'Ty and Samnang will look after you. The others will explain, but it appears my son is a person of consequence in the Khmer Rouge, and I have been seconded to Siem Reap. The town has fallen to the insurgents. I will try to contact your embassy from there; with any luck it should be possible.'

Yves held out his hand and Bill gripped it tightly, then, leaning down, he kissed the old man hard on both cheeks.

'We go,' Samnang repeated.

As they started single file down the garden path, Anne ran forward, hugging her small bundle of possessions. 'Is Narat back? Is he all right?' she whispered frantically as she caught Bill up. 'Did you see him?'

Samnang, looking back, put his finger to his lips.

'He's OK,' whispered Bill coolly. 'Now let's get a move on. It's late.'

Shifting the bundle to her hip, Anne fell willingly back into line. She barely noticed the jungle or worried about the darkness, or even the future. Samnang could tell Narat where to find her.

21

YVES DID NOT GO UPSTAIRS, BUT LAY DOWN IN THE hammock. It would be dawn in about an hour and he doubted that he would sleep. The sudden departure of the others had proved surprisingly painful. They had lived so fully together that now a shared existence felt cruelly snatched away. He imagined the little party hurrying through the darkness, too alarmed perhaps by what they were leaving to be intimidated by the jungle's more immediate dangers – dangers real enough that the Khmers, an indigenous forest people, engaged in daily propitiation.

It was essential that they escape from the region as quickly as possible. Bill almost certainly had been condemned, and, if so, the others would be under sentence, too. Insurgencies were of necessity ruthlessly efficient. Nor did they condone personal favours. His son would have begged this one only in order to save his father's life. And now a hitch had arisen: for, the others having managed to flee, the Khmer Rouge would assume, and rightly, that Yves would now do his best to help them.

He saw he would not being going home any time soon, and he began to resign himself to a lengthy incarceration at Siem Reap. The Grand Hotel would make a comfortable prison in this swelling sea of distress. He would get news of his daughter Esme, and Huoy would know that he was well, if she did not already. But he feared for his son. Sophatra was full of hope for the future, for progress and a new enlightenment. So, for that matter, was Bill Bolton. Both men were naive; both believed wholeheartedly in a particular philosophy of life, and they derived great strength from it. While Europeans like himself, older, possibly wiser, certainly disillusioned, watched sceptically from the sidelines as the younger faiths energetically produced their results. America had surpassed them all, but hegemony sat awkwardly on her young shoulders, as she protested, with self-righteous indignation, accusations of a lost virginity; and as Mammon, clothed in the immaculate robes of democracy, was sanctimoniously paraded before the world. When that god failed there was going to be big trouble. Yet it would happen. Again and again civilizations failed and the garden of Eden was reborn, the jungle re-emerged and the primal innocence of survival returned: the killing.

A faint haze of pink was visible above the tree line, and Yves decided to stay in the hammock a little longer. There was no real reason to get up; but soon he would do so, and then he would have a drink.

The Barangs had been walking for over an hour. It was impossible to know in what direction, but Samnang appeared able to see in the dark. They walked in single file, holding on to a cord to keep together, as in mountain climbing. The jungle was marvellously still, eery in its quietude.

'Jungle sleep,' Samnang whispered.

But some time before dawn had penetrated the overhead canopy, unseen birds and monkeys began to sing and chatter; and at first light, roars, barks and high-pitched shrieks exploded in sporadic outbursts. Everywhere there were bellies to be filled; the day's work had begun. A pointless existence, Anne had once observed; and Marjorie had answered that it wasn't, if animals housed transmigrated souls. Amused, Anne had declared this the only argument she had ever heard that gave animal life some meaning, other than as evolutionary antiques.

'You're forgetting the food chain,' Bill had interjected. 'Where would we be without it?'

Samnang had halted and was pointing ahead with his stick. Barely visible in the pale-pink light, a leopard lay stretched out on a low branch over the trail in front of them, presumably awaiting its breakfast. Without so much as a glance it sinuously bestirred itself, and in a long and fluid stretch leaped gracefully down, like a house cat jumping off the arm of a chair, and loped off nonchalantly into the undergrowth. Everyone was thrilled, and Bill thought what a fine shot it would have made, even with a pistol. The leopard was that close.

Salty, having noted the direction of the dawn, was surprised to find they were walking northeast, and not west towards the Tonle Sap. With the whole region flooded the lake shouldn't be too far away, and there would be a chance of finding a boat, maybe even people willing to help them. With a boat they could get across the lake, and presumably away from the fighting. Salty was on the point of saying this when, before them, a high stone wall appeared as out of nowhere, blocking the trail. Trees grew on the top, making a leaf-crowned palisade. Their exposed roots, silvery grey like the skin of elephants, reached downwards, gripping the stones beneath with long witch-like fingers in a vice that was at once the wall's destruction and its preservation.

'Dead end,' allowed Salty, not at all displeased. 'How about making for the Tonle Sap? Get ourselves a boat.'

But Samnang didn't stop. The path continued alongside the wall, and the Barangs followed behind him to where there was a breach, making an aperture that they could pass through.

Inside lay an extraordinary sight. Huge chunks of masonry – broken pillars, ruined towers, the remnants of galleries and terraces – once interconnected, now ragged and solitary sentinels, stood haphazardly about, covered by a verdant carpet of vines and undergrowth. It was as if the forest canopy had collapsed. Blocks of dressed stone littered the ground, and from behind the vines and roots of trees, delicately carved *apsaras* peeked out seductively. One of the galleries was relatively intact, the corbelled roof undamaged, the stone-balustered windows identical to those at Angkor Wat. On the exterior a bas-relief, clearly visible in the morning light, depicted a king holding a club, about to smite a cringing, gremlin-like demon.

But most spectacular was a gatehouse. Standing well inside the perimeter wall, and elevated on a low terrace, the huge tower, partially swathed in vines, was decorated with elaborate carvings. At the top, four gigantic stone heads with flattened Khmer noses and broad bow lips gazed out upon the jungle at cardinal points, smiling identical enigmatic smiles. Another head lay near by, at the foot of another truncated tower, broken into pieces.

'Ozymandias!' exclaimed Salty with a low whistle, and somewhat to Anne's surprise.

But Marjorie, who was standing beside him, didn't respond. Enfolded in the mysterious magic of this failed and forgotten place, she could feel, through her imagination, its disinherited ghosts moving in an eternal silence among the gravestones of a dead empire, and she was thrilled.

'Where do we buy the postcards?' Bill called out, pulling a vine away better to reveal an *apsara* twiddling a lotus flower in elegantly contorted fingers. 'Hey there, little girl!'

Of them all, however, Anne's delight was keenest. Anne knew uncharted ruins existed in the forest that blanketed so much of the country, but they were usually small and relatively insignificant. This temple was enormous, its size roughly on a par with Angkor Wat, its bas-reliefs of exceptional quality, while the colossal heads bespoke the reign of Jayavarman VII. Anne was standing before a discovery that could make her name. Suddenly she felt almost as if directed to this point, as if her life, previously so patchy and uncertain, was falling kaleidoscopically into place. Why shouldn't she stay on? She and Narat could live together at Shangri La; he could continue his political work from there, and she, in addition to helping him overthrow Lon Nol, could travel back and forth to the ruins with a guide – preferably Samnang – and map them in detail. But if she had to leave now, because it was too dangerous, then as soon as the fighting was over, even if it took months, Anne made up her mind then and there that she would come back.

Samnang took hurried leave, promising to return next morning with food, and the Barangs, searching for a place to sleep, decided on the stone-floored gallery. Depositing their bundles at the end blocked by fallen debris, they settled down on the gatehouse steps.

Bill, eagerly questioned at last, took care to conceal the very real danger they were in. The Khmer Rouge were just a bunch of nuts, he insisted dismissively. Total paranoids, who believed that every Westerner was CIA, since why else would anyone want to visit their ridiculous little country? Bill saw no reason to mention the telex, but said that despite his having provided them with his entire life story, the Khmer Rouge had remained moronically unconvinced.

'Surely Narat backed you up? He knows who you are,' blurted Anne, delighted by this chance to speak Narat's name aloud.

Bill merely replied that as they had been staying in Narat's house, he too seemed under some suspicion, which had made things a lot more complicated.

'But that's terrible! If Narat's in trouble, then it's our fault and we must help him. I think we should go back.' But even as Anne spoke, she knew it made no sense.

'If he's in trouble, the last thing he needs is us,' retorted Bill, with razor-sharp finality. He had thought Anne a smart, level-headed young woman, despite some silly left-wing ideas and a fair amount of arrogance. But lately she seemed increasingly off her rocker, and suggesting they should risk their lives for Narat was as lunatic a piece of bleeding-heart liberalism as he'd ever heard.

Marjorie, however, perceiving in Anne's outburst something nearer the truth, patted her hand in sympathetic understanding.

* * *

They built a fire early, so as not to attract attention after dark; and, boiling water collected from a nearby stream, they filled the two canteens and cooked their rice. Marjorie made a lotus-blossom salad, and after supper Salty produced his packet of marijuana and some dried banana skins, cut into little squares, for wrappers. It was almost like old times, everyone insisted, sitting on the terrace steps, passing their communal cigarette, having once again survived near disaster with barely a scratch. It inspired a kind of bemused triumph, and as night made its meteoric descent, peace also descended; the great stone faces overhead stared out blankly across the forest, smiling their mysterious Khmer smiles.

Samnang arrived at dawn to find the little party sitting bleary eyed on the gatehouse steps, drinking cold tea.

'Rescue!' he called out in English, grinning as he hurried forward; and pulling a paper from his shirt pocket, he handed it proudly to Bill.

'Yves got hold of a field telephone. He's talked to the embassy – a helicopter's being sent!' Bill waved the paper about like a flag, and a great cheer went up. 'It'll be here tomorrow morning at nine o'clock.'

Another cheer, some impromptu dancing steps, and Samnang was patted heartily on the back, as if it were all his doing.

Bill then read the details aloud.

> 'The helicopter will land near the Cessna, a landmark both parties can find. Samnang will return to take you there. He says you must be ready to leave by seven. Many Vietnamese are in the area. They are well armed and in possession of mortars, so the helicopter cannot wait. To cut its engine would be

too dangerous. You *must* be there, or it will have to leave without you. A second attempt would be both difficult and dangerous, since your whereabouts would by then be known.

'Godspeed, *mes amis*. I go to Siem Reap tomorrow for an indefinite period of comfort and recreation at the Grand Hotel.'

The day passed in heady anticipation. Anne, having purloined Samnang's biro, sketched in some detail a remarkable bas-relief of Loksevara, the Buddha's disciple, his multiple arms spread out like two fanned-out packs of cards, giving the impression of fluttering wings. Anne was happy. Life would be like this when she and Narat were finally together, pursuing equally worthwhile careers and comfortably housed at Shangri La. And into this blissful maundering was woven keen excitement at the impact her discovery would have on the archaeological world. She would be famous.

Bill lounged on the gatehouse steps, scratching his many mosquito bites and reading James Bond for the third and final time. Having survived a life-threatening adventure of his own, pitted against scheming and ruthless men, he identified with Bond's as never before and the story took on new life, much of it being Bill's own.

Marjorie and Salty occupied themselves gathering bamboo shoots in the forest for dinner, clapping their hands at intervals, as Ty had taught them, to scare off snakes. In ways, they were like two peas in a pod, thought Marjorie, aware none the less of a vein of melancholy in Salty that only increased her tenderness for him. Salty believed himself to be a child of nature born into a largely man-made world, and he could never be fully at home in either. He longed for unification, for a sort of oneness that in its essence was probably mystical. And unable to achieve it, part of him was forever in mourning. A bit like that cucumber plant, thought Marjorie, who understood such instincts because to a degree she shared them. But unlike Salty, Marjorie was highly adaptable, and she enjoyed a solid footing in that other, unnatural world.

During the night Bill was awoken by strange noises coming from outside the gallery. Careful not to rouse the others, he retrieved the pistol, now more or less permanently in his possession, and tiptoed over to the window. One of the balusters was broken, and Bill leaned forward and peered carefully out. He could see nothing at first, it was too dark; but there was no doubt about the sound: the muffled thud of feet was clearly audible.

If Samnang had been followed, Bill knew their situation would be dangerous in the extreme, because if they were ambushed their refuge would become a cage, a cul-de-sac from which escape would be impossible. Yet on no account must anyone be taken prisoner. Torture and death by bludgeoning would follow. Bill forced himself to confront a dire reality. Whatever happened now, four bullets must be kept in reserve, and he must be prepared – unflinchingly prepared – to use them. For the first time in his life, faced with no alternatives, he experienced bleak despair as, pressing his face against the balusters, he looked out anxiously in the direction of the sound.

The moon had tumbled from behind a cloud, flinging out myriad shadows like malign encroachments that, unfurling, overlapped, and grew in all directions. One of them ballooned into a monstrous silhouette, so that for a moment Bill considered, optimistically, the presence of ghosts.

But the silhouette was rapidly fleshed out.

To Bill's utter astonishment, a huge elephant was standing in the ruins, its tusks gleaming in the moonlight like a pair of unsheathed sabres. Bill gazed at the gigantic creature in stunned fascination and immense relief, his heart still pumping hard. The elephant was nosing with its trunk among the fallen stones, ponderous, yet seemingly methodical, as if searching for something. Was it a harbinger, scouting out territory, and could it have known this place earlier, before the herd had migrated to the Kulen hills? Elephants had notoriously good memories; they even bore long-standing grudges. Most probably this was an old male, on its own. But had it divined that the ruins were occupied by others? It was impossible to know.

The elephant, continuing its mysterious search, disappeared from view. Bill was about to return to bed, balmy relief beginning to flow through his veins and a pleasant fatigue enveloping him, when suddenly something crept over his hand, where it lay on the sill, covering it in a rough and eerie caress.

Seized by a kind of primal horror, he jerked his hand back. But the caress battened down, fastened in a grip around his wrist, and, locking his hand in an improbable handshake, seemed about to pull his arm through the balusters.

Appalled, Bill slammed the pistol butt down hard on the elephant's trunk with his free hand. The butt, hitting flesh, made no noise; it was like hitting a thick piece of rubber. The elephant made no noise either. The grip was relaxed and the trunk slithered off the sill.

But the elephant moved in closer, its great mass of flesh and high domed forehead filling the window. Bill was inches from a glinting malevolent eye. Set in heavy creases, the eye was fringed with surprisingly long lashes, the pupil ringed by the warning amber light of a glowing iris. The eye looked tiny, embedded in the massive head; but the power behind it was enormous – the unpredictability equally so.

The elephant seemed to study Bill, standing doll-like before it, to be sizing him up, forming arcane and primitive thoughts inside a savage brain that took its dominance and force of will for granted. Bill wanted to shoot straight into that staring eye. It was that sinister, glaring at him from the repulsive carapace of wrinkled flesh. But at bottom he knew that he was probably safe; they all were. There was nothing to be frightened of. The gallery's narrow entrance and stone-barred windows protected them. Their cage was again a refuge, and the jungle safely at bay.

But furious at having been so frightened, so unmanned, of glimpsing even for a second that impinging void of black despair, on a sudden impulse, he clenched his desecrated hand into a fist and thrust it through the balusters, straight at the bestial eye. The blow fell slightly short. The elephant lunged against the window, and Bill barely retracted his hand in time. But he refused to quit. Instead, he moved in closer, so that once more they were eye to eye. He raised his fist again. But this time he opened it slowly, like the blossoming of a poisonous flower; and grinning menacingly into the unblinking scrutiny, he gave the elephant the finger. 'Fuck you!' he silently mouthed.

He was breathing normally, even smiling, when he returned to his pallet. The elephant was still at the window, its great head blocking the moonlight. Bill wrapped his *krama* around him, like a blanket, and lay down; then, adjusting the bundle that made his pillow, he tucked the pistol beneath it and willed himself back to sleep. Tomorrow was a big day.

Next morning the bizarre nocturnal visit seemed unreal – a lurid nightmare or waking marijuana dream. But the undergrowth beneath the window was flattened, and there was a pile of elephant dung beside the narrow gallery entrance. Salty, off to collect water, said dried elephant dung made excellent fuel. A shame they couldn't use it now. The women, disappointed at missing the elephant, wished Bill had woken them up. But already everyone's thoughts were elsewhere, riveted on their departure, and Anne and Marjorie, in anticipation of meeting the outside world, made careful toilettes before depositing their bundles, ready to go, on the gatehouse steps.

Minutes later Samnang arrived, his *krama* full of bananas. He laid them on the steps, then pointed to seven on Bill's watch. It was now six thirty-five.

As the Barangs downed the bananas and sipped cold tea from the night before, Samnang, volunteering to carry the women's bundles, set about cutting a short bamboo cane and tying a bundle on each end, to make a shoulder board. He was laying the pole across his shoulders to test the balance when suddenly he froze, his eyes fixed searchingly on the aperture in the wall, his hand raised in a signal of alert.

'It's Salty,' mumbled Anne, munching the last of her banana. 'He'd better hurry if he wants a banana.'

'Or *domrei, domrei chlong*,' Marjorie said hopefully, not sure which word was 'elephant' and which 'crossing'.

When a flock of birds rose up, flying in elegant formation overhead, everyone laughed, except Samnang, who, with narrowed eyes, focused in the direction from which the birds had come.

'It *is* Salty. I can see him,' declared Bill. From the terrace, he could just see a figure emerging from among the trees, beyond the crumbling wall.

The others resumed their preparations, and only Bill and Samnang were still watching when, moments later, Narat, together with half a dozen young soldiers, entered through the breach in the wall.

'Khmer Rouge!' hissed Samnang, stooping quickly to retrieve his knife.

With a cry of joy, Anne leaped down from the terrace and, rushing forward, beaming her delight, took Narat by the arm, looping both her arms around his, and drew him involuntarily forward.

'You kept your promise. I knew you would!' she whispered. 'And I know how dangerous it is right now – mixing with us, I mean. I know we've caused you a lot of trouble, and I'm truly sorry.'

'Welcome to our humble abode,' Marjorie called out hospitably.

Bill and Samnang exchanged a rapid-fire glance.

The soldiers had remained beside the wall, glum and confused, clasping their unsheathed knives.

At the foot of the terrace Narat stopped, Anne still clinging devotedly to his arm.

'You must return to Domrei Chlong,' he announced coldly to Bill, pushing the shock of hair off his forehead with his free hand.

Bill was thinking fast. There was not much time. 'What about the others?'

'The others also. We wish only to do what is right

where every person is concerned. Each case will be heard individually. This has been agreed with Angka.'

'Narat, dearest,' murmured Anne, 'why not just leave us here? Say you couldn't find us.' She smiled beseechingly, aware their escape must not now be impeded, their rendezvous kept secret. 'As soon as everything settles down, I'll be right back. I promise.'

'You must come,' Narat repeated to Bill. He did not look at Anne.

Precious minutes were passing. Bill knew Salty would have seen the soldiers and must be lying low, doubtless arranging a tactical diversion. He decided on a gamble. 'OK Narat, I'll come if you'll agree to leave the others here till we can get a written promise of their safety. Angka wants things written down. Well, so do we. You can leave them under guard if you want, but they won't be going anywhere. That's for sure.'

'*Bill!*' cried Marjorie.

'I'll come too. I'll be your hostage,' Anne suddenly declared. 'Then there'll be no need for guards. Just leave the others here, as Bill says.'

Bill was dumbfounded in the face of such courage – or utter stupidity. But Narat's hand grazed Anne's gently, as the humane and thoughtful man struggled against the persona of a trained and determined soldier.

'A drink of water, Margie,' Bill told his wife, with a fierce look of warning. The extreme tension in his voice was evident, and Marjorie, her hands quivering, her eyes blurred with tears, dumbly obeying, retrieved the water bottle.

Bill took several deep gulps from the canteen, pausing between each one. He was girding himself in cold determination. Then, still holding the canteen, he leaped down from the terrace. 'One for the road,' he proposed hospitably, offering the metal flask to Narat. 'If you and I go on ahead, the others can follow later.' How much later was left open, for negotiation and a possible diplomatic compromise.

Narat, already facing a difficult dilemma, was further embarrassed by the hospitable offer of a drink. He was also very thirsty. Taking the proffered canteen, he gave Bill the tiniest nod, uncorked the bottle and raised it to his lips. His head thrown back, he drank lustily and with evident pleasure, quenching a deep and parching thirst.

As he did so, Bill shot him at point-blank range, squarely in the chest.

Narat fell backwards, a look of wonder and confusion on his face.

Then everything happened at once. Anne was shrieking, the soldiers rushing forward with their machetes, Bill shooting at them and Samnang pulling a frantic Marjorie back into the gatehouse. A dark badge was spreading over Narat's breast, and water from the canteen was spilling on to the ground, beginning to dilute the fine crimson trail already disappearing into the earth.

'Oh my God, oh my God. How could you!' shrieked Anne, kneeling over Narat's body. '*How could you!* Oh my God; it's not possible!'

The soldiers, no match for gunfire and their leader dead, quickly retreated, one of them limping badly, supported by his comrades.

'Come on, let's go!' shouted Bill, pistol still at the ready, his eye fixed on the retreating Khmer Rouge. 'Let's get out of here!'

'We can't leave without Salty!'

'He's waiting for the soldiers to clear off. He'll catch

up. Salty's a born tracker. He knows where we're going. Just get Anne, will you?'

Anne, weeping and traumatized, had to be torn from Narat's body.

'Hurry up, for Christ's sake!' shouted Bill. 'We haven't got much time.'

'Horrible! Oh, horrible!' Anne kept on repeating it in a keening litany, over and over again. 'How could you! Oh my God. How could you, Bill!'

'Anne dear, it was self-defence,' murmured Marjorie, lamely. Appalled and confused by the shooting, the instinct to protect her husband was paramount. But she was now desperately worried about Salty, and removing her *krama* as they walked, she hung it on a branch to mark the trail.

Samnang had jettisoned the shoulder board, and putting one arm around Anne's waist, clutching both bundles with the other, was gently urging her forward along the path.

'He wasn't armed. He wasn't even *armed*! It was murder, *cold-blooded murder*!'

'He was going to kill us,' shouted Bill over his shoulder. 'Take my word for it! It was him or us.'

But as he spoke, Bill realized with a sudden burst of pleasure that no explanation was necessary in the jungle. Freedom was total. And it crossed his mind that modern living would need a lot of adjustment to match in its exhilaration this rare moment of pure, undiluted and triumphant elephant joy.

When the whup-whup-whup of the helicopter sounded, they were near the edge of the savannah and could see the Cessna's badly rusted skeleton through the trees. A terrible fear swept over Marjorie. There was still no sign of Salty, and they could not possibly leave without him.

'Bill,' she pleaded, tugging desperately at his arm. 'Bill, stop! We have to wait!'

Samnang, his arms waving like a windmill, ran forward to alert the pilot; spotting him, the helicopter made a circle, hovered briefly, then dropped down like a hawk, the door open, the co-pilot beckoning.

Samnang indicated that the others were coming.

They emerged into the brightly lit savannah, the women literally pushed along by Bill, his arms around their shoulders and gripping hard; Marjorie was frantically imploring her husband, the propeller's roar blotting out every word, as the co-pilot waved, urging them to hurry up.

Anne, still in shock, was pulled into the helicopter first; then, with Bill's help, Marjorie. Samnang stood at a distance from the whirling propeller, and Bill motioned that they could take him with them. Samnang laughed and shook his head, and Bill, removing his watch, tossed him the Rolex. Samnang caught it, his face alight with joy. They saluted each other.

'Look out for Salty,' shouted Bill. Then, gripping the co-pilot's outstretched hand, he leaped into the plane.

The helicopter lifted weightlessly, its door still open. Samnang waved and grinned. The door closed, and the plane shifted sideways; then, buzzing noisily over the jungle, it swung back towards the plain, like a cradle, and levelled out in the direction of Phnom Penh.

Aftermath

THE BOLTONS RETURNED HOME TO A NATIONAL-FRONT-page welcome, their adventure compared to shipwrecked sailors scavenging on exotic isles and pioneers surviving in the American West. Salty's disappearance added drama and continuing suspense. A search was underway, directed from the American embassy in Phonm Penh, but the area was remote, in a state of disruption, and reliable information was increasingly hard to get.

A few weeks after their rescue, Bill, in Washington for the day, had a meeting at the State Department. His report of a substantial North Vietnamese presence far inland from the border, together with the existence of a fast-growing Communist-led insurgency, was carefully listened to. Bill, uniquely, had been behind enemy lines; and when aerial maps of the region were produced, he was able to pinpoint specific areas of the insurgency, and the presence of North Vietnamese troops, with some degree of accuracy. He came away feeling he had more than returned the State Department's favour, an impression confirmed a few days later by a note from President Nixon, congratulating him on his escape and praising his valuable contribution to military intelligence in the region.

Not long afterwards, the search for Salty was quietly abandoned; western Cambodia had fallen under rebel control, and what followed is now history:

In an effort to halt Communism and protect its South Vietnam allies, the United States, in the early seventies, dropped more bombs on Cambodia than it had dropped on Japan in the Second World War. An estimated two hundred thousand Cambodians were killed, and hundreds of thousands of refugees wandered about the countryside or sought shelter in the improvised shanty-towns of Phnom Penh. All of which helped to swell the previously slender ranks of the Khmer Rouge.

Then, having abandoned South Vietnam, America withdrew its support from Lon Nol's faltering government, closed its embassy and fled Cambodia, the US ambassador hurriedly evacuated by helicopter in much the same way as the Boltons had been. Six days later, the Khmer Rouge marched victorious down Phnom Penh's Monivong Boulevard, and the following day forcibly evacuated the city. Banks, schools, towns, hospitals and families were declared redundant. The populace must work on the land to build a new and egalitarian society, under the direction of the mysterious Angka, headed by the equally mysterious Paris-educated Saloth Sar – alias Pol Pot – whose dedicated efforts to create a new and better world would result in the destruction of traditional society and death of a quarter of the remaining population, through disease, hunger and assassination.

With Cambodia on its knees, in 1978 the North Vietnamese invaded, easily defeating their former allies, and the Khmer Rouge retreated into the forest. Sporadic fighting continued for the next twenty years, and for most of that time the West, refusing to acknowledge Vietnamese hegemony, recognized the Khmer Rouge as part of an 'official' Cambodian government. A Khmer Rouge delegate occupied Cambodia's seat at the UN, and in a secret jungle camp in Malaysia, British and American troops trained Khmer Rouge guerrillas in the manufacture and use of landmines. The Vietnamese retaliated, and soon Cambodia was seeded with them.

In 1989, weakened by the collapse of the Soviet Union, the Vietnamese retreated and civil war again broke out. The United Nations arrived to broker a peace. Departing four years later to international acclaim, it left behind a fragile but democratically elected coalition government (boycotted by the still-fighting Khmer Rouge), also massive corruption from profligate over-spending, and the biggest AIDs problem in Asia.

Four years later, Pol Pot died in his jungle camp and the surviving Khmer Rouge melted into mainline Cambodian politics.

All the factions continued to believe they had been right.

During these years the Boltons' lives continued much as before, but with certain key domestic changes. Hattie died in 1975, and Marjorie, now a vegetarian, took full charge of her kitchen. Resigning from her charitable committees and abandoning tapestry work, she found a job teaching in a local primary school, and loved it; and she became a Buddhist. She didn't tell Bill about this at first, but when finally she did, there was little reaction. Bill seemed either resigned, or else disinterested. For Marjorie, however, life was fuller than she could ever remember.

Bill, busy backing the development of new enterprises

and technologies, had rapidly lost interest in Cambodia, and in the eighties and nineties made a fortune in fast food, shopping malls and microelectronics. Enriching himself had enriched the lives of others, as he was fond of pointing out; and as the new millennium approached and the human genome was being mapped, Genetech, Bill's favourite venture, stood at the cutting edge of a magnificent and revolutionary future. Centre court had lost some of its appeal, but the void he felt between successful deals always helped to stimulate the next financial adventure. And when, with age, business adventures became less frequent, fishing and sailing helped to satisfy the need for challenges. The adrenalin rushes, although diminished, still delivered their therapeutic highs.

The Boltons rarely spoke of Cambodia, but Marjorie often thought of it, and for years she worried and wondered about Salty. What both she and Bill feared but never said was that Salty had been captured by the retreating Khmer Rouge, following Narat's death. A fate too terrible to dwell upon.

But little news came out of Cambodia. In 1976 a rare photograph showing Khmer Rouge leaders at a conference had appeared in the *New York Times*, and Marjorie thought she saw Chandrea in the second row. The lower part of the woman's face was obscured by the man in front of her, but Bill, too, thought it could be her.

Then, one evening soon after the millennium celebrations, the Merriweathers came to dinner, bringing with them a copy of the *National Geographic* magazine. In it was an article about the impending restoration of a large and little-known Cambodian temple. The temple was located near the final stronghold of the Khmer Rouge, and colour photographs included a full-page picture of a towered gatehouse – or *gopura*, as the article called it – crowned by four colossal and mysteriously smiling heads. The author was Anne Jameson. It took the Boltons only moments to realize this must be Anne Phillips, and they calculated she would now be sixty years old.

A few weeks later, sitting at the breakfast table on a sunny June morning, a dogwood blooming in the garden outside, its white blossoms pressing against the window, Marjorie opened a letter postmarked India.

'Darling, it's from Anne – Anne Jameson – our Anne.'

Lowering his newspaper, Bill faced his wife directly for the first time that morning. 'Well, hey.'

'I wrote to her, care of the *National Geographic*,' Marjorie now confessed. She had removed her reading glasses the better to gauge her husband's reaction, but it was difficult to interpret: a mixture of interest, surprise, also irritation, perhaps, at an unnecessary or unwanted intrusion. 'I asked her if she knew anything about . . . well, everyone.'

'I'm all ears,' declared Bill, laying the paper aside and settling back in his chair, hands folded comfortably over his stomach. 'Go on.'

'It's quite long,' Marjorie apologized. The typewritten pages suggested a formal or professional aspect. 'Here goes.'

> 'My dear Marjorie, I've often thought of you, but I had no address.'
>
> 'It would have been easy to get,' interrupted Bill.
>
> 'Hearing from you was such a joy, and I'm thrilled you liked the article so much. In all those years, you know, I could never forget that temple. It became

symbolic of the repeated ruin of that beautiful country. But I wasn't able to return until last year, and then feared terribly to do so. I wasn't even sure I could find the temple again, or bear to see it. But when the World Monument Fund agreed to back the project and undertake its exploration and preservation, naturally I couldn't resist.

'Getting to Domrei Chlong was almost as difficult as getting out of it thirty years ago. The roads to Siem Reap are bombed to bits, but there are flights now, and the Angkor temples are up and running, and there is a great mood of optimism about tourism – everyone building hotels like mad. The WMF laid on two Land Rovers and an anti-landmine team. Landmines are the most awful problem. They are everywhere, the peasants constantly being killed or losing a leg, simply trying to grow some rice. It's insidious beyond belief!

'Local people knew about the temple, of course, so I was able to find a guide at Domrei Chlong. But that story is in the magazine, so I'll go straight to news of the village. It has survived, if only just; but, alas, our dear Shangri La is no more – not a trace remains. And no one seemed to know me, or anything about us, except for one woman who'd been in our school. To think that she may be the sole survivor of all those dear little girls! She is the only one of them still in the village, at any rate. And Marjorie, she could sing – and did – "You Are My Sunshine". Her name is Typa. Do you remember her? I don't. She's thirty-five now, but looks much older.

'The village had a hard time, I'm afraid. Incredibly, it was bombed by American B-52s shortly after we left, most probably by accident, since why anyone would choose to target that remote place is beyond imagining. Twenty-two people were killed, and a lot more wounded. Then later on, when the Khmer Rouge took control, everyone was put to work as forced labour. Food was so scarce that workers received only two cups of rice a day. They were supposed to enlarge the reservoir – make it four times as big. The Khmer Rouge planned to feed the whole area from Domrei Chlong, and take out a cash crop as well. Yet ironically, people were starving.

'Ty, a wily politician if ever there was one, managed somehow to hang on. He paid lip service to the Khmer Rouge at the same time as trying to protect the villagers, who still respect him. He died in his bed about ten years ago. The reservoir was tripled in the end, but never quadrupled, and though the sluice gates are in disrepair, it's still used by some of the peasants for a second crop. I asked why so few of the villagers grew a second crop, now there was enough water, and I was told they didn't need a second crop, that only the poorest, with the smallest amount of land, did. So, as you see, despite all the dreadful things that have happened, the Khmers are still the Khmers, for better or worse.

'The pagoda was badly damaged and all the *bonzes* either died or were killed. But it's been restored now – quite a good job, I thought – and several *bonzes* are in residence, all of them young, of course.

'People said Chandrea became fairly important in the Khmer Rouge, but died in one of the inter-party struggles, though no one knew any details. As to pretty little Bopha and the valiant Samnang, reports differ. Families were separated, as I'm sure you know, and Samnang had openly backed Lon Nol, so almost certainly he died early on, while Bopha, like so many others, simply disappeared without trace. It is all so dreadfully sad.

'Now I must prepare you for something else. It's about Salty. Typa remembered the story, and she told me. It seems he was killed by an elephant. Apparently it happened that last morning. There must have been some sort of provocation, and it's thought he may have got between a cow and her calf, and she charged him. There was an elephant in the ruins that last night. Do you remember? We didn't see it, though; and perhaps there was a calf as well.

'Salty's body was found not far from the temple, at the foot of an acacia tree, and Samnang buried him there. I think Salty would have liked that, don't you? It was even the sort of death he might have liked. And he would have died very quickly, they say, dashed against that tree. I'm sorry to be the one to tell you this, even after all these years, but I hope you'll feel better knowing exactly what happened – and that he was already dead when we left.'

Marjorie paused. 'Yes, I do feel better. I've imagined some terrible things.'

'The village is pretty run down, but then it always was. The headman, a war orphan like so many others, was a great help, however. He found a guide for us, and produced Typa to answer my questions. I had an interpreter from the WMF. The headman clearly has some European blood; he even knew a few English words. He told me he had always known them. But he did not know his parents' names; only 'mama' and 'papa'. I find that so poignant. His own name, of all things – can you believe it – is Jayavarman. I loved that! He has a wife and children, but I didn't meet them.'

Bill had stood up.

'I've been married for twenty-five years now to a fellow art historian. His name is Daniel. We have two boys, one in medical school and the other a solicitor in Manchester. Dan and I spend a lot of time in India. Hindu art is our great and unifying interest. It has ties with Angkor, of course; so doubtless that was the catalyst. But I'll stop now, this letter is already far too long. I loved hearing all your news, and I very much hope that we will keep in touch. With all best wishes, Anne.'

Bill was standing at the window, his back to his wife, looking into the staring white faces of the dogwood blossoms. 'She never mentioned me,' he said.

'There's a postscript,' responded Marjorie in a comforting voice. 'It's handwritten.'

'I was in a very bad way when we left the jungle in that helicopter. But even before that I was totally out of my head. And if I'd stayed on, which I confess I foolishly planned to do, I'd be long dead, and doubtless made pretty miserable long before that. I got a lot of things wrong; I know that now. But so did almost everyone, it seems, and maybe there were no clear-cut answers, although I find that very hard to believe.'

Bill's cancer was by now well advanced, and the following spring, one week after the human genome had been successfully mapped, he was dead. His will, published several months later, included, in addition to the usual property transfers, a number of charitable bequests, among them a half-million-dollar donation to Cambodian landmine relief and a gift of fifty thousand dollars to the village of Domrei Chlong, to be used as the village headman saw fit.

Bolton's philanthropy was widely praised.

THE END

Acknowledgements

Without the help I received in Cambodia, this story could not have been written. I particularly want to thank Khin Po-Thai, whose knowledge of Cambodian traditions, flora, fauna and agriculture was both comprehensive and meticulous, and whose introduction to villages of the northwest proved invaluable. I am also indebted to Som Sophatra, who answered many questions, and to his family, who made me welcome as a guest in their home.

Sir Leslie Fielding not only answered several political and social queries, but supplied a vivid first-hand impression of Cambodia in the late sixties, and threw me a lifeline of encouragement when I needed it most.

In addition to my patient and supportive publishers, I thank Barry Langridge and Roy Head at the BBC, Melissa Jenkins and Alice Walker (World Monument Fund), Robert Turnbull, Dickon Verey, Jane Dorrell, Hilly Beavan, John Pritchard and Kethy Tiulong; also Philippa Harrison, Ronald Hayman, Lauro Martines, James Michie and Julia O'Faolain.

Interpretation, point of view and any errors are entirely my own.

A ROPE OF SAND
Elsie Burch Donald

'WRITTEN WITH A LIGHT, DEFT TOUCH THAT BELIES THE EMOTIONAL PUNCH THAT IT PACKS'
Kate Atkinson

A chance encounter in a French town brings dark memories flooding back to fifty-five-year-old Kate. As a student at Sweet Briar College, Virginia in the 1950s, she joined a grand tour of Europe along with three classmates and their chaperone, Miss Grist. At the last minute, the mysterious and wealthy new girl, Olivia Hartfield, surprised them all by joining them.

Revelling in the unparalleled freedom of the old world, Kate and her friends gradually form a privileged and sophisticated clique as, one by one, three intriguing but very different young men latch on to their party. But nobody is quite as they appear, and as facades crumble, this journey will prove eye-opening in ways the girls couldn't have possibly have imagined. On a remote outing a tragic and sinister event occurs. Now, thirty years later, the question is still open: what really happened that day?

'A PERFECT HOLIDAY READ. ITS ABSORBING NARRATIVE COMPELS THE READER TO TURN THE PAGES, AND YET ITS DESCRIPTIVE WRITING OFTEN INVITES RE-READING FOR THE SHEER PLEASURE OF THE PROSE. SET IN FIVE COUNTRIES (MOST SPECTACULARLY EGYPT), AND IMBUED WITH THE SPIRIT OF HENRY JAMES, THIS NOSTALGIC CHRONICLE OF A LOSS OF INNOCENCE STILL DRAWS REFLECTIVE THOUGHT LONG AFTER THE BOOK'S CONCLUSION'
Guardian

'YOU HAVE TO READ ON, AND YOU CAN'T ASK FOR MUCH MORE THAN THAT'
Spectator

9780552772112

BLACK SWAN

RANDOM ACTS OF HEROIC LOVE
Danny Scheinmann

'TENDER AND INSIGHTFUL'
Observer

1992: Leo Deakin wakes in a mysterious South American hospital. His girlfriend Eleni is dead. Dazed and bruised, Leo's only certainty is that he is somehow responsible for her death. Sapped of all passion and drive, he feels his life is over. But Leo is about to discover something that will change his fate for ever.

1917: Moritz Daniecki has survived fighting in the Great War. But at what cost? Abandoned in the Siberian wilderness, he is determined to return to his beloved Lotte, the memory of whose single kiss has sustained him throughout the war. What lies before him is a terrifying journey over the Russian Steppes. If he ever makes it, will she still be waiting?

9780552774222

BLACK SWAN

MADWOMAN ON THE BRIDGE
and other stories
Su Tong

'RESTRAINED AND MERCILESS, SU TONG IS A TRUE LITERARY TALENT'
Anchee Min

Set during the fall-out of the Cultural Revolution, these bizarre and delicate stories capture magnificently the collision of the old China of vanished dynasties, with communism and today's tiger economy.

The madwoman on the bridge wears a historical gown which she refuses to take off. In the height of summer, to the derision of the townspeople, she stands madly on the bridge. Until a young female doctor, bewitched by the beauty of the mad woman's dress, plots to take it from her, with tragic consequences.

From the folklorist who becomes the victim of his own rural research, to the doctor whose infertility treatment brings about the birth of a monster child, to a young thief who steals a red train only to have it stolen from him, Su Tong's stories are a scorching look at humanity.

'SU TONG WRITES BEAUTIFUL, DANGEROUS PROSE'
Meg Wolitzer

'SU TONG IS AN IMAGINATIVE AND SKILFUL STORYTELLER'
New York Times

'OVERWHELMING AND IMAGINATIVE VIRTUOSITY'
Rick Moody

9780552774529

BLACK SWAN